Hanging Flynn

A Tale of the Fairypocalypse

ADDISON LANE

Hanging Flynn
A Tale of the Fairypocalypse

Cover design by Lee Milverton

Addison Lane
www.addisonlane.net

Lee Milverton
www.leemilverton.com

Printed in the United States of America

First Printing: November 2011

ISBN 978-0-9839538-2-1

Library of Congress Control Number: 2011942327

DEDICATION

Special thanks to Mom, Dad, Jayce, Jamie, David, Adrienne, and Sandra. This is to everyone who supported and advised me on this journey.

Chapter One.

An airship slowly cut through the sky from the east. Now and then, it disappeared behind wisps of clouds as the late morning breeze pushed last night's storm out to ocean. It was the noon air ferry from Lancaster. Fergus Irvine had never been to Lancaster before; he'd never been further than the water ringing New Peiling. He leaned back, bobbing on the waves, and watched as the airship was momentarily obscured by the towering, craggy silhouette of the city, stretching up so far into the clouds that he couldn't even see the white buildings at the top.

The water drew him closer to the rocky shoreline, but he wasn't worried, because due to the tiny island that housed the airship docks, this particular strip of ocean wasn't dangerous. He'd been coming here to swim since he was a small child, and he'd swum in much more challenging areas around the city, too.

Even if there was a storm, water wasn't such a big threat to a hybrid with a *kelpie* spirit.

"Fergus, could you please come on already? I have to go to class."

He righted himself to see a dark-haired young man on the shore. Flynn pushed his black ringlets out of his face and scowled.

"Just go by yourself. I swear, Lady Gemini isn't gonna eat you," Fergus called.

Flynn, however, either didn't hear him, or he didn't want to hear that answer, because he didn't reply. Sighing, Fergus began to swim for the rocks, scrambling up onto the path between them.

"Turn around," he instructed, picking up the threadbare towel he'd brought along and doing his best to dry off before pulling on the jeans and jumper laying over a nearby rock. They were wet from the spindrift, but he was damp from the shabby towel. At least, he thought, it was late spring, so once the sun came out, he'd be all right. He scrubbed at his messy brown hair and then shook his head, sending drops everywhere.

"Watch it," Flynn said, holding up his hands to block the errant splatters.

Fergus snorted. "Whatever. Like a little salt water'd kill you."

"You never know," Flynn said, tucking his hands into his pockets and pulling out a copper watch. "Jeez, I've only got 20 minutes."

"You'll make it," Fergus said and began picking his way up the path towards the docks. "You gotta get over this old lady phobia."

"But you know she's right 90% of the time. Remember what happened last time?"

"When she said that Sarah girl was gonna dump you?"

"And then she did half an hour later. Just like that."

Fergus shook his head, glancing over his shoulder at his roommate and best friend. "Weren't you having problems already? Seems like a coincidence to me."

"Yeah, well, I don't like the kind of coincidences she heralds."

Fergus sighed. Flynn had been afraid of going to the marketplace alone for nearly a year now, ever since he'd had a run in with Lady Gemini. Lady Gemini was a seer of no small talent. She was very good at picking out the exact type of fairy-soul a hybrid might be sharing for those who couldn't work it out on their own, but few wanted her to say more than that. This was due to the fact that she was a hybrid with a *banshee* soul, which meant that her predictions were eerily accurate and mostly dire.

Though Fergus brushed off Flynn's paranoia about running into her, he had to admit, she was known as the best fortuneteller in New Peiling for a reason. He'd rather not have her running into him, eyes rolled back into her head, weird scar stretching her face, and spouting out doom and gloom. He'd long since decided that he was just going to run if she ever started stumbling his way. He wasn't sure why Flynn couldn't adopt the same plan, but ever since that fateful day, he wouldn't go near the docks without Fergus at his side.

The dockside marketplace was probably the only really good thing about lower New Peiling. The rest of the area was made up of slums cobbled together out of the remains of buildings that had once stood in direct sunlight before the Cataclysm. Now, though, they were just the rotting remains of another time, kept in the dark nearly 24 hours of the day and shouldering the layers of the city above. Unsurprisingly, nearly all of the hybrids made their homes in the lower city. Most humans avoided it as a result, but since the docks housed the ferry that went to the airship port, it was the city's entry point for supplies, which meant that the fruits, vegetables, fish, and meats sold there were the freshest in the city. It was enough to make the denizens of the upper city brave the admittedly dubious express lift and the hybrids.

On a Thursday morning, it wasn't very busy. Fergus tucked his hands in his jeans, watching Flynn look around for the gnarled form of the old fortuneteller before going over to inspect a pile of carrots. He stifled a yawn, turning back to the sky. The airship was a little larger on the horizon, which meant that it would soon be noon, and he'd be due at the Magpie to tell Felix that this would be his last afternoon of washing dishes and clearing tables. He was a little sorry to be giving his resignation.

Felix was a great boss. He employed a number of the homeless kids around lower New Peiling, giving them wages that he probably couldn't afford, along with a meal a day to keep them from starving. If Fergus believed in saints, he might have thought Felix was one. But now things were picking up with his band, Everyday Resources. They were getting more gigs, and though the gigs didn't pay exceptionally well – especially when split four ways – it was almost as much as he made at the Magpie, and he figured he'd been there long enough. It was time for some other hungry soul to get a chance to eat.

Besides, he also had his job as shop keep at Beathag's, the number one magic shop in all of New Peiling. Fergus had been working both at Beathag's and the Magpie for a few years now, ever since his mother had disappeared. He'd lived with her in the apartment he and Flynn now occupied until one day, four years ago, he'd returned from school to find her gone. She'd also been a hybrid with a kelpie soul. Maybe there was something wrong with her fairy-soul, but she wasn't easy to deal with on the best of days, and in the last few years before she left, she frequently erupted into fits of violence. When he found her gone, he wasn't entirely surprised. He'd dropped out of high school shortly thereafter. That was when Felix and Ursula (the owner of Beathag's) had taken pity on him and given him jobs. Even with their help, without Flynn, he never would have made it.

He'd met Flynn not long after his mother had abandoned him. Actually, he'd found Flynn sleeping on the stoop of his apartment, so he'd invited him in for the night, and he just never left. Together, the two of them managed to pull together enough for rent and food. Fergus wasn't entirely sure where Flynn worked, but he thought it might be an apothecary near one of the universities of magic, which worked out, since Flynn was enrolled as a part-time student there. Besides the markets, the magical universities were the only things in lower New Peiling that rivaled the offerings of the upper layers. Luckily, they were also free. Fergus had no head for magic, though, and he hadn't finished high school, but he did enjoy watching Flynn work on his potions and spells.

The only magic that Fergus knew was music, and it was the only thing that got him through some days. He spent a lot of time at Beathag's jotting down lyrics on pieces of napkin, though his favorite place in the city to write was in upper New Peiling, in Erstwyre Park. It took nearly an hour on the lifts to get to the top, and though his mother had brought him there a lot as a child, as he'd grown and begun to show signs of being a hybrid, he'd begun to feel anxious about visiting. The cops were always on the look out for anyone who seemed like they might be from the lower city, and they were all too happy to come up with phony misdemeanors to ban that person from ever stepping foot on the top layer again.

Fergus visited the park more than most hybrids. He was a fan of sunlight and fresh air, which were in short supply in the slums. It wasn't as often as he would have liked, however.

"Aren't you going to get anything?" Flynn asked, returning with a small paper bag in his arms.

Fergus shook his head. "Nah, I won't have enough until after tomorrow's gig. I mean, I'm kinda short on rent this month anyway."

"That's okay. I just got paid, so we should be good," Flynn said, digging an apple out of the bag and rubbing it on his sweater. "Want one?"

Fergus wrinkled his nose.

"Carnivore." Flynn took a bite of the apple and began to walk towards the city.

"Are you gonna come?" Fergus asked, falling into step beside him.

"I'll try."

"Free beer."

"Curse your silver tongue," Flynn said around a mouthful of apple. "Okay, I'll double try, but I've got a study group thing tomorrow evening, so I'll have to come after that."

"Good enough."

They left the daylight behind, walking deeper into the labyrinthine streets of lower New Peiling. A curious mix of Victorian style street lamps and neon signs lit the streets. That was not all that illuminated the buried heart of the city. Here strange, magical things grew. Dimly glowing toadstools protruded from the sides of buildings, and patches of luminescent fungi peeked from the cracks of the walks. Soon the buildings turned into a cobbled collection of apartments built around and upon the remains of a dead city. Dried, ancient ivy clung to the walls, and romantic tumbles of decaying brick drifted into the streets. Tattered signs cropped up here and there with newer directions affixed to them.

They passed an abandoned building, smashed up between two newer apartment complexes, and Fergus thought he could see a rotting curtain flutter: drifters, willing to risk the roof caving in for a free night of shelter.

Fergus and Flynn also lived in an apartment constructed on the remains of an older building. The original architecture was damaged, leaving lions without snouts and the imprints of what might have been curling flowers and vines. It had been made of pale stone – perhaps some sort of public hall – but it had been cut down to only half its size in the Cataclysm. Two brick buildings now rested on the remains of its foundation. A fragment of the original wall was visible within the entryway and even within their living room, and though badly damaged on the outside, the inner sculptures were still mainly intact.

Fergus took one big step and cleared the stoop, opening the door for Flynn and following him up the stairs. They stepped over their old neighbor, who was where they'd left him that morning - half-drunk and half-conscious, draped across the stairway.

"You should get to your real bed, Mr. Farrier," Flynn called from the top of the stairs.

Mr. Farrier let out a loud snore.

Fergus took the rest of the steps two at a time and passed Flynn, walking up to the door and pulling out an antique key. He jangled it around in the lock for a couple of minutes until he felt it catch and give, and then he pushed the door open, ushering Flynn through.

The apartment was dark. He fumbled around in his jeans pocket for a match to light the lantern beside the door and, having shed light over the interior, shut and locked it. He could hear music coming from the apartment above and Flynn opening cabinets in the kitchen. Next to the kitchen door was a dimly glowing fish tank. He paused next to it and gave it a tap, peering in at two clownfish and three angelfish. None of the angelfish had names, but the smaller clownfish was called "Toby." Fergus gave the tank another tap, but as expected, Toby ignored him.

"Did you already feed them?"

"Yeah, of course," Flynn replied.

Fergus continued into the kitchen and opened the icebox, pulling out a nearly empty bottle of milk and giving it a discriminating sniff before tilting it back and taking a swig.

"You didn't buy milk, did you?" he asked.

Flynn shook his head.

"I'll get some tomorrow night on the way home." He put the rest of the milk back. He felt a little disappointed that Flynn hadn't bought any. Milk was pretty expensive; it would eat a considerable chunk of tomorrow's earnings. "Too bad we can't just live on beer."

Flynn gave a little snort. "Yeah, remember when we tried that? But hey, maybe Ursula will give you a little bonus if you sweet talk her."

"Yeah, 'sweet talk,'" Fergus muttered. "We'll see what kind of mood she's in."

Ursula had owned and operated Beathag's for as long as Fergus could recall, and before she'd hired him, she'd done it all by herself. He wasn't sure how old she was, but she looked like she was in her late 20s. It was a mystery to him just how she'd gotten on before him, because she had the obnoxious habit of answering questions with questions and possessed no sales persona to speak of. She did, however, possess other gifts, which she sometimes bestowed on him in the supply closet before handing him a little extra and sending him home, but Fergus had learned early on that these "bonuses" weren't something he could rely on.

Ursula's moods changed by the hour, and most of what she did was on a whim. It certainly wouldn't trouble him if she was in that mood, but he thought he should consider other means of obtaining cash.

"You should wear that blue t-shirt. You look good in it. Matches your eyes."

Fergus gave Flynn a little shove. "Would you shut up?"

"Fine, fine, fine," Flynn replied, holding his hands up.

"And wipe that stupid grin off your face. Aren't you supposed to be at class?"

"Oh, damn! Right!" he exclaimed, accidentally banging a cabinet door shut. "I may be out late."

"Okay," Fergus replied with a shrug, stepping back to let Flynn rush past. "See you whenever, then."

He barely caught sight of Flynn as he hurried out the door. He paused in the kitchen door and turned to the tank of fish.

"He's always got somewhere to be, huh? Guess I do, too."

The door to his room was hanging open, towel draped over the top. He only shut it when he was sleeping. Flynn's door was shut, though, as usual. Fergus already knew what lay beyond: a room much tidier than his own. The bathroom was across from Flynn's room. Fergus stepped inside and kicked the door closed before going about forcing the rickety old pipes to drudge up some warm water. This effort alone – the twisting and jerking and fiddling – could take up to five minutes. Several people must have showered recently, because it took nearly ten before the water was both warm and clear. He splashed his face in the sink as he waited for the shower to warm up a bit more and stared into the grimy mirror, watching water dripping down his cheeks.

For the most part, Fergus resembled the human denizens of New Peiling. He had longish, dirty brown hair, which was presently sticking out at strange angles, wide blue eyes, and freckles dotting his pale cheeks. Only one thing really separated him from looking wholly human: in dim light, as well as from certain angles, his eyes looked entirely white. Otherwise, he was just an average 20-year-old, if from the lower rung of the social ladder.

He rubbed the water from his eyes and stripped out of his damp clothing to climb into the shower. The shower itself was as old and unkempt as the mirror, and he nearly slipped on the tiles.

"Close," he muttered to himself as he took up his washrag.

After ten minutes in lukewarm water – even in the clammy atmosphere of the lower city, Fergus's kelpie soul couldn't stand *hot* water – he was feeling cozy and scrubbed as much as seemed reasonable. Climbing out of the shower, he picked up his damp clothes and took them to his room where he dumped them in the pile of dirty clothes dubbed "most recent" in his head before going over to open the narrow window opposite. He jerked it open a couple of inches, enough that he could see the lights going off behind the curtains of the strip club next door. The music was still thumping overhead. He sighed and plopped himself onto the palette he called his bed, pulling a pair of mostly clean jeans out from a pile of clothing and slipping them on.

His foot knocked against his guitar case, and he paused for a moment before pulling it closer. He didn't have time to play, but he thought he should at least lean it against the corner, so that he didn't step on it later. He then sought out the blue shirt Flynn had mentioned – even if he was joking, every little bit helped – to put it aside for later, before pulling on a grey hoodie and going back out into the street.

The Magpie wasn't much of a walk from the apartment. It was a squat brick building a few blocks towards the outskirts of the lower city. There was a weird, phosphorescent patch of green growing on the wall under a hand-painted sign with a picture of a black bird with white and blue markings. Fergus pushed the door open and stepped into the dark pub. It didn't open until one, but Felix was already busy at work, wiping down glasses behind the bar. Fergus walked over, sliding onto one of the hard-backed stools.

"Morning, Fergus," Felix said, looking up and studying him for a moment before chuckling softly. "Looks like you have something on your mind."

Fergus gave him a contrite smile. "Kinda. Well, yeah. I mean . . . "

"Guessing this is your last day?"

He nodded.

"I thought it might be coming. I still remember when you first came in – a scrawny kid with crazy hair. Well, the hair hasn't changed too much."

Fergus reached up to try to comb it with his fingers.

"If you ever need work again, you always have a place here. How about a drink to celebrate?" Felix put down the glass and rag and pulled out a bottle of whisky, pouring a little into two tumblers before sliding one to Fergus.

"Thanks. Gonna miss this place."

"Don't say you won't be back."

Fergus smiled, clinking his glass to Felix's with a brief, "cheers." The whisky burned the back of his throat, making him grimace, but he still took an extra drink before answering. "Of course, I will. Anyway, if you hire me back, I wanna be a barkeep."

Felix put down his empty glass and swatted at Fergus with the rag. "We'll see about that."

Fergus finished the whisky and stood. "I'll take the empty kegs out."

"Good man," Felix said, returning to lining up the glasses behind the bar.

•   •   •

They had a few more rounds before Fergus left for the evening, so he was tipsy when he stopped by his apartment to grab his guitar en route to the garage the band rented for practice space. The rest of Everyday Resources was already there, sitting on the floor and chatting idly. Fergus put his guitar in a stand and flopped next to the bassist, Terry Bridges. He had a wild mop of reddish hair and grey eyes. Fergus wasn't sure what sort of hybrid he was, because he rarely talked about himself. Beside him sprawled the lead guitarist – a girl with dark, curly hair named Evelyn Ross, whom he knew to be a *púca*, and who had talked her way into the band by getting cozy with the drummer, Raja Youssef. Raja had electric blue eyes and came from a place so far away, Fergus couldn't even imagine it. He was sitting with his arm around Evelyn's shoulders.

Fergus felt it was just lucky that she could play.

"Hey," Fergus said.

"Hey," repeated Terry and Evelyn. Raja nodded.

"You want to talk about the set list for tomorrow?" Evelyn asked, extracting herself.

"What about it?"

"Well, I was thinking we should switch 'Lucy's Hymn' for . . . anything else. It's so downbeat."

Fergus frowned and blew his hair out of his face.

13

"You and Lucy have been split up for like over a year now. I mean, even Emily is old news by now," Evelyn persisted.

"I know," Fergus replied a little irritably.

Watching Evelyn and Raja getting all cozy irked him. Evelyn's remark wasn't helping. He hadn't had a girlfriend for several months. His last, Emily, had been the jealous type, and even though he had paused things with Ursula while he was dating her, she refused to believe him and demanded that he quit the shop. Seeing as how Beathag's was his highest paying source of revenue, he'd refused, and she'd dumped him.

"How about 'Magnet'?" Terry suggested, edging himself between Evelyn and Fergus.

"Yeah, that'd be okay," Fergus replied, pulling out his guitar and running a finger over the strings. Without the amp, it sounded hollow and thin. He adjusted the pegs. "I've got a new one, but it won't be ready by tomorrow. We can still practice it today, though," he said, picking up his satchel and rooting around for an ancient spiral bound notebook held together by rubber bands.

"What's it called?" Evelyn asked as he passed the notebook to Terry who glanced over it before handing it to her.

"'Lancaster.'"

"You should set your sights higher."

"Yeah, and when you find that buried treasure, you let me know," he replied with a little frown.

He wanted it to happen – he wanted to leave New Peiling – which was in part why he felt even more annoyed at her. However, a trip to Clohaven, Lancaster, or even the farmlands, which were under two days travel, cost an arm and a leg. Since Fergus could barely afford to pay rent and eat, travel was a much longed for, but far out of reach, luxury. His guitar gave an angry little *twang*, and he cringed.

Terry began tuning his bass. "Lancaster's no better than New Peiling. If you're gonna go somewhere nearby, at least go to Clohaven."

"I'll keep that in mind. Okay, listen up. This is how it goes."

• • •

It was well into the night when Fergus returned to the apartment. The lights were off, and he couldn't hear any movement from Flynn's room, so he settled onto the couch with his lyric book and stared at an empty page for a while before deciding he was hungry and going to root around in the icebox. He drank the rest of the milk and stuck the bottle on the counter at the end of a long line of jugs and metal cans. The neon sign next door lit the room a dull red. It had gotten colder, and the whole unit felt drafty, so he turned on the oven and leaned against it, wondering when Flynn would be home.

His thoughts passed from Flynn to band practice. He'd done a reasonable job of reeling his temper in, but he still felt ruffled. Fergus didn't want to rename the song. He didn't want to go to Clohaven. Clohaven was where, as far as he knew, his runaway dad lived.

His mother didn't keep pictures. She had been very bitter about it. Fergus had no idea what his father even looked like, but he thought he would know if he ever ran into him. At least, he should know, and if that ever happened, he wasn't sure what he'd do. Maybe punch him. Maybe push him over a ledge. Well, maybe not the latter, but he still didn't want to see the man who'd abandoned him before he was even born. He thought of writing a song about that, but then snorted. He felt he was past the stage of writing things like, "Fall into the ocean and drown, useless human."

Fergus turned off the stove and collected his lyric book, putting out the lamp, and retired to his room to stare at the ceiling. He watched the red light blinking against the ceiling until he fell asleep.

Chapter Two.

The problem with mornings in the lower city was that without natural light coming through the window, it was hard to wake up. Even though he didn't have work, Fergus tried to get up around the same time every day. Otherwise, with the lack of daylight, it was easy to lose track of night and day, of time in general, and sink into depression. Depression was a major issue in New Peiling's slums. It was hard when life was hand-to-mouth, uncertain, even violent, and the shadows persisted throughout the day. For many, it seemed the only escape was to die. No one with any actual power was invested in fixing this, however, and so it wasn't rare to see people fishing bodies from the bay in the mornings, and it probably never would be.

The neon sign was becoming increasingly annoying the more awake he became. He groaned and pulled his pillow over his head. Upstairs, his neighbor began playing music. He could feel it vibrating through the mattress. With a curse, he sat up and stared blearily at the pulsating light on the other side of the fish-patterned curtains he'd had since he was a kid. He squinted at the offending glow the way he squinted at it every morning before deciding that yet again, glaring at it wasn't going to get him anywhere.

Rolling out of bed, he went to take a shower. He considered making toast, but felt guilty since he was going to have to lean on Flynn for rent anyway, so he left with an empty stomach, taking a stroll towards Beathag's. The shop was closed, as he suspected it would be. Ursula never opened before noon on Fridays. He peered through the glass door, but he couldn't see anything beyond the shadows of the shelves. Rousing Ursula early was a poor idea, so he continued on his way.

His final pay from the Magpie was in his pocket, and he thought he could probably go ahead and pick up some food at the markets, but decided against it. If he went in the evening, near the end of market hours, he could probably get some discounts. He nodded to himself and started to change direction when he saw an old woman standing on the curb. His breath caught in his throat. He stopped and stared at her crooked back apprehensively.

However, the old woman didn't turn to him, and after a moment, began to hobble off towards the docks. Fergus shook his head. Maybe Flynn's phobia was contagious. He gave himself a mental slap; he couldn't be jumping out of his skin every time he saw an old lady standing around. It wasn't like Lady Gemini was the bogeyman. She was just some crazy old bat with a penchant for pessimism.

Whether it was her or not, the old woman soon disappeared from sight, and he put her out of his mind, instead turning his thoughts to visiting Erstwyre Park and hammering out the kinks in "Lancaster."

The lift smelled like spoiled tomatoes, and he wondered if someone had been sick recently. It wasn't a rarity, given how long and rocky the ride was. He tried not to look too closely at the floor, but instead stared out of the glass side as the lift jolted to life, carrying him and a handful of others up through the layers of New Peiling.

They passed a number of stationary lifts. Except on the very top layers, the lifts tended to only run when five or more people boarded to save on energy. He wasn't surprised to see one or two passengers standing inside the still glass boxes, waiting for enough people to join them that they might go up or down. It was a stroke of luck that he'd managed to be the fifth onto this one.

The people around him looked anxious. Probably they needed papers from the city hall on the top layer, or maybe they just weren't used to being shaken about quite so vigorously. Fergus shifted away from a greenish looking young man and held his breath.

The lift finally reached its destination, grinding to a halt and swaying violently for a moment. He impatiently moved past the others to step out into the fresh air. It was a sunny day and breezy: perfect for spring. He took a deep breath and smelled newly clipped grass and flowers. It'd been weeks since he'd been up here, and he'd nearly forgotten what fresh air smelled like. Feeling cheered, he crossed the square with its large marble fountain, heading towards the rows of apple trees that led to the park's entrance.

He walked along until he found a nice grassy spot in the sun and flopped onto it, linking his hands over his eyes. The ground was damp from the morning dew and cold, but the sunlight was warm. He wondered what it would be like to live up here – to live anywhere where he could see the sunlight regularly.

"You, what are you doing on the grass!?"

Fergus cracked open an eye to see a grumpy looking man in uniform approaching. He sat up, cringing.

"This grass is still growing! You can't lie on it!"

"Sorry, sorry," he said, quickly getting to his feet.

"Get moving," the man ordered, pointing to the paved path.

Fergus bit his cheeks, counting to ten before giving a tight nod, and skulked off to the designated path. He walked along for a few minutes before locating a bench by the duck pond, but his mood was soured. He kept imagining shoving the rude park official, or telling him off. At least in his mind he could get away with it. Jabbing violently at the paper didn't make him feel any better, but rather rendered the page illegible with inkblots. After ruining several sheets in this fashion, he decided just to go back down to the lower city and get something to eat.

The lift was more crowded on the way down, and he found himself crammed up against one of the glass walls, hoping desperately no one close by became ill on the ride. He closed his eyes and tried to think of anything else as they went from the gleaming white buildings of the upper city to the fancy brick buildings of the top-middle layers to the grimier, but still well tended homes of the lower-middle, and then down through the increasingly soiled, dark layers of the lower city. Not for the first time, Fergus thought there was no lack of symbolism, if unintended, in the journey down to the bowels of the city.

Fergus let out his breath as he filed out of the lift with the others and then gave himself a sniff to see if he smelled like decomposing vegetables, but happily, he thought he smelled a little like the park. He felt buoyed by the thought, and there was a renewed spring to his step as he headed to the docks. If he just got one thing to eat, he could still come back later to do some actual shopping.

He shuffled past the stands of fruits and vegetables to the carts of fresh fish. There were fat lipped bass and small, angular sunfish, thin, silvery whiting and a plethora of shellfish. The whiting was cheapest, and he had just caught the fishmonger's eye to request some when he felt a tug on his sleeve. The color drained from the fishmonger's face. The man took a step back, and Fergus's stomach did a violent little flip. Turning slowly, he found a tiny old woman with a queer scar leading out from her left eye. She wasn't looking at him. She couldn't, because her good eye was rolled back, staring somewhere in the depths of her skull.

"It has come to pass," she said, voice raspy, and released him.

Without another word, she began to totter off in the direction of her houseboat on the west end of the docks.

Fergus stared after her, lost on her meaning and struggling with a sudden sense of unease. He gave himself a shake, trying to rid himself of the weight that had settled in his stomach. The man behind the cart was making signs to ward off evil. Fergus attempted to ask him about the fish, but the man shook his head wildly, making fast-paced, complicated gestures with his fingers. Fergus turned hopefully to the next stand, but the attendant had shrunken back and was sitting with her back to him.

As he turned, he found everyone in the vicinity was either staring at him or backing away. He found his appetite suddenly lacking and began to edge away from the gawkers, walking and then jogging back towards the city.

He wanted to tell Flynn. At least, Flynn would be able to sympathize with how disturbing it was. He ran up the steps, fumbled with the lock, and flung open the door. The apartment was still and silent. He put on the lamp and walked past the fish, which were bobbing hopefully at the top of the tank, on his way to Flynn's room. He hoped Flynn was home and just taking a nap, but knocking on the door resulted in silence. Fergus stamped his foot in frustration, cursing, and retreated to the living room.

He watched Toby swim in circles and then chase one of the angelfish without paying much attention, busy trying to think of what he should do, then telling himself there was nothing he *should* do, because she was just an old woman, and what she said could mean anything. He was just searching for meaning in it, buying into the local superstition.

He took a deep breath, steeling himself, and went over to shake some fish food into the water. He stepped back, watching the fish eat their flakes, and steadied his breathing. It was a cold reading. She'd been doing the spooky eye thing for so long, of course she could do it at will. Probably, she was hoping to drum up some business by scaring a random passerby, trying to lure him back to her home for a full reading.

"Right," he told himself. "That's all it is."

•   •   •

Six o'clock rolled around, finding Fergus on the sofa where he'd parked himself to wait until Flynn got back. It didn't look like he was going to be home before Fergus had to leave for the gig. He sighed, deciding he'd have to save the story until later, and tried to concentrate on the show.

In less than an hour, he'd be on stage before a jostling crowd. It would be hot and loud and thrilling. He closed his eyes, exhaled, and gave his guitar a last strum before sliding it into its case. Standing, he went to splash his face in the sink, put on a fresh shirt, and change his lip ring. Fergus jotted down the details for Flynn and left the note by the collection of bottles and cans on the counter before heading out.

He arrived at the same time as Terry, who gave him a curt nod. His eyes looked bruised and his face a little tight. For a second, Fergus thought about asking him if he was all right, but Terry was already stepping inside, disappearing backstage. Raja and Evelyn were already there, waiting.

"You look tired, Terry," Evelyn observed without even glancing at Fergus.

"Hello to you, too," Fergus muttered.

"I'm fine," Terry replied, waving one hand and taking a seat on the ground. "Had to work late last night is all."

Evelyn raised an eyebrow, opening her mouth.

"So remember: 'Magnet' instead of 'Lucy's Hymn,' okay?" Fergus cut in. He thought Terry gave him just the briefest thankful smile.

"Yeah, we know already. We're ready to go," Evelyn replied, bending down to open her guitar case. She clapped her hands. "Up and at 'em, people. Let's go, let's go, let's go!"

"Cut it out," Fergus muttered, and Raja gave her a little nudge.

"Relax, Fergus. It'll be fine," she said, brushing her hair over her shoulders. "How do I look?"

"Whatever. Let's get out there and set up."

•   •   •

An hour and a half later, Fergus was sweaty, tipsy, a little hoarse, and generally feeling good. He stumbled out of the bar, zigzagging in the fashion unique to drunks. Terry walked with him for a few blocks, as Fergus loudly sang (forgetting the words right and left) to fill the silence. While Terry seemed amused, he soon departed, leaving Fergus to cross the avenues on his own.

It was late, and even in a place as lightless as the lower city, it was dark. Most of the daytime lights were out, and it was only thanks to his fairy-soul that he could make out the streets at all. Perhaps it was because he was drunk, or maybe it was because it really was that dark, but he missed Ursula's approach. She spilled out of the shadows, lazy and winding. A moment later, her arms encircled his shoulders and mouth brushed his ear, making him jump.

"Did you have your fortune told?" she purred.

"Fortune told?" he parroted. It took him a moment to work out what she meant. "Oh. No, she just ran into me, rambling something."

"Was it really mere babble?"

Fergus paused, pursing his mouth.

"Do you know who came to see me of all people?" she asked.

"No, who?"

Ursula chuckled, drawing back and sliding one hand over his throat. "Guess."

". . . Flynn?"

She shook her head, catching a tooth against the side of his neck. He shifted uncomfortably.

"I don't know. My mom?"

She snorted.

He glowered, feeling his buzz dying.

"That pretty little pup," she said, tapping his shoulder with each word.

"Emily?" he asked. "Wait, really?"

"And do you know what she called me before she left?"

Fergus cringed.

"That's right," Ursula said, patting his cheek.

He cleared his throat. "Well, I dunno why she would. I haven't talked to her in months."

"Perhaps she had heard a fast-paced rumor, or perhaps she is simply a petty little creature."

"I'm surprised you didn't hear it first."

"Oh, I did, but I wasn't so concerned – precious thing. Will you tell me what the fortune lady said?"

"Something about something starting."

"Disappointing."

"Sorry." Fergus tried to step away, thinking now would probably be his chance to escape if he wanted to pass out on his own cot and enjoy the rest of his happy tipsiness.

"I wonder if you wouldn't have a drink with me, hmm? I'm very bored tonight."

"What about Dominique . . .?"

She brushed her fingers against his cheek again, and he felt a faint sting – the hint of claws. "Didn't I ask for *you*?"

Fergus considered. He was tired and had to work early in the morning – at her shop, no less. On the other hand, there might be money involved, and he was short on rent. Plus, it wasn't like there weren't other rewards to be had, and he didn't want to provoke her into cutting his shift for "his sake," so he sighed and untangled himself to wrap an arm around her shoulders.

"Do you think cats or dogs are better?" she asked, one hand clasping his wrist.

He raised an eyebrow and snorted softly. "Cats are reliable in their own way, I guess."

"And?"

"More talented in their ways, too," he added, rolling his eyes.

Ursula smiled with a slow-growing kind of satisfaction. "Good boy."

• • •

He returned to the apartment late the next afternoon to find the building blocked off. A handful of police officers were wandering around inside the barrier, and a crowd had grown on the other side. Amongst them was a girl with long black hair and eyes nearly as dark. She turned to Fergus as he approached.

"Emily," he said, not trying to disguise his bewilderment.

Emily smiled, but he thought it looked like she'd been crying. He didn't have a chance to ask before her nose wrinkled and her lip curled back in disgust. "You reek."

"That's great. What's going on here?"

Her disdain evaporated, and she looked away, twisting her hands in the folds of her dress. Emily never fidgeted unless something was really bothering her. When they were dating, she'd only done it during fights or leading up to a big argument.

Fergus looked away from her twisting fingers to the officers. Realization began to sink in, coiling tightly in his stomach. He looked up to the living room window of his apartment and saw a police officer standing there. His brain shut off. Pushing past Emily, he climbed over the barricade, trying to wave off the policemen. They stopped him long enough to verify his address, and a middle-aged man with a beefy face escorted him up the stairs to his unit.

They passed through the living room with the faintly glowing fish tank – Fergus followed the way the fish swam to the top, bobbing hopefully – and down the hallway. Both his and Flynn's doors were open. A group of officers in white gloves blocked his view of Flynn's.

Fergus smelled the whisper of blood.

His heart hammered in his chest. The policemen stepped aside, and he recoiled, hitting the opposite wall and slumping down. Flynn's feet dangled in the air on the other side of the old officer's knees.

Fergus put his head in his hands and thought he might puke.

• • •

Emily draped her jacket over his shoulders as they sat in the empty lobby of the precinct one level up. A haggard woman with a smoker's voice lumbered over to them.

"There was a note," she said, holding it in thick, gloved fingers. She wouldn't let Fergus hold it, but read it out to him: *I'm tired*.

Fergus didn't think it sounded right, but she ignored his pleas to read it again.

"You're just in shock," Emily said, rubbing his shoulders. "It's just shock."

She kept quoting statistics about hybrid suicides, and he wanted to shake her until she just shut up, because Flynn wasn't depressed. He always had something to do, somewhere to go, someone to meet, and when he didn't, he was happily sitting around with Fergus, drinking, playing cards, swapping stories, or just reading in comfortable silence. He was quiet in his way, but Fergus had lived with him for years. They were like brothers. If Flynn had been hurting, Fergus knew he would have noticed. Yet Emily kept insisting he wouldn't have.

Soon a young man came out, introducing himself as a grief counselor, and began repeating Emily's words.

Fergus glared between them. Fine, maybe *other* people were in denial because someone they loved was secretly depressed and wound up killing themselves, but that wasn't Fergus, and that wasn't Flynn. Flynn wouldn't kill himself.

"You're just in shock," Emily repeated for what felt like the hundredth time. "It's just shock."

"No, it doesn't make sense."

"Fergus," she replied. She still sounded pitying, but a little frustration had crept into her voice. She put her hands on his shoulders, leaning over him. "Just come home with me tonight, okay?"

He looked up into her dark eyes and felt too tired to continue arguing, so he stopped speaking entirely and simply did what he was told: signed the papers for the identification of the body and turned it over to the city. He wondered what would happen now. It wasn't like he could even dream of affording a proper funeral, and Flynn had no family to speak of. *They* would just as soon have thrown him into the ocean as let the city handle things.

He wanted to stay, though, at least overnight, because it seemed sad and brittle for Flynn to be left alone now. Even so, he found himself at Emily's, drinking her flavorless soup and lying on her sofa. At least, she stopped trying to comfort him. She just turned on the radio and left him to read quietly in her room – in the room he had shared with her only last winter. Fergus stared, sleeplessly, at the pale yellow walls, the moldings around the ceiling and corners, the bookshelves, the glass cabinet built into the wall, and the big orange and navy blue paintings between the windows. It smelled sweet and cloyingly familiar.

He left at 2:30 A.M. from the fire escape, walking nearly all the way across the city to his apartment. A guard was posted outside his flat.

"An investigation is ongoing," the man grumbled, rubbing his eyes.

"Why? You said it was a *suicide*," Fergus demanded.

"An investigation is ongoing. We will let you know when you may return."

Frustrated, Fergus turned and stalked away.

Across from Beathag's was a 24-hour convenience store. The gaudy blinking lights clashed horribly with the traditional stone facade of the magic shop, and despite Ursula's considerable influence in the lower city, even she couldn't seem to have it uprooted. Fergus dallied, numb and detached, between rows of snack foods and minor household items and dusty displays of sunglasses that probably hadn't been touched in decades. He stood before the glass window to the cold goods and squinted at his reflection, his eyes stinging from the fluorescent lights.

He chose the cheapest, highest proof bottle he could find in his disoriented survey of the spirits and then sat outside on the curb and drank it. It was noxiously sweet. He vomited, but washed back the taste with more unpleasantly fake lime flavor. There wasn't going to be milk this week. Scoffing, he ran a hand over his face, wondering if that even mattered. He couldn't imagine just going back to live in the apartment his mother had abandoned him in and Flynn had died in. It seemed ludicrous. But if he didn't return, where was he going to go? He suddenly recalled that he'd forgotten to ask the guard to feed the fish. He wondered if they would die, too.

It was at that point that Ursula finally came to him, though without a scrap of pity in her expression. She looked between the vomit and Fergus for a moment before frowning at the annoying blinking sign and sighed. She didn't sit down or crouch, but rather stood above him with her arms crossed imperiously.

"Come on," she ordered, grabbing him by the collar and pulling until he stumbled to his feet.

The bottle of neon green liquid slipped from his grasp and smashed on the street in a flurry of glass, pooling around his feet. Fergus cursed.

"You're an idiot," Ursula said bluntly and stalked back across the street to her shop. Fergus veered and tripped on the curb, scraping up his hands, but managed to enter the narrow confines of Beathag's without help.

"Flynn's dead," he dumbly informed her.

"Yes, I am aware. You've only said so five times. Don't touch anything – you'll never be able to work it off."

He stood, obeying because it was easiest, until she turned on a light and beckoned him.

"Shower first," she instructed and followed through by divesting him of his clothing and shoving him into a tiny room that could hardly fit the enormous footed tub pressed against the wall. She tinkered with the taps until the water came pouring down like rain through the spout overhead, and Fergus toppled in, resting his forehead against the side of the tub, unmoving. He thought he might be sick again. Ursula made a sound like a growl in the back of her throat, but after a moment, he felt a washrag running down his back with surprising gentleness.

"He didn't kill himself," he slurred.

"Why do you say so?"

"Because I knew him better than anyone."

"I wonder."

"I did," he snarled, lifting his head in a spray of water.

Ursula wrinkled her nose and wiped the droplets from her face. "I didn't think he had either," she replied in a way that was so matter-of-fact that Fergus found himself irritated rather than relieved. "But he still is gone, and so I say, 'I wonder.'"

"What do you mean?"

Her fingers dragged over his scalp, scraping and stinging. Goosebumps ran down his neck. She hummed to herself, working soap into the scratches she'd just bestowed, and his eyes prickled at the pain. Fergus sucked in a soft breath, closing them before the suds could attack those, too. For a moment, he didn't think she would answer at all, but as she pushed him under the water to rinse out the soap, she spoke.

"I will be plain," she said, her voice muffled by the roar of the water. "He is not dead of a natural reason, and so you should leave it at that. I'll help you find a new place. Leave everything of him behind."

"Do you know something?"

"Only that asphyxiation is not a pleasant way to die, and the person who could kill a *tarbh uisge* that way is not to be messed with."

Fergus said nothing for a moment, but couldn't stay silent. "Was he involved in something?"

She forced his head back under the water. He choked, water going up his nose and down his throat before he could jerk free. He surfaced, eyes and nose streaming, to find Ursula regarding him coolly.

"I wonder if a pony can be so arrogant as to think it is stronger than a bull," she sneered.

He glared at her, and she glared back, unwavering. Too tired to fight her, he sighed and leaned his cheek on the cold shoulder of the tub once more, closing his eyes.

• • •

Fergus awoke in the tub. The water was clear and cold around him. He dragged his wrinkled body out and dried off. Despite sleeping in a very cramped place, he felt reasonably good. There was a plate of grilled fish left out for him, which he gladly ate as he searched the paper with a morbid brand of hope for articles about Flynn. Ursula was out, and the front of the shop had the closed sign up. He wondered if she was assuming he would open for her, but eating the fish reminded him of Toby, so he pulled on his dirty clothing and walked back to his apartment. A new officer was standing out front.

"Can I at least get some clothes and feed the fish?"

He was grudgingly permitted into the apartment, though the man followed him the whole time, hovering just behind him. Fergus packed a bag with a few changes of clothing, his toothbrush, and a book Flynn had loaned him. On the way out, he shook some flakes into the fish tank before asking the officer if he would make sure they were cared for and jotting down a list of instructions. He returned to Beathag's and put his things on top of his guitar in the bedroom before resigning himself to opening the shop.

Ursula still wasn't back.

Chapter Three.

Fergus slumped against the counter, feeling annoyed. The ancient grandfather clock behind him was ticking away at about half a second too slowly. Given how many of these delayed ticks had passed, he was thinking a lot of time had gone by. The unfortunate thing was that most of Ursula's customers were students, and so most had known Flynn and heard what had happened. Fergus had taken the opportunity to hedge as much as he dared to try to see if any of them might know some secret about Flynn that he did not, but most of them only had condolences to offer.

A pretty redhead walked in, looking through jars of gemstones. It wasn't long, however, before she made her way over to the counter. He lifted his head, readying himself for the inevitable. He did his best to not be snappish as he glossed over her personal monologue on Flynn and started reading off specials for the week, but she wasn't so easy to dissuade. After a minute, she leaned on the counter, her top slipping down until he could see the satiny rim of her bra cup and the shadowed slope of her breast. He was wondering how it was that she could be offering those kinds of condolences and trying not to make a study of her pink, wet lips when Ursula made her abrupt reappearance and with a pointed look, draped herself on him.

"Did Fergus tell you our special items for today?" she purred, staring at the girl without blinking.

"Ah, yes. I think . . . Yes, I will buy half a kilo of the powdered nettle," she stuttered, stepping back from the counter quickly.

"Go prepare it," Ursula commanded, and Fergus wasn't sure whether he was relieved or annoyed (though he wondered if he ever didn't feel this way around Ursula) and went back to scoop the herb into a vial. As he returned to the counter, Ursula took it from him, dropping it into a brown sack and holding it out unceremoniously to the girl, who quickly grabbed it, clutching the parcel to her chest, and retreated with an uneasy glance over her shoulder.

"Just what did you do to her?" he muttered, shaking his head.

"How rude," Ursula replied, blinking up at him, wide-eyed, from her lounging spot on the counter.

He moved on to a more important question. "Where were you?"

"Making a deal for glowing moon snail shells. They should arrive by the end of the week. I'll need you to crush them up later, but not immediately. They go off quickly once powdered."

"Uh huh."

He stared at her skeptically, she stared back blankly, and he knew that once again, he wasn't going to win, even if they both knew that Ursula never required that much time to haggle. He sighed irritably.

"You should keep an eye on who tries to get close to you," she finally said, turning her eyes to the front of the shop.

"Because they might know something?"

"Because they might *want* something."

Fergus said nothing for a moment, drumming his fingers on the counter, before shaking his head and blowing hair from his face. "I don't think she wanted anything dire."

"Because you're an idiot. Be careful of who you let close to you, or I'll have to find myself a new pony, and I don't dislike this one."

He snorted, but despite that felt a wave of something warm and effervescent wash over him. He brushed the feeling away; getting worked up over Ursula was more dangerous than letting a little college girl make advances.

"Did you find me a place?"

"Do you want to leave so soon?"

"Not really."

"It will happen soon enough, but I may need you to mind the shop for a few days. A number of traders are due in the port, and I want to secure transactions before the scavengers arrive. They are terribly vexing."

"Yeah, sure. No problem," he muttered, drumming his fingers on the counter.

"What if we closed up now? Would you come out with me for dinner?" she asked, finally looking back up at him with dark green eyes that seemed slitted at her present angle.

Fergus reached out to brush a stray lock of hair from her face and nodded, though he found it a little odd that she was offering this kind of treat out of the blue. Still, free food was free food, and maybe with a little wine, she might explain the secrecy she was trying to impose on him.

Of course, then she chose a place by the water, and the rushing waves and smell of brine called to him as strongly as the steak in front of him, or her foot navigating his ankle. He couldn't seem to concentrate on any one thing for more than a couple of minutes. He was having a hard time recalling that there was anything that he wanted to ask about in the first place.

"I saw you went out," she said, delicately slicing a piece of fish drizzled with something that smelled citric and creamy.

"Mm," he replied, sawing through the steak and trying hard to peel his eyes from the dark water over the side of the pier. He swallowed roughly, dousing it with wine, and cleared his throat faintly before adding, "Just to get some clothes and stuff."

"Did you go into his room?"

"No, the officer was shadowing me the entire time."

"Was it a human?"

Spray crashed against the rocks under them, splattering his cheek with a thin film of cold water. It took him a good minute to realize he'd been fixating on that when he should be answering.

"Yeah, of course. Why wouldn't it be?"

"Just curious," she drawled, resting her chin on the palm of her hand and pushing the fish around in its sauce. "Nothing strange, then?"

"Should I have noticed something strange?" he asked, biting another overly large piece of steak and wondering how long it'd been since he'd had red meat. It was so good. Richer than anything he was used to. He'd never seen a cow in person before. He wondered how long it took to ride the ferry to the island where most of the farming for the city took place. "You have to go through the Fada Pass to get there, don't you?" he asked and then colored as he realized he'd said it aloud.

Ursula chuckled. "To the country? Yes. Are you thinking of becoming a farmer, Fergus? You know, you can't eat your livestock."

He glared at her.

"Don't be cross," she murmured, her toes finding their way to his knee and brushing the inside of his thigh. She released her chin to refill their glasses. "When I was young, I thought of owning a vineyard."

"Why didn't you?"

"I almost did," she replied, taking a sip of wine. "My other aunt owned a small one, but the aunt taking care of me owned Beathag's, and she died first – without children, mind you."

"You could've sold Beathag's and gone to the country anyway."

"Maybe, but maybe not. Beathag's is perhaps more important than you can wrap your little mind around. Besides, Auntie Gertrude had a son, so he owns the farm, but now and then, he sends me a bottle," she said, fingering the rim of her glass.

Fergus thought she might be a little tipsy. Either that or he'd recently gone up a few notches on her ever-changing list of favorites. Maybe she wanted some information in return. Probably that was most likely, but he knew less than she did by his reckoning. He put down his glass to better study her.

"I hate when you get that suspicious look. Do you think it suits you? It doesn't," she snapped, not quite looking at him. "Did that girl from before give you her name?"

"Yeah, Jane, but that's all."

"Where she lived?"

"Are you jealous or something?" he asked, cocking his head.

She turned back to him, smiling slowly. Her foot found its way higher. "What if I am?" she asked.

"I'd be surprised," he replied, a little ruffled that she'd called his bluff.

"You're not terrible to look at. You amuse me well enough. Does that trouble you?"

He felt his face growing hot. Thoughts of water and meat suddenly faded into the background. He shook his head dumbly.

"Let's have the rest packed to go," she suggested, withdrawing her foot and holding up a hand to summon a waiter.

As they returned to the inner city, Fergus realized that he was the drunker of the two of them, because he felt unsteady and pleasantly foggy and were it not for Ursula's slow but consistent movement in the right direction, he thought he probably would be tripping over himself and sleeping in an alcove. It wouldn't have been the first time. Luckily, it seemed she wanted nothing more from him than what left him tired and draped across her bed.

However, he was sober enough that he woke when she got up and started shuffling around the room and then again sometime later when she had not yet returned and finally a third when she returned, crouching down and letting something slip – heavy and hard – onto the floor. She crawled back under the sheets, cold and demanding, pressing her frozen feet to his shins and curling against him.

•   •   •

As promised, Ursula left after breakfast, placing him in charge of the shop for most of the day. He hadn't seen daylight recently, and the hours were starting to blur. It felt like a great deal of time had passed since that moment when he'd crouched in the hallway outside Flynn's room, trying to get his bearings, but unable to focus on anything but the space between the floor and his best friend's toes. They'd been a funny blue-grey-purple color. He shuddered, shaking his head violently to rid himself of the thought.

He was almost grateful when one of the officers appeared in the shop. It was, he thought, the old man who'd escorted him into the apartment the first day.

"The investigation is over. You may return to your apartment."

For a moment, Fergus just stared at him. Return already? Not that he was having a vacation here, but the idea of going back and being alone in the flat filled him with a distinct sense of dread.

"Everything there is now yours by law," the man continued. "We thank you for not hindering the investigation and remind you of our counseling services if you . . . "

Fergus nodded through the rest. Everything was his? Like he would want it. At least, with only three and a half rooms besides the bath, there wasn't much to own. The idea of going through Flynn's things, however – especially going through them alone in that room – left him feeling weird and cold. Fergus realized that he had forgotten to press the officer about the final verdict, but when he went to the door, the man was already out of sight.

He returned to the counter, slumping down and staring blankly at an odd patch of light reflecting from a jar of toads' legs. Part of him thought he should go now and have a preliminary look through the room before anyone could obstruct his search. He might be able to find something the officers had missed, maybe something that Ursula wouldn't be keen on him having, and yet despite her warnings, he wanted to know. No, needed to know. He *needed* to know why Flynn was dead. He resolved to go, standing up and tossing his apron over the counter. He locked up, putting the closed sign on the door.

He felt uneasy – jittery and breathless – like he would shake apart if he just stood still, so he ran until he arrived, and then he was too tired to feel the horrible unstable feeling. Toby was looking hungry when he stepped through the door, so he fed the fish, tapping on the glass, though they ignored him. Their tank looked a little grimy. He thought before he left, he should probably stick an arm in and let it soak until the water cleared up (one benefit of being a kelpie: easy aquarium maintenance). He went into the kitchen. The icebox was bare, so at least there was nothing that needed to be tossed. The cabinets, too, were empty save for some stale bread (which he did throw into the bin), some oats, and condiments. It looked a little like they'd moved out of this room already.

Fergus was procrastinating. He knew he was, and he knew that if Ursula came back to the shop and found it closed, she would come here and be angry, so he couldn't really afford to be fooling around. But his feet did not want to make their way down the hall to the now empty room. Slowly, step-by-step (and there were about ten of them), he forced himself to go. It was surprisingly tidy inside. He thought the officers would have turned everything over and left it that way. He was thankful that they hadn't, though it made the funny mark on the carpet all the more obvious, like everything in the room was trying to shy away from the stain. He tried to walk up to it, but found himself giving it a wide berth.

Fergus started with the antique CDs, for which players no longer existed. He stacked them neatly on the bed. He turned to the old hand-painted burlesque prints, slowly pulling them down one after the other and stacking them next to the CDs. Under the bed was a mess of socks, not a single one seeming to match, and dozens of notebooks, all filled with the same familiar tight spikes and dips of words. It seemed that the most recent was from about four months ago. Had Flynn simply stopped writing, or had someone taken the most recent ones? If he had stopped, maybe that meant something, because it seemed like the notebooks went back a couple of years, and there were more in the closet.

Maybe Flynn *was* depressed, Fergus thought, flipping through an entry about a pretty girl that he'd had a one night stand with only to realize the older guy on the couch hadn't been her brother, but a live-in boyfriend, and only barely making it out with his nose intact. Fergus laughed to himself, recalling the story, which Flynn had told over a game of Black Jack and a bottle of wine that was well past its prime.

He thought he would keep these. At least, some of them. He put them in neat stacks on top of the posters to go through more carefully later. Then he lay down next to them on the bed, across the pillows, which still had a nice peppery scent, underlying the sour smell of old sweat. He watched dust unfurling in the bleak light coming from the lamp by the door. There was a faint bumping sound beyond the plaster ceiling, the muffled sound of a female voice, and then fast-beat music that had never come out of any traditional instrument, accompanied by a squeaky, off-tune voice.

He laughed hoarsely. "She never gets sick of it," he murmured to the empty room. "I swear to God, she played it 20 times in a row the other day. Maybe we should complain." His voice broke. He bit his lip.

Molecules of dust were still gently drifting down, down, down through the gritty light, undisturbed in their meandering tracks. The bass vibrated through the floor, and he could hear shrill laughter. He closed his eyes tightly, feeling a little like his stomach was trying to cram itself up and out of his throat. Just below the skin, everything was burning and tingling. He pressed his knuckles to his eyes, taking shuddering, empty breaths.

•   •   •

He woke up, and the lamp had gone out, leaving the room in darkness save for a slim ray of red light from across the way. The music had gone silent, too. Fergus sat up. He felt heavy – too heavy to remain erect – and after a moment, he shifted to press his forehead against the hard spiral binding of one of the diaries. He wanted to sleep longer, but at the same time, he felt asphyxiated and stranded in the empty room. His fingers restlessly pressed at the edge of one of the notebooks, perhaps remembering a nervous habit of Flynn's, for the edge was well worn.

He forced himself to sit up and after a moment pushed himself to his feet, leaving the darkened room and then the apartment. He stopped at a deli a few blocks away, still feeling weighted and lost. He stared dazedly up at the menu. The letters ran together. He rubbed his hand over his face. Still, the words swam and made no sense to him.

"Sorry about Flynn," the man behind the counter grunted. He leaned over the glass, clasping grimy, meaty hands together, and giving Fergus a sympathetic look under heavy brows.

Fergus smiled wanly, forcing his head to jerk up and down once, and thought of leaving then. Instead, he just ordered a tuna sandwich and one with everything and took the two bundles back with him to the shop as a peace offering. Ursula was sitting on a stool behind the counter, filing her nails. She glanced up at him with a look of disdain as he walked over to place the gift in front of her before looking back down at her nails.

"They say it all belongs to me," he said, unwrapping his and taking a bite. For all the sharpness of the vinegar and smoothness of the cheese and freshness of the lettuce, it tasted like sand. He swallowed roughly, studying the insides of his sandwich. "Dunno what I'm supposed to do with it, though."

"Sell what you can. Put the rest out on the curb, or just leave it there for the next person."

"They didn't take the rug."

"They probably don't need it."

He fingered a leaf of lettuce. "Yeah, guess not."

"I'll have someone remove it, if you like."

He nodded dumbly, still staring at the sandwich. Ursula sighed and picked hers up, delicately unwrapping it and taking a bite. She didn't look terribly impressed. Fergus tried, as well, to eat more of his own, but swallowing was hard, and the effort made his stomach twist.

"Maybe he did do it."

Ursula lifted an eyebrow.

"Maybe he killed himself. You're right. It would be really hard for someone to murder Flynn like that, and there were all those journals he'd kept, but none lately. So maybe he did it."

She said nothing in response, but watched him cautiously, slowly chewing.

"Everyone wants me to believe it. I bet even you do." He turned to her, finding her silence aggravating. "Well, say something!"

"You don't believe it," she calmly replied, wrapping the sandwich back up and setting it down. "Gut instincts are usually right." She paused. "This is what you want, right?"

"No, I don't want you to just say what you think I wanna hear. I want you to say what you think!"

"Flynn was only a customer to me. I was never close to him. I don't know what circles he moved in. I know practically nothing about him, so isn't it natural that I'd defer to you?"

Fergus opened his mouth and then shut it. For a moment, he could only scowl, but then he thought of something. "Where did you go last night?"

"Upstairs for a drink. I couldn't sleep."

"Really?"

"Wouldn't it be better to not ask if you don't want to accept the answer?"

"Fine."

At least, thanks to his frustration, his hunger returned, and finishing the sandwich turned out to be little problem. They made small talk for the rest of the afternoon until she set him to grating burdock root in the backroom. He had to admit, it was a little cathartic, though he caught his knuckles on the serrated bumps a few times in his vigor. He came out with the jar tucked under one arm and the knuckles of the other in his mouth.

"You have a visitor," Ursula said, nodding to the front of the store. Fergus turned and blinked in surprise at Terry's russet-haired, lanky form framed by the doorway. He was looking away, outside.

"Terry?" He walked over and was rewarded by a halfhearted smile.

"Thought you could stand to take a walk."

"Go on," Ursula bid him, going to toss out her sandwich.

•　　•　　•

They walked down to the docks. Terry didn't say anything the entire way. Fergus wasn't surprised and thought it probably was just the guy's way of showing that he'd been thinking of him. It was pretty nice of him. Just what he needed, even: he'd wanted a distraction, and here it was.

"Well, thanks for that," he started to say as they reached the busy markets.

The vendors were fervently bent on their last sales of the evening. The sun was long gone, hidden behind the black clouds rolling in from the west, and Fergus could feel that it would storm from way down in his bones. The water broke against the docks with increasing violence, sending foam into the air, which caught in his hair and on his cheeks. He wiped it away and looked hopefully towards the city where, at least, the effects of the storm could mostly be avoided.

Terry didn't budge. His pale eyes were fixed on the cloudy horizon and his mouth set in an unpromising line. Fergus shifted, trying to catch his gaze, leaning over a little to do so.

"What's wrong?" he asked, frowning.

"I knew Flynn."

Fergus said nothing, unsure of how to take this revelation.

"I knew him from above. We went to the same schools."

Fergus thought this explained a lot about Terry. There was a difference in disposition between hybrids born from another hybrid and raised in the slums all their lives and those raised by humans and exiled to the lower city. Flynn had always been upbeat about it, but he never went to the higher levels, and he would hardly even look at the lifts when they passed by. Still, Terry was more what Fergus was used to – reticent, surly, and secretive.

Probably things he'd learned in trying to hide his true identity from the family who would inevitably throw him out.

"There aren't that many schools, so it's not surprising. We weren't close, either. But his parents found out he was a hybrid and threw him out about two weeks before I left. I followed him down here, but I lost his trail. Well, that's not so important."

He had a grim set to his jaw that Fergus felt said otherwise, but he didn't argue, still waiting to see exactly where Terry was going with this.

"I didn't see him again until I met you. I don't think he even recognized me. We hadn't ever talked before. I only went after him because I didn't know what else to do. But seeing him again . . . he seemed the same as always." Terry paused, at last lifting a hand to run through his quickly soaking hair. Drizzle was starting to come down, making the air thick and wet, and it was hard to hear over the crash of the waves. "I do a lot of different jobs, so I hear a lot of different things. Maybe more than your Ursula."

"What kinda things?"

"There's a lot of turmoil right now. Surprised? We don't get much of the news from above here. Not the same way, at least. You know our governor? Callum Whitehurst? His term is nearly up. He's no hybrid sympathizer, but compared to his competition, he's our patron saint. You see, his competition is Paige Harriet, who hates hybrids with a burning passion. She's got a lot of people behind her, too."

"So what? Most people hate us. What's new about that?"

"She's rumored to have ties to Evalach."

"Eva-what?"

"Didn't think you'd know. The Knights of Evalach. No one is sure when they formed, but they've been active for about four months now, at least."

"Active doing what?"

"They're vigilantes, Fergus. Do you remember three months ago when Bunting's burned down, and those kids were caught inside? That was Evalach. They've done more than just that. They say they're only after 'dangerous' hybrids, but that could mean anything."

"Why are you telling me this?"

"Evalach isn't the only organization on the move. Hybrids have theirs, too. Niamh and Bandersnatch."

Fergus stared at him in utter confusion.

Terry ran a hand over his face, wiping away the drizzle. "Bandersnatch is bad news. They seem to be led by a masked man who calls himself, 'Badb Catha.' Some would say they're hedonists. They do whatever they want without thinking about it. I don't know a whole lot about it, but supposedly they know how to strip other hybrids of their powers – how to take other hybrids' powers."

"What? How?"

"I don't know. But it apparently adds to their lifespan and their own powers. That's what people say, at least."

"What happens if someone takes your powers?"

"You die. That's what happened to all the hybrids who've been exorcised, at least. If the fairy-soul is removed, the body dies of shock, and the human part of the soul is also destroyed."

"Oh. So . . . these Knights and Bandersnatch . . . are at war?"

"Not exactly, though you'd think that's who Evalach would want. But it seems like either they don't know about Bandersnatch, or there's something else going on."

"I don't get it."

Terry shook his head. "Just listen, okay? About two months ago, a hybrid started getting attention on the upper levels."

"How?"

"Not all hybrids are stuck down here, you know."

Fergus scowled a little. "Yeah, but why should we care what the ones sucking up to the humans do?"

Terry ignored him. "This person calls herself Fand. She's the leader of Niamh. It's mostly hybrids who're on good terms with the humans."

"Again, why do we care?"

"Do you really need this history lesson?"

Fergus's scowl grew.

"You know why hybrids exist, right? Because of the Cataclysm, fairies that had been in the human world were also killed, only their souls didn't go anywhere. They were just wandering around lost. The Cataclysm didn't just change the surface of the Earth; it tore down the wall between the fairies and the humans. The fairies' souls needed new bodies, so they turned to the humans. It's why things are like this – because the souls latched onto children, since their personalities were not yet fully formed and their spirits weakest. It caused a rift.

"The humans said the Cataclysm was the wrath of God. The hybrids said it was because humans destroyed nature with their greed. For decades, the two groups were at odds. Often violently so. In New Peiling, the fighting lasted until Whitehurst became governor and reorganized the city's security."

"Guess I slept through this part of history," Fergus muttered and pushed his dripping hair from his face. The storm was making him increasingly jumpy, but he tried to ignore it. "So, why is Niamh important, then?"

"You probably know that there are places all around where actual, full fairies live. It's not like we're treated great here in the human world, but most of the hybrids who try to rejoin the fairies are killed on the spot. Niamh believes that there's a way for us to become full fairies and return to the homeland. That there is a way to find Tír na nÓg."

Fergus raised an eyebrow. "That sounds pretty much impossible."

"Maybe. I don't know. But maybe it's not. Niamh seems to spend a lot of time researching the Cataclysm and ways to restore our bodies. A lot of students are involved with it."

"Flynn?"

"I'm not really sure, but it's not impossible."

"So . . . you're saying the Knights killed him? Or Bandersnatch?"

"I don't know."

"Then why . . .?" Fergus asked, waving one hand wildly.

"I like the band. It's probably the only good thing that's happened to me . . . maybe ever. So I don't want you to go off and get yourself killed. Getting involved with any of them is bad news."

"Even Niamh?"

"Maybe so." Terry let out a soft sigh, squinting against the rain. He reached out, putting a hand on Fergus's shoulder. "Flynn didn't seem like the kind of guy who'd want you meddling in this. So just don't, okay?"

Fergus nodded slowly. "Okay."

"We have a gig in two nights. Don't forget," Terry said, releasing his shoulder and fading away into the haze of rain.

Fergus sighed, feeling rain dripping down the back of his neck and soaking the toes of his trainers. His socks were soggy, his head was killing him, and he didn't have a clue about what he should do with this new information, so he turned and trudged back to Ursula's.

Chapter Four.

Fergus packed up the apartment. He sold the posters, the clothing, and most of the furniture. He kept Flynn's bookcase, because it was better than his own, and the journals. The rest he either sold or stuck out onto the curb until there was only the couch, his bed, the bookcase, and the aquarium in the flat. Ursula offered to let him bring the fish over, but the tank was heavy, and he hadn't gotten to that yet, just as she hadn't found him a new place. She was, however, spending more and more time upstairs, and so Fergus began to think she had perhaps forgotten that offer and was now assuming that he'd take up the quest on his own.

It wasn't easy to find a place in the lower city. There were plenty of abandoned buildings and rooms, but one had to fight tooth and nail to maintain their possessions to stay there. It would be nice to stay with Ursula, but her fancies changed on a whim, and just as she had vacillated towards him a few weeks ago, she seemed to have renewed her relationship with Madam Dominique – the proprietor or proprietress (no one was entirely sure which, though most went with "proprietress") of the burlesque house, the Labyrinth, above Beathag's. Dominique was probably the only semi-serious relationship Ursula had maintained for any period of time.

So he was all too aware that any night he was allowed to stay over was borrowed time. He asked around at practice, but Terry was more nomadic than Fergus had ever reckoned on, and Raja and Evelyn were staying in one of her friends' basements. It didn't look terribly hopeful. Still, he didn't want to return to the old apartment, and he didn't want to live on the street when Ursula inevitably tossed him out, so he kept at it. He needed a better job, he decided. He had a little extra money from clearing out the apartment, but it wouldn't last him more than a month in a decent unit. He wasn't a big fan of his options.

And then, at last, Ursula supplied an answer.

"Oh, they call him all sorts of things," Ursula remarked, waving a hand dismissively.

"He's weird."

"He's normal enough for our kind. When you talk like a human, it annoys me," she scowled. "It pays well, doesn't it? And wouldn't you still be able to help around here?"

"I guess."

"You've done this sort of thing before, too, for Felix at the Magpie. All you have to do is bring things when he calls for them, take them away when he dismisses them, and tidy up."

Fergus frowned. More money would be great, and it sounded like an easy job, but that was only how it sounded. When he thought about it, working for a guy who called himself "the Count Palatine" made it seem like it would be a great deal more complicated. Anyone who gave himself such an ostentatious alias was bound to be picky, arrogant, and temperamental, and Fergus had an issue with those things. However, he *would* have enough money to live somewhere nicer and plenty of time for music. He spent the afternoon crushing moon snail shells and warring with himself over it, but at length, he agreed to meet the Count.

•   •   •

The Count Palatine was a short, tow-headed man with freckles running from one cheek to the other. His head was a mop of unkempt curls, his green eyes all but actually twinkled, and his cheeky grin made Fergus want to hit him. He ground his teeth and restrained himself, but despite Ursula's sharp elbow to his ribs, he couldn't force a smile. Grinning obnoxiously, the Count looked him up and down, rubbing his chin. Fergus's mouth twitched, but only turned into a deeper frown, especially when the Count stood on tiptoes to look straight into his face.

"I can see why you're Ursula's flavor of the day," he remarked, finally stepping away. "But do you have any social graces?" he asked, brows rising.

Fergus opened his mouth, eyes narrowing sharply.

Ursula cut him off. "Of course . . . Once he's warmed up a bit. Are you implying that I'd keep a thug for a companion?" she smiled, crossing her arms over her chest.

Fergus let out a soft snort, shaking his hair into his face, and tried again to smile, so that they'd at least stop talking like he wasn't even there. He felt a little like he was being paraded about, like a pony at a fair; it did not please him.

"You've worked in hospitality?"

"Yeah, at the Magpie for about three years."

"And I suppose you've been at Beathag's as long?" the Count remarked, glancing sideways at Ursula.

Fergus couldn't see her reaction, but he nodded.

"What can you do?"

Fergus watched him swirling his spoon around the remains of his coffee, finding that easier to focus on. He cleared his throat a little awkwardly. "Um, sing, I guess. Play guitar. I'm kinda strong."

"Can you make drinks?"

"He can learn," Ursula interjected, patting him on the shoulder and smiling intently.

"Guess you are pretty young. Fair enough. I'll take you on for a trial period. This is my address," he said, holding out a lavender and silver card. Fergus struggled not to make a face as he took it, glancing over the details. "Be there by eight tonight."

Fergus forced his mouth to twitch into something like a smile and nodded.

"And do something about his . . . attire," the Count said to Ursula, pursing his mouth.

Ursula laughed. Fergus glared. The Count left.

"Well, I suppose we should replace those rags."

"Rags?!" he snarled.

"You've probably been wearing those jeans since you were 15."

"I've grown since then, you know."

"Well, it's on me, so don't complain."

Fergus gave in and – after finishing his coffee – allowed her to take him to a boutique nestled in an alleyway near the docks. The trousers felt tight in all the wrong places, and he was sure the shirt was cutting off his circulation, but Ursula said it suited him. He still felt like a kid forced into Sunday clothes, but then she slipped through the curtain behind him, and he felt it was worth his while.

•   •   •

Fergus was in a better mood by eight, as he boarded the glass lift that would take him up two levels to the Count's penthouse. He was even starting to feel a little excited as he exited and followed Ursula's map up the street to the brownstone across from a large glowing fountain with mermaids at its center. He was greeted by a stern looking brunette in a black dress and apron, who introduced herself as Deirdre. They nearly matched, he realized. They were soon to be a perfect set, as she took him to the kitchen and stores to show him what was where on a tour ending with an apron. Unlike hers, it didn't have frills, but he was nonetheless filled with misgivings as he tied it on.

He eyed the multitude of closed doors reproachfully as they returned to the kitchen. "What's he need all these rooms for anyway?" he asked, but Deirdre ignored him. He sighed.

Deirdre was pretty, though, putting aside the fact that she looked like she might slap him at any minute. She had a long, slim face and a full mouth that almost seemed too large for the rest of her features, but it worked for her. Moreover, at least on this first evening of work, it seemed he wasn't going to be asked to directly serve his new employer. Instead, he was put to work peeling and slicing vegetables and washing dishes, which Deirdre seemed to return endlessly. It was worse than even the busiest nights at the Magpie.

"Is he having a party or something?" Fergus asked, the sleeves of his black dress shirt rolled up to his elbows and his forearms submerged in suds.

"No, this is normal. He just fired a staff member, so Audrey and I are making up the slack until you become acclimated."

"Audrey?"

"You haven't seen her yet. She's shy."

He nodded, and she dumped a fresh load of silverware into the water. He bit back a groan and doggedly continued scrubbing.

"So, who's up there?"

Deirdre gave him a look, crossing her arms over her stomach. "He sees many notables from all over the city and abroad. It's unwise to pry."

This only made Fergus more curious, and so when at last the supper dishes had all been brought down and washed, and only coffee and sweets were out, he slipped from the kitchen to poke around. The dining room was not on the same floor he soon found. He had to go through a dark corridor from the kitchen, up a narrow flight of stairs, and past a room emitting steam and a hint of ginger, which he thought was the shower. The door was open, but he elected not to peek inside, just in case. He heard the hum of laughter coming from down the hall. Stuffing his hands into his back pockets, he made his way towards it.

A sliver of light escaped the room at the end of the hall. He slowed his steps, shuffling as quietly as he could as he approached the door. It wasn't really shut, but it wasn't really open. Fergus got the impression the Count didn't care about privacy in his own domain. Still, it was closed enough that it did feel a bit like spying. That didn't stop him. He was at a very poor vantage point, but he could still see the Count sitting at the top of the table with at least five guests to either side. He didn't recognize any of them, and it took him a moment to work out what was going on.

It seemed the pretty woman to the left wasn't simply leaning over to hear a secret, because the Count appeared to be nibbling on her neck. That was a little licentious, but not really shocking – not compared to what the Count was doing to the man on the other side. If Fergus was seeing what he thought he was seeing, it appeared that he had his hand down the front of the man's trousers. The man had a glassy look – his cheeks reddened, and mouth parted – and for a moment, it seemed that their eyes met. That strange, feverish gaze gave him a trill of alarm, and Fergus stumbled back just in time to feel a gentle pull on his elbow.

He turned to see a short girl with a round face and averted eyes. She was turning a funny shade of red. He started to ask if she was okay, but she held a finger to her lips. She had a bottle on the tray balanced on her other arm, and after a moment, she nodded for him to step aside and slipped into the room. There was a short exchange – laughter and a little cry of surprise – but Fergus didn't look to see what was happening before she returned, empty-handed and staring at the floor. She gestured for him to follow her as she slipped back down the corridor.

When it seemed they were a safe distance away, he finally ventured, "Audrey?"

She nodded, mousy-colored fringe falling in her face.

"Um, thanks," he wagered, figuring it would've been bad if he'd been caught by Deirdre.

"It's fine," she mumbled, still intent on his feet and shifting subtly back from him.

"Um, what was . . .?" he asked, unable to help himself.

"Dignitaries," she paused briefly before adding, "from Lancaster."

"And . . .?"

She turned red, her cheeks seeming to inflate, and Fergus felt sorry for pressing her. He held up his hands apologetically. "Don't worry. None of my business, right? So how long have you worked here?"

"Two years." She pursed her mouth and then said, "Come. If Deirdre finds you've left the kitchen . . . " she trailed off, shaking her head.

He laughed uncertainly, rubbing the back of his neck. "Yeah, good idea."

•　　•　　•

Later, as he lounged in bed with Ursula, he recounted the scene. She snorted.

"Gave you a shock, did it? Well, it's just as you feared. He's a *gancanagh*, you see, but he doesn't really fancy women – not one bit. Still, he can hardly keep them off him. He goes through a good many wives to reach their husbands. Probably, he was thinking that he might land himself a reasonable trade route if he pleased the both of them with his 'entertainment.' Well, no one's entirely sure what he has his hands in, but generally speaking, he's in the airship business. Even the Air Guard is rumored to be supplied by him."

"He's that important?"

Ursula nodded. "And because he has a good bit of sway over travel in and out of the city, he's managed to weasel his way into a good many other ventures – like politics. It would be best if you didn't let your curiosity get the better of you again."

Fergus nodded, putting out his cigarette, and rolled over to sleep.

He was jarred awake by shouting coming from outside the room. He pulled on a pair of jeans and crawled over the stacks of books to the door. To the left lay the kitchen, bath, and sitting room, and to the right, the shop. He tiptoed down the corridor to the right. As he had guessed, one of the voices belonged to Ursula, but the other voice, deeper and huskier, was a woman made tall by stiletto boots with bronze skin and long black hair pulled up into an elaborate coif – Madam Dominique.

"So, then you'll just have me in the afternoons, is it? Like I'm a bloody cup of tea?"

"If you're going to be like this, I won't have you at all. How long have I entertained you, and why do you think anything has changed?"

"Because you're living with the kid."

"Did you want to live with me? You certainly never made a peep about it before now."

"Well, no, but . . ."

Fergus slipped behind a shelf of dried snakes and turtle parts. He couldn't recall a time when he hadn't known of Madam Dominique. Moreover, he'd been acquainted with her since he'd started working for Ursula. He'd even gone to a show once or twice and had held meaningless conversations with her. Besides the fact that she owned the burlesque house over the magic shop and was uncertain in gender, all he really knew about her was that she had an on and off again relationship with Ursula, which he'd been aware of for as long as the rest.

It wasn't that their relationship was unbelievable, but at the same time, to walk in on their lovers' quarrel was awkward, and it also made him jealous and angry. He could feel dark, hot emotion closing his throat, pressing against the walls of his chest, and he bit his tongue and closed his eyes for a moment to keep from storming into the scene. It sounded volatile enough already.

"So the poor, homeless urchin moves in, and I'm shuffled off to the side after all these years. Is that how it is?"

"You're the only one who thinks so."

"Well, it certainly feels that way!"

There was a pregnant pause in which the two stared at each other, but said nothing. Ursula was, as Fergus knew from experience, a champion in this realm, and it seemed her title wasn't going to be challenged today, because as she stood there looking calm and haughty, Dominique turned away with a sound of disgust. For a moment, Fergus's heart caught in his throat. He thought he'd been spotted, but luckily, it seemed both were too embroiled in their own anger to spot him. He let out a soft sigh of relief and thought he certainly was doing a lot of sneaking around lately.

"Don't tell me you regret *that* of all things."

"Of course not."

"Then tell me what it is. Why don't you just kick him out?"

"Because it pleases me to keep him around."

"*Pleases* you? *Pleases you?*" Dominique demanded and stepped closer, so that he could hardly see Ursula around her. Fergus shifted, hands tightening into fists. He could just make out the top of her face; her eyes were wide and uncertain for once.

"What are you doing?" she demanded.

"I'm asking you what part of that uneducated, unrefined whelp 'pleases you' so much that you've kept him on like this. What, *that*?"

Ursula snorted, but said nothing.

"Unbelievable. On that alone . . . "

"It isn't that alone, or I would have tossed you both out already." Her green eyes shifted, catching Fergus's gaze for a moment, and he cringed. Dominique missed the shift in attention.

"Well, obviously, you're in the mood for slumming it," she growled.

Even Fergus was surprised at the sound of skin striking skin. Ursula's eyes were slits, and he could see her nursing her hand, breathing heavily.

"Never presume that you may speak to me like that. Whatever I do is my business, and I would think after seven years, you'd recall that much."

There was a moment of silence. He imagined that had they hackles, they'd be on end. The quiet was broken by a loud crash as Dominique knocked a whole rack of vials from the counter.

"Well, that's not going to be cheap," Ursula remarked.

"You're lucky it wasn't you."

"Hey!" Fergus found that he had rather unfortunately cried out without thinking. There was no point in trying to hide, so he stepped out into the open, feeling very vulnerable under the full force of Ursula's and Dominique's glares. Unsure of how to react, he fell back on anger. "I don't care if you've just got some twisted sense of humor or what, but you have no right to say that to her."

"Fergus, it's fine."

"Oh, I see. So now you're writing the rules on what I can and can't say to the woman I've been with since you were in grammar school."

"Yeah, I am, 'cause if you don't know better at your age . . . "

"Fergus, stop."

This time, they both went silent, turning to her. She looked angry. Fergus had never seen her angry before, not to mention this angry. He bit back his next remark. Dominique also remained quiet.

"I do not require an idiot knight-in-shining-armor," she said to Fergus. "And I do not require a boorish cry baby either," she added to Dominique. "Both of you displease me. Leave."

Fergus stared at her for a moment, but she obstinately looked away, so he shrugged, muttered a soft, "whatever," and went outside without even his shirt or shoes. Dominique followed, joining him a moment later. The stairs to her place were in an enclave just to the side, but she did not immediately climb them, but rather paused to scowl at him.

"What do you want?" he snapped.

"I want you to go."

"Well, I want *you* to go, so – I dunno – how about *screw you*?"

Dominique's eyes narrowed. "Uncouth dog," she muttered, starting up the stairs, but she made sure to continue her grumbling audibly the entire way. "Doesn't even realize when its master has betrayed it. It'll probably end up just – the – same."

The door slammed, and Fergus was left with those bitter words, half-naked in the street. He sighed and sat on the curb. He didn't have anywhere else to go, so he simply waited for Ursula to come out and let him back in. There was plenty of time to stew on Dominique's words until then.

He started noticing peculiarities: how Ursula had waylaid him the night of Flynn's death, the way she had come to collect him outside the liquor store, how she had avoided questions and demanded he stop asking them, and how she had let him stay with her for so long. She wasn't normally this charitable, and the more he thought about it all, the more he began to wonder. Did she have some role in Flynn's death? And if she did, would she go through the trouble of hiding it? She'd never invested that much in his wellbeing, or his opinion, before.

He couldn't think of a single reason why she'd try to shelter him, so he figured Dominique must have made the implication out of spite. Yet he found that once the doubt had taken root in his mind, it was hard to shake. By the time Ursula came out to tell him to get back inside, get dressed, and get to work, he was feeling very confused and suspicious.

He stared at her for a long moment, but in the end said nothing and went inside.

Chapter Five.

Fergus did not bring it up. Though he did see Dominique outside now and then, they had arrived at an unspoken agreement to simply ignore each other. There was a kind of smugness about her – she knew she'd sown doubt remarkably well – and it made him want to punch her, so he thought it better to pretend he never saw her around. Things settled down, the way time tends to ease things, though it didn't hurt that Fergus was never required to do more than dishes at the Count Palatine's house, nor that Ursula was being nice to him again and had not thrown him out. Everyday Resources was going well, too, though Evelyn and Raja kept showing up to practice late, which Fergus found annoying.

He was sitting on an old folding chair, the back rusted out, and tuning his guitar. It was about 7:15 P.M., and he and Terry were alone. Fifteen minutes ticked into 20, and Fergus started to feel really irritated.

"Tighten 'em much more, and you'll snap the strings," Terry remarked as Fergus's guitar let out a loud, angry *twang*.

He blinked, looking up. "Oh, yeah," he muttered, adjusting it.

"Used to be that only I was ever late," Terry said, running his thumb along the bass guitar's strings. They let out a low thrum of sound. "And that was only for work."

Fergus stopped adjusting his guitar and rested his arms over it, studying Terry. "It's weird to see you annoyed," he said at length. And it was weird. It was so weird that he forgot to be angry himself. "Everything okay?"

"Yeah," Terry replied, fiddling with the pegs. "Just the job I'm doing right now's stressful."

"What kind of job is it?"

"Strong arm work at the docks. My boss is just . . . particular and short-tempered."

"Tell me about it," muttered Fergus.

Terry hummed, which made him look up and frown.

"What?"

"People are noticing. She's kept you for nearly a month. First time ever."

"Yeah," Fergus replied, and his frown deepened.

"Are you growing tired of it?"

"It's not really that."

Terry lifted an eyebrow, and Fergus sighed.

"It's just hard to trust her sometimes."

"Well," Terry paused before adding, "yes."

"I mean, it's not like it's a surprise. I've known her reputation for years. I've worked for her for years. Just, lately, I feel confused."

"Have you fallen for her?" Terry asked, not bothering to hide the hint of dread in his voice.

"No," Fergus replied defensively.

"You always let yourself get confused. Probably why women walk all over you." Terry paused. "Probably why they like you so much."

"What does that mean?"

"Fergus Irvine, tortured rock star. Women like that."

"I'm not tortured," he scoffed.

"No," Terry agreed, "but you are moody. Especially when you like a girl."

Fergus didn't reply, but glowered at the worn out toe of his trainers.

"I heard she got you a better job."

"Yeah, it pays well, at least."

"Are you going to stop working for her?"

"Probably not. She still seems to want me on."

Terry nodded and put his bass aside. "I've worked for that guy before."

"What? Really?"

"He can be hard to deal with."

"So far, I'm just washing dishes."

"He won't forget about you forever."

Fergus considered this for a moment before asking, "You don't think he wants . . .?"

"He always wants. Question is whether he takes."

Fergus sat up, feeling alarmed, but before he could ask what exactly Terry meant by "take," Raja and Evelyn finally arrived.

He stood, remembering to be angry. "Do you know how many times you've been late recently? In the last week, even?"

Evelyn blinked, staring at him wide-eyed for a moment, but her expression quickly turned stony. "We had things to do," she replied, crossing her arms over her chest.

"Do them when it's not time for practice," Fergus snapped and was surprised to hear Terry echoing him.

Raja and Evelyn both blinked at that, ignoring Fergus to stare at the redhead. At length, Evelyn muttered, "Sorry," and took out her guitar. Raja said nothing, but idly tapped one of the cymbals, staring off into space. Fergus turned back to Terry, giving him a thankful nod.

•　　•　　•

Despite that, they did not make it a point to come earlier, and three days later, Fergus found that he had to abandon practice altogether to get ready to go to the Count's where he would be helping out with an actual party. Deirdre had asked him to poke around for extra help, and so he'd asked Terry who didn't look incredibly eager, but agreed nonetheless. He wasn't sure what the gala was about, but it seemed it was the first time that he'd actually be serving, so Ursula had gotten him a new shirt to go with his black trousers. She was already dressed in a black cocktail dress when he returned to the shop and hardly said a word to him before she left. He didn't even have a chance to ask if she wanted to go together. Feeling a little ruffled, Fergus braved the remnant steam and got ready.

When he arrived, the doors hadn't yet opened. Deirdre was sitting out back smoking with Terry with an unusually aggravated look on her face. Audrey was nowhere to be seen.

"Yo," Fergus said, lifting a hand in greeting.

Deirdre said nothing, but Terry gave him a nod and shifted the carton to knock a cigarette free, offering it to him. Fergus thankfully took it and stood against a lion statue, observing the other two. They both looked very smart in their black, formal attire. Terry's hair looked redder than usual and Deirdre's face whiter, like a doll's. She took a long drag and spewed it out through her nose, looking up at him at last.

"Terry has done a party like this before, so he'll be babysitting you for the evening."

Fergus nodded uncertainly, glancing at him. She stood, and Terry put out his cigarette on his trainers, tucking it back into the carton for later. Fergus did the same. Inside, they were met with an entire troop of new faces, being ordered about by the cook – a grim old woman whose features were half-hidden in folds of skin. Her hoarse voice echoed through the kitchen as she argued with a younger man who looked considerably more distinguished. Fergus noticed that she had pulled back her frizzy hair, and her apron was lacking the usual smears of sauce and grease stains. Still, she looked like she had come in from the street compared to the guest chef in his clean white outfit.

They were arguing over the contents of a large pot, but Fergus didn't have time to see what it was before Deirdre shoved him into the cupboard with Terry and told them to tidy themselves.

Terry took the trouble to try to fix Fergus's mop of hair and straighten his collar. He even produced a tie, which Fergus could only assume came from Deirdre, and tied it for him. He felt weird when they stepped out, but no sooner had he emerged and started fiddling with the tie than Deirdre was right there, smacking him on the hand, telling him to leave it, and pressing a crystal tray of sparkling champagne flutes into his hands. She then directed him and Terry to go upstairs to the dining area immediately.

"You may hear some interesting things tonight," Terry said, "but think twice – no, three times – about just who you share them with. Even small secrets can come back to haunt you. And above all, avoid the large, freckled man with long ears. His name is Trevor Fennis, and he's said to be an important member of *that* group."

Fergus opened his mouth to press, because there probably was going to be more than one guy with freckles and big ears, but they'd already reached the room, and Terry pushed opened the double doors and slipped inside. Fergus was left behind, but he didn't even notice. Inside was a sea of red and gold, practically glowing under dozens upon dozens of small candles in globes crisscrossing the room. There was something foreign and heady in the air, and it made him feel a little lightheaded. As he took his first stumbling steps into the room, he nearly ran into one of the guests and sent his tray splashing all over. It took a rather impressive display of juggling to keep them both dry.

"Not bad," said a deep voice.

Fergus looked up at the man he'd nearly doused: a man nearly twice Fergus in width with a fraying tuft of blonde hair slicked to the side, freckles, and strangely elongated ears. He smelled strongly of garlic. Fergus's apology caught in his throat as he stared at the man he could only assume to be Fennis.

"It's all right, son. You may speak. You must be native to this level. You don't see those kinds of manners below."

"S-sorry," Fergus managed, swallowing his irritation. "Would you like a drink?"

"Don't mind if I do." Fennis took one of the flutes, dwarfing it in a large, knotted hand.

Fergus took the opportunity to really look around. Encapsulating the reds and golds from above and below were sheets of semi-transparent fabric presumably set up to resemble the night sky and grass. Not fake grass, either, but lush, thick grass even better than Erstwyre Park's lawn. Fergus stared down at it in amazement, wondering how much it had cost to bring in, or if it could even be real.

Fennis was already disappearing into the crowd, his other meaty hand clasping the shoulder of some greying dignitary, and Fergus let out a sigh of relief. He scanned the room for Terry, Deirdre, or Audrey. Instead, he spotted Ursula, who was getting very cozy with an athletic looking blonde man, and he found himself immediately seething.

Before he could stalk over, however, he felt a tap on his shoulder. He expected to see a coworker, but was entirely surprised to find a pretty redheaded girl looking up at him. Her dark curls were half-pulled back on one side, but cascaded freely over her shoulders. Her nose was dotted with freckles, and it was a very nice nose, too. She smiled at him under heavy lashes framing light blue eyes and twisted a lock of hair around one finger. He didn't recognize her, but he felt like he should have.

"May I have one?" she asked, indicating the tray of glasses.

"Oh yeah, sure," he mumbled, handing her a flute of champagne and turning red.

She smiled, taking it, but didn't leave.

"Can I get you something else?" he asked.

Her expression faltered. "Jane," she suddenly said. "It's Jane. I came to your shop. I wanted to give you my details, but . . . " she trailed off, glancing over her shoulder towards Ursula.

Fergus blinked, failing to comprehend, and then it hit him. "Oh. From the shop. Yeah. Uh, hi."

"Hi? That's all?" she asked, pouting. Her mouth was very small and round and glossy.

"Uh, funny meeting you here?" he tried. "Aren't you a student?"

She laughed, tossing her head back, and he could see the curve of her breast pressing against the embroidered front of her dress; he thought she suddenly looked a lot more familiar.

"Yes, I am," she agreed, tilting her head to the side. "But my family had business dealings with the Count Palatine."

"Airships, huh?"

She gave a vague nod.

He gave her a serious study this time, looking for a mark – something that might reveal if she was a human or a hybrid. That's when he noticed that she had taken off her shoes, which were dangling by the straps in her other hand. She smiled at him over the rim of her glass.

"You might be stepped on," he pointed out, feeling obvious and stupid.

"Already have," she replied, "but it's rare to be able to curl your toes around grass like this. You should take yours off, too."

"Don't think he'd approve."

They said nothing for a moment. Her eyes were lowered to the glass, and he thought he could see golden flecks in her lashes.

"Do you want to go outside?" she asked, head still lowered.

"I'm kinda working," he mumbled, rubbing the back of his head.

"Hmm. Well, I suppose he would be angry if he didn't have a chance to show off his staff. He's very selective, you know."

"Oh?"

"They say that woman with the black hair – the one who manages everything . . . "

"Deirdre?"

"Yes, her. They say she's the subject of at least two important paintings debuting this year. Another left for Clohaven to model in the big department store. He'll be modeling for the Count at the big airship fair next spring, too."

"Huh."

"Perhaps this is your big chance."

"Not interested."

"Really? What are you interested in?"

Fergus stared at her for a moment, frowning, before muttering, "Music."

She blinked. "Music? What kind of music?"

"Uh, rock, I guess. There's a band. We . . . "

"Oh, wait, I remember! Everyday Resources, right? Flynn told me about it."

Fergus cringed.

"Oh, sorry," she said unapologetically. "I was going to come to a show with him, but curfew on this level is early."

He wrinkled his nose, thinking, *Human*.

Perhaps she caught the expression, because she frowned at him, but her face softened as she continued, "Well, whatever he's agreed to pay you for the evening, I'll double it if you'll come for a walk with me."

Fergus recoiled. "I dunno what you've heard about me, but it sounds like you've got it wrong."

She blinked. She was either a very good actress, or quite honestly surprised that he'd taken offense. "What . . .? Oh, no! No, I just wanted to walk with you and talk where others won't pry . . . "

"Look, I earn a living honestly. I work for it, like everyone else from down there, and . . . "

He was cut off as Terry suddenly appeared at his shoulder, subtly moving in front of him. Jane schooled her expression as she met his eyes and smiled. Terry was likewise cordial, but the hairs on the back of Fergus's neck were prickling.

"Fergus, at least pretend like you aren't just here for the ladies," Terry remarked with a forced joviality.

"Oh, he wasn't bothering me at all," chuckled Jane.

"Well, I've run out of drinks, and that side of the room is still thirsty, so . . . "

He nudged Fergus away from Jane, and Fergus felt relieved. Casting a quick, thankful smile Terry's way, he allowed himself to be sucked up into the crowd.

Chapter Six.

Unfortunately, it seemed getting lost in the crowd for the rest of the night was out. He managed to slip through the throngs of people without interference for about an hour before his tray was once again empty, and he had to head back to the kitchens, or he would have, except Jane was persistent. He'd seen flashes of her hair through the crowd for the last 30 minutes, and he was pretty sure she was following him. It was flattering, but he also couldn't shake the inexplicably uneasy feeling he'd had since the altercation with Terry. So he tried to go the other way whenever he spotted her, but at last, she outmaneuvered him. Before he could make it through the doors, she appeared, barring the way.

"Is this déjà vu or something?" he muttered.

"No, it's a certain repeat," she cheerfully replied. "Here we are once more."

"Here we are," he echoed.

"I think you're avoiding me."

"I'm just working."

"Well, my glass has been empty for at least half an hour," she replied, one hand going to her hip and holding the empty flute out with the other.

Fergus took it and put it back on his tray. "I'll be back with more in a minute."

"No, that really isn't good enough. You *have* been avoiding me, leaving me to go parched, and now you owe me."

"Owe you?"

"Yes, you owe me a dance."

"I'm work—"

She held up a finger to his mouth, shaking her head. "If you just dance with me this once, I'll leave you alone for the rest of the night."

Fergus looked over his shoulder.

"No one is watching. It's just five minutes tops."

He sighed. "Okay, but if I get fired . . . "

"I'll tell him to hire you again. He can't expect you to resist my charms, can he?"

Fergus lifted an eyebrow, wondering if she was just trying to be cute. He snorted softly, but put his tray down on a nearby table and held out his hand.

"Apron, too. This is a society event, you know."

He gritted his teeth, but did it, dropping the apron down next to the discarded tray and holding out his hand once more. He really hoped Deirdre didn't come by and find it. Jane took it and made a beeline to the center of the dance floor.

"Do you know how to do a box step?"

"Nope."

"Follow me. I'm sure you'll pick it up in no time," she said, putting one of his hands on her side before lightly placing her other hand on his shoulder. He looked down as she stepped backward and then did his best to follow the steps, though her cleavage was distracting.

"Is it really so bad?"

"What?" he asked and stumbled, just missing her bare feet.

"Dancing with me."

"Not really."

"Then why wouldn't you go for a walk with me?"

"Because I'm working."

"Okay, but why wouldn't you *really*?"

He frowned, saying nothing, and followed her steps as she moved to put them at an angle. She was pretty. It wasn't like pretty girls just threw themselves at him all the time. He was pretty sure that Ursula was a total fluke. He just didn't feel happy about Jane's interest. Besides feeling belittled, there was the fact he'd met her in the near immediate aftermath of finding Flynn hanged in his bedroom. It was hard not to associate the two things. On top of all that, he got the feeling this girl's doe eyes and marshmallow fluff sweetness was an act. It didn't sit right, and it made him uneasy. He didn't know how to say it, though, or that he even should. Actually, he knew he really shouldn't.

"I don't know," he finally replied.

"You certainly thought about it long enough to not come to a conclusion."

His mouth formed a tight line as he pointedly looked down at their feet. He had an idea of how this dance went by now, but he felt stubborn and didn't want to be helpful in any way, even if it was just to take control of their steps. However, even though he felt like being difficult, he didn't want to just say she rubbed him the wrong way. He couldn't think of anyone – man or woman – who would appreciate that.

"It's just that I've heard so much about you," she continued with a sigh, leaning a little closer. "And Flynn – he talked about you all the time, so it's like you're . . . "

"Stop it," he snapped, abruptly planting his feet.

"I'm sorry," she replied, "trying" to steady herself and falling against him in the process. He didn't shove her away, but simply stood as though indifference alone could set him apart. "You're probably more upset than anyone. At least, if you felt the same way . . . Maybe he never mentioned me. Even so, we were . . . very close."

Fergus's eyebrows knitted, his head tilting slightly. Flynn hadn't ever mentioned her, but then, there were nearly as many nights that he'd been out until dawn or later as Fergus had. That he might have had some kind of semi-steady thing in the background wasn't surprising, but this girl? She didn't really seem his type. He figured Flynn would prefer a bookish girl with glasses and an over-fondness for library stacks. Maybe like Audrey if Audrey wore spectacles.

Knowing that Jane might have really meant something to Flynn and watching her be so solicitous made him feel even more uncomfortable. But then, what if he was just misreading her friendliness? If she was telling the truth, she might have been almost as close to Flynn as he was, and he couldn't help but harbor a tiny fellow feeling for her. He didn't really know what to think, but his body beat his brain to a reaction. His face softened before he had a chance to school it, and a relieved smile filled hers.

"I know you don't want to talk about him, but I really do. If we could . . . "

His mouth twitched downwards, because he really *didn't* want to, but at the same time, he knew how she felt. He sighed and reluctantly nodded.

"Really?" she asked, face lighting up.

"Yeah, really. Guess you already know where I work, so . . . "

"How about tomorrow afternoon? No, wait. I have class. The day after?"

"Yeah, sure," he mumbled.

"Great! Well, I suppose the song is over, so I'll let you go back to work. Fly away, Mr. Irvine. Get to work and all that."

He rolled his eyes, but his treacherous mouth twitched into a smile as he slipped away.

His platter was gone. Terry was in its place, looking grave. He took Fergus by the arm as soon as he came close, and he thought probably he was about to mention Jane, or that Deirdre had found out he'd been slacking, but all he said was, "We're needed upstairs," and nodded to the door.

He wondered why they were being summoned. As they walked, his mind started supplying ideas, like maybe the Count had brought someone up and made a mess, which was okay as long as it was *just* wine or food, or maybe he hadn't forgotten about Fergus and was planning that "taking" Terry had implied before. He felt a jolt of panic, but before he could demand an explanation, Terry turned off into a corridor Fergus had never been down before.

It was too dark to easily make out his surrounds, but a number of surrealist paintings lined the walls. There was just enough light illuminating them that Fergus kept catching glimpses of strange faces and beasts out of the corner of his eye and jumping. Even without a decent light source, he could see that the paintings were large and grandiose. He wondered why they were tucked away in the shadows.

"He's strange," Terry suddenly said, glancing back at him. "He painted all of them, but he's never bothered showing them, nor selling them. Instead, they're all just stuck in this back corridor."

Fergus moved closer to the wall to get a better look, but Terry was briskly moving ahead, and it was hard to keep up and study the paintings. Mostly he caught strange organic smudges and wild twists of color. However, as they neared the end of the hallway, one scene caught his eye. Despite the poor lighting, the contrast in the painting made it stick out. The background was mostly black; if there was any variation, it had been swallowed up by the gloom. The central image was presumably a rendering of the Wild Hunt. Misshapen creatures were running around a track. He thought they must have been going around and around for quite some time, because there was considerable dirt piled up on the sides of the track.

Their bodies were grotesque and bestial, but a number of them had human faces: surprisingly elegant faces. A lone man stood in profile just beyond the hunt's ghoulish fairy cast, looking regal and glowing against the mire of paint. Fergus's eyes widened as he recognized the reddish-brown hair, the straight nose, and strong chin. He took an abrupt step backwards, mouth opening soundlessly as he turned to Terry, pointing at the painting.

"Yeah," he said, "it's the only one that's not finished. It was a part-time thing I agreed to sit for, but I cancelled my employment and moved out before it was completed."

"Moved out?"

"I lived here for a while – the way Audrey and Deirdre do now. He's got space for a dozen servants, but he's picky, so he only invites his favorites to live in full-time."

"Why'd you leave?"

"I joined Everyday Resources. And I just got kinda sick of his demands."

Fergus nodded, not quite sure he followed, but pretty certain he was better off not knowing the details.

"C'mon. We have to hurry," Terry said and led the way to the door directly ahead of them, perpendicular to the corridor.

Fergus tore his eyes away from Terry's naked form and took a few jogging steps to catch up. He stumbled as he approached the door. Coming from within was a familiar and unpleasantly intriguing smell, like taking the plastic off a container of steak. Fergus immediately felt a little sick and also a little hungry and then a little sicker. Terry was apparently unaware of his situation, though, and opened the door without pause, walking straight in. Thankfully, the smell was only a little stronger with the door open, but Fergus still felt weird and tingly. He didn't want to enter the room, but someone was barking his name, and somehow his feet found their way through the door.

He wasn't sure what he was expecting. Blood, gore, maybe something like a meat locker scene in a horror story, but the room was incredibly tidy. There was a large four-poster bed with rich blue drapery pooling down to the floor, clasped back with silver rope. The bed itself was covered in pristine white sheets. There were a couple of sofas and a table to the side near a large picture window with window seat. Between these and the bed was an elaborate antique writing desk of a dark wood with carvings of lions, which matched the bed. On the other side was a closet and before it an easel on a white sheet, which was splattered with old paint.

He couldn't tell where the smell was coming from, but it was strong. He searched for dark leaks creeping out from under the bed or the closet, but the room was immaculate. The Count was washing his hands in a basin beside the bed with his back to them, but when he last stepped aside, Fergus could see where the smell was generating. He had his sleeves rolled up and was drying his hands on a white towel that was quickly becoming pink. The water in the basin was a distinct red. He didn't address Fergus; he didn't even acknowledge him. Instead, he spoke directly to Terry.

"The rubbish is already waiting out back. I just need you to take it to the docks and dispose of it. Make sure no one traces it back to me. Understood?"

"It's going to cost you," Terry replied in an absurdly calm way.

Fergus was pretty sure he wasn't confusing the situation. They were definitely becoming involved in a criminal activity, and if they got caught, they would take the fall for whatever horrible matter was in this so-called rubbish. Eyeing the Count's pink stained hand towel, he had plenty of ideas – none of them pleasant. He wanted to protest, but he felt as though he was in a dream – like his mouth was stuck together and his feet rooted to the spot. He just stood and watched as Terry and the Count haggled until it was decided, and Terry turned and gave him a little nudge, jolting him out of his stupor. He stumbled backwards out of the door as Terry shut the door.

"No."

"What?"

"No. Whatever he wants, we shouldn't do it," Fergus insisted, feeling annoyed at the pleading edge that had seeped into his voice.

"We're just dumping rubbish into the bay. It's not a big deal."

"It's not just rubbish."

"You're being paranoid."

Fergus shook his head.

"Fine if you don't want to help, but you know, you *are* a kelpie. This is probably part of why he hired you – to carry things."

"I don't want to be involved in this kind of thing!"

Terry turned to him. "Keep your voice down and listen. He's gonna know you know something's up. What are you going to do? Quit? Refuse to help? Make it obvious you wanna defy him? What do you think will happen to you if you do? Maybe you didn't know what working for him would entail, but it's a messy business, and once you're in, you gotta think good and hard about how to get out again. You can't just say, 'no.'"

Fergus stared at him, mouth slightly ajar, and then he snapped it shut, brows furrowing. "I'm not afraid of him. Just let him come after me."

Terry grabbed him by the arm, dragging him away from the room, down the hall, and flinging open a door seemingly at random. It was dark inside, but Fergus could see sheets had been tossed over the furniture, and the air was thick with dust. He wrinkled his nose to keep from sneezing.

"God help us if he didn't already hear all that," Terry muttered, shutting the door and letting Fergus go with a rough shove.

He righted himself, still glowering. "I don't care if you already did something illegal for him, but you shouldn't do it again. Why would you? Are you scared of him?"

"Yeah, I don't want to end up hanging from the rafters. Is that okay with you? Listen, Fergus."

Fergus stepped back, the anger on his face lessening as he tried to work out if Terry was intending to hit him or not.

"I know life's been tough. Your parents ran out on you. Flynn's dead. You're pretty much penniless. You've had all the cards stacked against you since the beginning. But you're also lucky. You know why?"

"Why?"

"Because up until this point, you've managed to live as a normal citizen. Even though life was tough, you could just focus on getting by, and that's all you needed to do. You think that something like this is evil without question, but it's not. You obviously don't know about this city's politics. You don't know how bad it's gonna be if Evalach takes control. They're already way too powerful, and they'll have us all sent off on a ship to nowhere if they have their way. They don't think of you as a person. To them, you're a monster, and they won't think twice about getting rid of you, me, Ursula, and everyone else you care about. You think you can handle them with fists? You'll be dead."

Fergus said nothing, brows knitting, mouth stretching further and further down, but he was caught off-guard, and he didn't know how to retort.

"Sometimes, you gotta do things that aren't easy for the sake of everyone. You've been sheltered like a little kid, but now you know things are going on, and you don't have a choice. You're involved."

He shook his head, mouth twitching as he tried to find the words to make Terry see that he was being unfair. Not just unfair, but crazy. But everything he came up with sounded childish and petulant in his head, and Terry looked so resolved and mature, he found he couldn't say anything.

"All we can do is try to keep them in check, and sometimes, this is the only way to do that. So I'm gonna go finish this job. You don't have to come."

"There's gotta be a better way than this," Fergus replied quietly.

"Well, you stay here and think of it."

Fergus cursed. Maybe it was the lingering scent of blood, but he was entertaining some violent fantasies. He wondered: if he banged Terry's head against the wall enough times, would it knock sense into him? Moreover, could he really let Terry go alone? He scowled at the redhead. Why did he have to be so persistent in the first place? He *deserved* it if he got caught. Yet even though Fergus wanted to believe it, he knew that if Terry went to the docks alone, he'd be doubling the chances of being picked up by the cops. If he was caught for something like this, he probably was going to end up executed, and Fergus didn't think he could live with that.

He sighed, exhaling a half-hearted curse. "Fine. I'm not staying here."

The smell was far worse in the kitchens. Deirdre directed them to two normal looking mid-sized crates. For a moment, Fergus wondered if he was making a big deal over nothing. Then he lifted one of the crates, and the scent of garlic and meat was so overwhelming that he almost lost his dinner. Head spinning, he barely managed to catch the box against his knee, letting out a cry of pain as it connected.

He didn't feel like talking during their grim task. He wouldn't know what to say even if he had. He limped the entire way, nearly dropping his load several times, and by the time they got to the docks, he wondered if Terry wouldn't have been better off on his own after all. His brain was burning from the tantalizing scent of fresh blood. He felt drunk and dizzy, but there was also the heady, delirious sensation that he could do anything, and at the center of that was hunger. Horrible, mind numbing hunger.

It was like he'd felt the first week after his mother had left, and there was nothing left in the cupboards and no money to buy anything to eat. He'd been depressed, he recalled, just lying on the floor watching a spider build a web under the couch. The only illumination had been from the aquarium. He'd wondered if he was going to starve to death on the living room floor and if that wasn't what his mom wanted after all, and then with even greater bitterness, he'd hoped she would return and find him dead and be crushed.

However, he'd learned then that survival won out over self-pity, and in the end, he'd gotten up and gone and begged outside the markets until an old fisherman had given him some half-rotten fish, which he'd stuck in the freezer, and with them he was able to sustain himself long enough to figure out a real plan to continue living.

It was like that, only deeper and more demanding. He didn't realize his hands were empty of the parcel until Terry was violently shaking him, hissing at him to snap out of it. He looked down. Blood had seeped out from between the boards and made a ragged line between his fingers. He started to lift his hand to lick it off, but froze, shaking his head sharply, and then bent down to thrust his hand into the ocean water. It was icy cold, but as the scent washed away, he returned to his senses. He took a deep breath, standing, and fumbled for the rest of the cigarette he'd had on him earlier. Terry gave him a light.

"You okay?"

Fergus nodded, sucking down as much of the acrid smoke as he could and then coughing a little, punching himself in the chest. "Yeah, fine," he managed.

"I'll tie things up back there. Just go home and sleep, okay?"

Fergus nodded, not once looking at Terry's face, and crammed his hands into his pockets, skulking off to Ursula's.

He was surprised to find her home when he got there. It didn't seem like the party was going to end until dawn, and she rarely left an event early. However, there she was, sitting in the faded red and bronze striped armchair in the back room. She was still in the black evening dress she'd had on at the party. He noticed the details for the first time. It was high collared and flared from elbow to wrist, countered by the rather short hem of the skirt. Sitting with her knees drawn up, he could easily see the shadow of lacy underwear beyond her skinny ankles.

One arm was on the chair and the other crossed over her stomach, as though she'd been wrapped up in thought for some time. Her thick, dark hair was falling over her face and eyes, and her lashes looked even thicker and heavier than usual. Maybe it was the light, or maybe it was her make up, but her face looked very white.

She turned to him, pursing her lips, and he noticed they looked bruised and swollen – the lipstick smudged. A trill of anger went down his spine. She didn't look too happy with him either. Her mouth formed a severe line, eyes narrowing. However, she didn't speak, just stared at him. He didn't speak either, but stared back at her for a few minutes, leaning on the doorframe and loosening his tie.

He still felt dizzy and strange in his own skin, and rather than find out whatever she was angry about, rather than get close enough to smell someone else's cologne on her, he wanted to just go to bed. He really wished at that moment that he had his own place, so that he didn't have to see her, didn't have to share a sleeping space, and more importantly, didn't have to feel obligated to her and thus guilty for wanting her to be gone.

She turned away, letting out an annoyed little sigh. "It seems that man has finally taken a real interest in you," she remarked with a lofty, disdainful air.

"What man?"

"The Count. He apparently wants to ask you to be another live in. He suddenly thinks you're 'interesting.'"

"Oh." Fergus didn't know how to feel about that. Given what he'd learned about Terry's experiences, he really didn't want to move into the penthouse. Some angry part of him wanted to say he did just to make her angry, but it felt like too much effort to go out of his way to pick a fight with her.

She continued, apparently reading his face, "Well, certainly, it's up to you. I suppose you are moving in different circles these days."

"What does that mean?"

"I wonder," she shot back, turning to him.

"Really, tell me what you mean."

"A pretty little thing, that redheaded girl. That *Jane*. You know, she's a rather lucky one. Her parents died before they found out she was a hybrid, and she inherited quite a bit, I hear."

"So she isn't human."

"It all comes together so perfectly," Ursula drawled, but her brows were pinched in anger and her nostrils flared. "The kelpie and the *selkie*."

"You're assuming a lot, looking like you just rolled out of someone else's bed."

She lifted an eyebrow, mouth thinning.

"I am gonna move out, but I'm not moving in with him or with her."

Her brow furrowed further, mouth parting in what almost looked like distress. "*Why?*"

"Because I can."

She unfolded from the chair, stalking over and poking him in the chest. "I don't want you to."

"I don't want you to be messing around with other people," he replied, taking her by the wrist.

Her jaw dropped, and she blinked rapidly. "What?"

"You heard me."

"That isn't how it works."

"Well, if you're gonna act like you've got a say in what I do, I think it's only fair."

She glared.

"You don't own me," he added softly.

"Who would you rather belong to?"

"Myself."

She snorted. "And who has been taking care of you all this time?"

"Myself."

"How ungrateful!" she spat, jerking her hand free.

"Yeah, well, I don't feel very grateful right now," he replied, reaching out to rub the smudged lipstick from the corner of her mouth. He felt like he could kind of sympathize with Dominique at the moment, but if he threw down any of her wares, he really wouldn't be able to pay it off. He laughed darkly. "I hate you sometimes."

She said nothing, but looked injured.

"Don't make that face at me now."

Above all else, that made him want to shake her. Another part of him wanted to lace his fingers in her thick locks and kiss her until she just stopped with all of this. Suddenly, he felt tired – too tired to even feel woozy or agitated. Just tired. He ran his hands up his face, through his hair, and stepped away from her.

"Where are you going?" she asked.

"I dunno," he replied.

He didn't want to lie beside her feeling sick and exhausted and wondering just what she had been doing when the Count caught up with her to ask if he could have Fergus. He didn't want to be working for a guy who made him take "rubbish" down to the docks for some skewed sense of the greater good and who was only interested in him for reasons he really, really didn't want to think about. He didn't want to be all that was left of Flynn, and he didn't want to think about the fact that the only person who had been like family to him since his mom had run away was ash now. There was pretty much nothing in his life that he wanted at that moment, so the obvious choice was to go for a walk until the feeling subsided.

She asked again, but he ignored her, leaving the shop with no particular direction in mind.

Chapter Seven.

Toby was tilted at a funny angle, fins waving weakly without propelling it forward. Its gills were flaring in the way fish tossed on land struggle to breathe, and it bobbed along in a circle in the spot it usually migrated to when it suspected food would appear from the sky. Fergus frowned and walked over to the aquarium, lifting the lid and getting out the scoop. He could see Toby's orange-striped body under the green netting, but despite the fish's sluggishness, it was exceptionally difficult to catch.

"C'mere, you stupid fish," he grumbled, but try as he might, he couldn't seem to catch it. The scoop slipped out of his fingers, but instead of floating, it dropped to the very bottom of the tank. He cursed.

"You should just use your hands."

He jumped and turned. Flynn was standing there – dark curls going every which way, near black eyes crinkling in amusement – watching him with a faint smile. It was the smile that said he knew Fergus was doing something the wrong way, but rather than be impatient, he kindly suggested something else.

"I don't think you're supposed to touch them with your hands. I think it'll kill them."

"I don't think yours would. You're a kelpie, aren't you?"

Fergus wasn't sure he'd have any more luck this way, but he reached in, snatching at the fish. He could feel its small, slick body pass in the space where his fingers and palm met. Closer, then. He made a second grab and could feel Toby struggling in the cage of his hand. He pulled it out, opening his palm, and fell backwards under the weight of Flynn's body. He struggled, trying to get out from under him.

"Fergus," Flynn gasped. His face was blotchy and swollen. His mouth and eyes were bruised. Fergus struggled his way free, backing into the wall.

"Take him to the docks," Terry instructed.

He turned, smacking his head against a very real wall, and blinked.

Sitting up, he rubbed his cheek. Everything was aching and stiff. It felt like the cold had seeped straight into his bones. He leaned against the wall, head tilting back, and stared up at the dark space over the buildings where the next plate started. There were spongy, phosphorescent things growing at the top of the building, spreading out horizontally, but crooking upwards. Tiny green motes, like snowflakes, drifted down from them, disappearing outside their circles of light.

He rubbed his face against the sleeve of his dress shirt. It felt grimy and soiled, which made his face feel even dirtier. His mouth was dry and fuzzy. He felt around for his wallet, opened it, and realized that it was empty. He'd spent the last of it on a small carton of milk – last night's dinner. He closed his eyes, feeling dizzy and nauseated. He wondered if Ursula had been feeding Toby and the fish properly. Then he wondered how many days he'd been wandering. Without a schedule, without running into anyone he knew, he'd lost all track of time, and it was impossible to tell time in the depths of the lower city. All he knew was that he felt awful and unclean and cold and probably the reason he was so queasy was because he was hungry.

He just wasn't sure he wanted to see anyone he knew right now. He definitely didn't want to go to Emily like this, thinking about Ursula still made him feel listless and miserable, and the penthouse was out of the question. Deirdre would probably turn him away at the door anyway, and he doubted the Count would have much more sympathy. Thinking about Terry reminded him about the job at the docks, which gave him a different kind of sick feeling. He missed Flynn, but that obviously wasn't going to do him any good.

Very slowly and awkwardly, he got to his feet and started walking. He didn't think about it, but operating on habit, returned to the old apartment.

It wasn't hard to break into the building. He kicked the front door until the wood cracked and swung free. Feeling around under the banister, he found he still had a copy of his key taped there. No one had moved in yet, and it was dusty and squalid. He paused, listening for the sounds of any drifters who might have broken in, and then locked the door behind him. It was strange to see the unit empty.

Though he'd grown up in this place, it felt completely alien without anything in it.

He made his way to the shower and stripped down before turning on the water warmer than usual. He dumped his clothing in first. There wasn't any soap, but he still tried to scrub them as best he could and then stuck them over the rod to dry, stepping in himself and just standing there in the darkness and steam without thinking.

He didn't have a towel, and his clothing was far from dry, so he just stepped out and went to Flynn's room, lying down where the bed used to be. He wasn't entirely sure why he'd chosen Flynn's. Maybe because it had also been his mom's, and he'd come here to hide under her bed when he was small and there was a storm brewing outside the sanctuary of the inner city. When she'd left, he hadn't gone inside until Flynn moved in. He'd held his breath when they'd brought in the bed frame, found in a nearby alley, because he hadn't wanted to smell her lingering perfume. After a week, it hadn't smelled like her anymore, but rather like Flynn, and he'd felt easier coming in.

It still smelled like Flynn, even with all his things gone – like loam and cedar and a hint of pepper. He hadn't really defined the scent before, but as he lay on the floor, his mind drifted that way, and the more he thought about Flynn, the lonelier he felt until his throat grew tight and his chest began to ache. He rolled onto his side and stared at the wall. It was cracked, the plaster coming off in chips, which had formed a little pile on the floor.

He reached out, pushing down on a piece and snapping it in two. He did the same to a few others, chalk coating his fingertip. And then he noticed something was sticking out just a little from a crack between the floor and casing. It looked like a grocery receipt. He carefully caught the tip under his middle finger and drew it out.

It seemed like it was just a scribble on the back of a receipt for milk, beer, bread, and oatmeal. He stared at it blankly for a moment. It was definitely Flynn's handwriting. There was a drawing of a circle with a bunch of funny looking symbols inside. Stretching between the symbols were lines going in seemingly random directions almost like a map. He started to crumple it up when he realized there was something in the side margin. The writing was so tiny, he almost missed it. He held the paper closer to his face, squinting.

Tír na nÓg.

"Huh."

He didn't know what it meant, but somehow, it suddenly seemed a lot more valuable. He carefully folded it into a little square and then clenched it in his hand, feeling the corners poking into his palm. He imagined that the press of paper against his skin was a connection to Flynn, and focusing on that, he drifted off once more.

•　　•　　•

When he awoke, he was cold, but completely dry. Trying to rub warmth into his limbs, he considered his situation. Probably he was just going to have to hope Ursula was out and go retrieve his things. Maybe he could squat in this apartment for a while. He could stay until it seemed like the landlord was making motions to move someone in again. He sat up, and the square of paper fell to the floor. He picked it up, blinking at it for a minute before he recalled what it was, and then went to check on his clothes. They were still damp, but they weren't soaked. He stuck the note into his empty wallet and pulled on his boxers, which were dry, at least.

It was warmer inside the house than outside, but that wasn't saying much, so he went into the kitchen to turn on the oven and sat next to it with the door cracked, looking out the window into the alleyway behind the building. His mind started to drift, going to a safer place this time. He could remember sitting like this with Flynn one Christmas morning. The heat had failed in the apartment, so they'd torn pages from old school books, balling them up and trying to toss them through the opening. They both had pretty bad aim, but Fergus had won with three out of eight going in on the first throw.

He missed when the front door opened, but he did hear the footsteps. He nearly jumped out of his skin as he tried to scramble to his feet. Terry loomed in the doorway. Fergus blinked up at him with his mouth parted.

"I didn't think you'd come back here, but I guess Evelyn was right."

Fergus settled back against the cabinet, wrapping his arms around his legs, and said nothing.

"You know we've all been looking for you for days, right?"

"What?"

"You've been missing for days, Fergus. Where the hell have you been? You look god awful."

"Thanks. Why have you been looking for me?"

"Ursula freaked out after the second day. Said she'd come here and there was no trace of you. A lot of people have been looking for you since then. She even made Dominique look, and Audrey and Deirdre, too, because she thought you might have gone to live there or something, and Audrey got really upset that you were missing. Raja and Evelyn have been looking, too, since you didn't show up for practice. Guess that's why I started looking . . . " Terry paused, sighing. "But here you are. What's the deal?"

Fergus shook his head. It seemed so complicated, and Terry was one of the main reasons he felt confused, so unloading on him was pretty much out.

"I missed home," he replied, running his thumb over the curve of his forearm.

"So you went MIA at both your jobs, missed practice, ran away from your girlfriend, and were entirely unreachable for nearly a week. Makes sense."

"I don't want to hear it from you."

"So what now?"

"Dunno."

Terry sighed and came over to crouch in front of him. "Guess you're in shock." He peered into Fergus's face for a moment, mouth softening into something a little more sympathetic. "I got an idea. Put your clothes back on. We're going out."

"Where?"

"You'll like it, so just try to cheer up and come on."

He wasn't sure about that, but he *was* hungry, and he thought maybe Terry would spring for food, because he actually would like that. Of course, that was a very hopeful estimation, but it didn't stop him from anticipating as he put on his clothes. He thought with some regret that he should have stuck them by the stove instead, because they were stiff and still a little grungy despite his efforts. At least, he hadn't been wearing jeans.

He splashed warm water on his face, and finding the remains of a tube of toothpaste set to scrubbing at his teeth with one finger and wiping his face off on the tails of his shirt before he re-emerged. Terry pushed away from the wall and led the way out of the apartment.

• • •

They didn't talk. Fergus wasn't in the mood, and Terry seemed to only be in the mood when he wanted to say something awkward, so Fergus was glad that he wasn't being talkative either. They made their way further into the city, to an area that was so dark, even with the street lamps, it seemed anything not directly within their spheres of light was covered in pitch. More of the magical fungi grew here, but the shadows sucked up the glow entirely, creating bright blots of pastels framed in black.

Fergus avoided this area most of the time. The residential sector ended about three blocks in, and after that, it was mainly nightclubs and strip joints leading into an area where factories from a different age once thrived. It was a good place to be stabbed.

Terry led them straight to one of the empty warehouses.

"What are we doing here?" Fergus asked, planting his feet.

A couple of guys were standing near the door. One had a particularly grotesque scar going from the top of his lip to his brow, which Fergus could only see because someone had stuck an exit sign over the door, which allowed a tiny bit of visibility. They didn't take any notice of Terry or Fergus.

"Meeting Evelyn and Raja for drinks."

"Uh, this doesn't really seem like their normal hang out."

"There's a producer from the upper levels here tonight. It's a long shot, but we figured we should at least try to find him."

Fergus considered this and then nodded, stepping towards the door. He wasn't sure why a human producer would stray this deep into the lower level, but if there was one, he definitely wanted to find him. As they neared the door, the two men finally acknowledged them, shifting into an imposing stance until they caught sight of Terry, and then they warily stepped aside to let them in. As Fergus opened the door, he was met with an explosion of thrashing guitar, thudding bass, and bodies smashed almost to the door. He couldn't make out people – just a writing mass of silhouettes stretching back about forty meters from the stage, which was the only thing that was lit.

Fergus squinted, trying to see the musicians against the single spotlight propped up on the side of the stage. The same thick, woodsy scent from the party was heavy in the air, only stronger. Fergus coughed and tried to squeeze his way inside. He found going around the perimeter yielded some leeway. Around the outside of the makeshift pit there were some tables set up, though at least two of them were being used for masses of bodies who obviously were not just relaxing. Fergus didn't bother averting his eyes; he couldn't make anything out anyway.

It seemed natural to approach the stage, so he did. This logic brought him to the "bar," which was made up of a few tables with coolers. Evelyn was standing next to the bar and Raja beside her with his arm around her waist. Fergus rerouted, going straight to them.

"Fergus!" she said, surprise lighting up her face. "Where the hell have you been?"

He shrugged, stuffing his hands into his pockets and looking away. "Around."

"Jerk," she said, punching his shoulder. "Glad you're alive. Hey, we're looking for a guy called Boulanger. Dunno much about him, except he's got green hair."

Fergus turned to the crowd. "Yeah, dunno if that's gonna help."

"Just keep an eye out! What do you wanna drink? You look like hell."

"Two of whatever's hardest."

Evelyn turned to shout to the bartender, and Fergus turned his attention to the stage. A moment later, two shots were pressed into his hands. They burned as they went down, tasting a little like rubbing alcohol, but he hadn't eaten properly in at least 24 hours, so he could feel the effect almost immediately and happily welcomed the warm, detached feeling starting in his fingers and toes and radiating up. He felt a little less concerned about his situation and considered asking for a third, but he doubted Evelyn was going to fund a bender.

"I know these guys," he shouted to his band mates. "I went to school with the singer."

He wasn't sure what their reaction was, because he started pushing his way through the crowd towards the stage. It wasn't like they were going to find this producer guy. Given how many people were here and how dark it was, the chances were stupidly slim, so he figured as long as he was here and buzzed, the only reasonable thing to do was get as close to the stage as possible and let the bass shake loose his bones and deafen him a little more. Being able to feel the music was probably one of the best sensations in the world, after all.

He managed to press his way up to the stage, though he soon found himself crushed against it. He grunted, trying to push back against the crowd, but even he wasn't strong enough to force a space, so he just gave up and went along with the beat. The song ended, and the singer – a guy with fake red hair and a tattoo on the side of his face named Emmanuel – swaggered to the front of the stage.

"How's everyone doing? No one trampled yet, right? We are Frisk. Okay, so I gotta a question for you – how the hell did you all hear about this? Seriously, is it underground anymore with this many people? Just kidding. I love you all."

The crowd surged forward, whooping and whistling and shouting. Fergus grunted as he was smashed even harder against the stage.

"Whoa, awesome. I feel it. Okay, next we're gonna . . . " Emmanuel stopped, looking down, and blinked. "Is that who I think it is? Fergus Irvine? Oh my God, dude." He leaned down, holding out his hand. "C'mere."

Fergus took his hand. In part, because the pinch of the stage against his sternum was getting really painful, but also because there was supposedly a producer somewhere in this audience, and it was free PR.

"This guy here? Do you know him? Fergus Irvine – front man for Everyday Resources."

Fergus held up a hand. From the stage, with the spotlight blinding him from one side, it was impossible to make out the crowd, but there was a lot of shouting. He couldn't tell if it was just because people were excited, or because they really did know him, but imagining it was the latter gave his ego a little boost. Though he'd never been particularly close to Emmanuel, he suddenly found himself being swept up into a crushing hug. He returned it. It felt far better than it should, and for a moment, something felt a little raw in his chest, but it was easy to cover it up with tipsiness and the adrenaline from being in front of hundreds of screaming people.

"How about it, Irvine? You know our music? I'll sing one you should remember. You know how to scream, right?"

Fergus snorted, leaning towards the microphone. "Yeah," he replied before straightening. "Loud as you want."

"Now that's what I wanna hear," Emmanuel smirked and then raised a hand, summoning a crash of cymbals.

Fergus did remember the song. Emmanuel had written it about three years ago when Frisk was still called Rabid Puppy. They'd played it at some school event, prompting every member of the band to be suspended for three days. Though he couldn't recall the exact title, he could remember most of the words. He'd liked the song, even if it wasn't very thoughtful. Mainly it was about starting fires in trashcans and fights in the street. He knew the part that Emmanuel wanted him to do – three shouted lines of, "Burn 'em in the street." By the time it was his part, his memory for the chorus had been refreshed, too. For a few moments, he forgot about Flynn and Ursula and Terry and politics as he sang along with Emmanuel.

His former classmate pressed the microphone at him for each shouted line and then drew it back for an additional, "Yeah!"

And then he found the mic being pressed into his hand for the second-to-final, softer repeat of the chorus. He fumbled it and then stood for a moment, staring out at the illegible sea of twitching bodies. The drummer did an additional beat, and Fergus took a breath. He felt more at ease than he had for at least two weeks as he sang out, "If you're just gonna sit safe in your room, don't blame us – don't blame us if you're consumed. The fire isn't gonna stop, cuz it's fueled by my head. Don't hide away and leave it unsaid. Cuz the streets are on fire, on fire, on fire!"

He passed it back, and Emmanuel threw his arm around his shoulders, finishing it up with the final shouted rendition of the chorus.

"Whoa, that was so awesome! God, we haven't sung that in forever, have we?" he asked, turning to the other band members. The guitarist was mopping his head with the back of his arm, but grinned and shook his head "no." The drummer did a little drum roll. "All right, everyone, give it up for Irvine. Go see Everyday Resources, okay?"

Fergus took this as his cue to leave and slid back down into the audience. The band was already starting the next song, and two girls, shouting words he couldn't hear, crushed him against the stage. He managed to gently pry them off, though every time he peeled one away, the other was on top of him, so it took a few minutes. Finally, he made it back to the bar, eager to see what his band mates thought. Terry had disappeared, but Raja and Evelyn were still at their post by the bar, which Fergus belatedly thought made sense if they were intent on finding this Boulanger guy.

Evelyn rolled her eyes, but after a moment, she smiled. "Well, at least, if Boulanger really is here, he heard about us."

Raja gave him a pat on the back. "Good work, man."

"Thanks. Where's Terry?"

"Dunno, he ran into some guys and went out back. Said the Fairy Dust was making him sick."

"Is that what the smell is?"

"Yeah, well, at least it'll mean people probably will remember your part fondly."

"What, it wasn't good?"

"Nah, but that song . . . "

Fergus laughed. He felt something unwind in his chest. "I'm gonna find Terry and get some air."

They nodded and turned back to the stage, and Fergus made his way around to the front door, which took a lot of time. Now that people had seen him on stage, as soon as he was close enough to make out his face, they started mobbing him. With no lack of effort, he managed to push his way outside, and by that time, he thought that maybe he was done and would rather retire to a more relaxed establishment for a victory drink.

Then he heard Terry's shout.

Chapter Eight.

Perhaps Ursula would have been able to see in this level of darkness – maybe a *cait sìth's* eyes would be able to pick up the vague hints of light – but Fergus found himself shrouded by darkness without time to adjust. He stumbled and hit something that sounded like a garbage can, tripping over the contents. His knees and palms stung as he got to his feet and kept running in the direction of the shouting. At first, he couldn't see what was going on. He ran straight into someone, and though the man seemed pretty big, he still went down quite suddenly, causing Fergus to sprawl on top of him. Fire suddenly sprang up from something one of the men was holding, illuminating the scene.

Terry was gripping one of the other guys by the arm, and in that hand was a broken bottle. The fourth, who had lit the scene, drew back his hand and smashed his bottle against the wall of the warehouse. There was a funny smell, and then fire danced across the bricks, climbing upwards and swallowing the strange growths on the side of the building. Fergus let himself be distracted a moment too long, and the man underneath him rolled suddenly, pinning him to the ground and putting a thick fist to his face. The world swam, and he disjointedly reached out to push at his attacker or grab his hand. He missed and was rewarded with a second punch. He could taste blood. Terry was shouting something, but Fergus was busy trying to struggle out from under his opponent.

The second guy grabbed Terry and was trying to force him against the burning wall, but Fergus had to ignore that, because the man on top of him suddenly grabbed him by the hair and smashed his head against the concrete. White sparks filled his vision, and his arm flailed convulsively, momentarily stunned. The pain woke him back up. He saw red. His coordination returned, and he reached out to grab the guy by the front of his jacket. He shoved as hard as he could, dislodging him, and then swung around so that he was on top.

Without hesitation, he punched the guy and felt the pop of his nose giving way. The man screamed, hands going for his face, and Fergus snarled and abruptly gave the guy a taste of his own medicine, lifting him by his collar and then cracking his head against the concrete. His eyes rolled back, and his attacker stopped struggling.

Humans, Fergus thought. For such a big guy, the man had gone down too easily to be a hybrid. His attention returned to Terry, who was shouting and thrashing. Part of his hoodie had caught fire, and the second guy was trying to help push him into the flames. Fergus went for that one, grabbing him around the waist and throwing his weight backward, pulling them both to the ground.

Suddenly, he realized what Terry was shouting: *Evalach*.

Fergus redoubled his efforts, but his new opponent was better than the first. There was a method to his movements as he wrestled to come up on top, and though Fergus was easily stronger, he just kept wriggling in the right ways, so that Fergus found himself on his stomach, face pressed to the ground, and one arm wrenched behind his back. He grunted and started to struggle, but the pressure on his elbow stopped him. A string of the most violent curses he could think of came out of his mouth, but were cut off as the guy took his other hand to press down against the side of his head, putting his weight into it.

A terrible scream erupted nearby, followed by the man on top of him being tossed aside. There was a funny pop in his arm, and a dull pain radiated from his elbow. He scrambled to his feet. The screamer was rolling around on the ground, howling and trying to put the flames out of his clothing. Terry started to stalk over to him, but before he could, four more figures came around the side of the building. They took one look at the man on the ground and started for Terry and Fergus.

"We need to warn the people inside . . . !" Fergus started to shout, but was cut off as one of the Knights tackled him around the middle, knocking him dangerously close to the fire. Instinct paired with anger, and he kicked the guy off, scrambling away from the blaze just in time for a second to grab him by the hair and yank back. He twisted around and punched as hard as he could. The man grabbed at his crotch and stumbled backward. It wasn't his favorite move, but Fergus was pretty sure these guys were planning to kill him and Terry and leave them here. Plus, there were the people inside who had no idea that the Knights of Evalach were party crashing with fire.

Terry, meanwhile, had made short work of another and was in the process of throwing a third and turning with a terrible kind of grace to shove him into the flames. Fergus could smell blood and burnt meat, and it made his head spin with hunger. Terry was already grabbing another, but Fergus was so busy with the guy he'd just punched that he missed whatever transpired between them. He didn't miss the sharp cry, though, nor how it abruptly cut off.

Fergus grappled with the last guy, who was proving to be a lot more difficult to manage than Fergus had thought. Obviously spooked by whatever Terry had done over his shoulder, he was struggling like a wild animal. Fergus managed to push him off, stumbling back a few feet. On top of the horrible hunger, his head was throbbing, and he was seeing spots in the corners of his eyes. He tripped, went down on one knee, but shoved himself back onto his feet. The man lunged at him, and Fergus put out his arms to try to shove him away, but he was too slow. Pain burst from his stomach. He stumbled back and looked down to find glass sticking out of him.

There were screams coming from nearby, and the smell of smoke was growing stronger. He could hear footsteps pounding as people poured out of the warehouse. He stared dimly in the direction of the entrance, but all he could see were a few dark figures sprinting off the other way. He looked back to Terry. The bottle man was lying at his feet, eyes open. Fergus looked back down at the glass jutting from his body. Terry was in front of him rather suddenly, blocking out the firelight. His hands fumbled at the shard. Fergus didn't want to look, but he couldn't stop.

He blinked at Terry in bewilderment and started to say something, or maybe he was already saying something, but the words weren't coming out properly. He tried to cobble together a proper sentence, but it seemed he was really only succeeding in gasping. Perhaps the word he was searching for was, "wait," but Terry seemed to miss it, because he wrenched the glass free. Fergus could see the blood covered splinter against the firelight, rivulets dripping down towards Terry's hand. It didn't look like the coated area was very long, so he hoped that maybe it hadn't been so deep, but blood was already starting to well and drip through his fingers. Letting out a rasping breath, he gritted his teeth and tried to clasp the wound tighter.

"Probably needs stitches," Terry remarked. "We'll go by her place. She'll have the right supplies."

Fergus figured this meant Ursula, and he didn't want to go. However, he also didn't want to stand around with a gaping wound in his stomach, so he allowed Terry to give him a shoulder, and they limped. Terry led them through the city, finding alley after alley to lead them back towards Beathag's without running into the stampeding crowd. Fergus had to admit, Terry knew the lower city far better than he did. He couldn't seem to recognize a single landmark. These thoughts were short-lived, though, as his brain idled and then picked up elsewhere.

He wondered if Raja and Evelyn were okay, but it was a vague kind of worry, because each step seemed to pull directly on the cut, and he could feel the blood soaking into his trousers, slowly dripping down until it was at his thigh, his knee, his ankle. By that point, he was stumbling, more dragged than aided, and the world was slanting in an unpleasant way.

"How much further?" he kept asking.

"Almost there," Terry kept replying.

But it felt like hours before they arrived at Beathag's, and by that time, Fergus could barely make his legs move at all, nor even lift his head on his own. The door wasn't locked, or maybe it had been, but Terry forced it open. That part went by in a flash. Whatever went down between Terry and Ursula also melted away beyond the buzzing in his ears. Just trying to look at them from his place on the bed caused agonizing pains to burst from his eyes to his brain, and so he closed them. Maybe it had been deeper than it seemed. He couldn't recall exactly, and it had been pretty dark, even with the flames encompassing the warehouse in the background.

With a sense of detachment, he wondered if he would die of shock and then laughed weakly, head lolling to the side. Weight descended on the mattress, jostling him just enough to be unpleasant. He could smell Terry more than see him, because he smelled like blood and ash, and it was stronger than Ursula's perfume. His thoughts kept racing and abruptly cutting off, leaving him confused until the next one took off.

A rag was held to his face.

"Breathe in," Terry instructed.

•   •   •

He awoke to sunlight burning through his eyelids and the pounding of his temples. A soft groan escaped him, unchecked, as he dared to crack one eye. For a moment, he wasn't sure where he was. There was a shift on the bed, and Ursula's face loomed over him, her dark hair falling around it, painting a sharp contrast between hair and features. She said nothing, but studied his face for what seemed a prolonged measure of time before he finally spoke.

"Was that for real?"

She didn't smile. "It was."

"Where's Terry?"

"Your guess is as good as mine, isn't it?"

He closed his eyes again, but opened them in surprise as she gently touched his cheek with a cold hand. Her eyebrows were knotted in what he could only guess was confusion.

"It's still a mess outside. They couldn't curb the fire, and it spread. They only got it under control an hour or two ago. When last he dropped by, he said to not worry about the attackers, but . . . the police came by a half hour later asking about two men." She pursed her mouth. "They apparently don't have much to go with: both tall, one with longish red hair, one nearly black. Except they said the dark-haired man had white eyes."

Fergus pressed his palm to his forehead and cursed.

"Perhaps one got away from him, hmm? It's not a lot to go on, but the people down here will know.

I'm not sure how long it will be until the Knights offer enough to betray you."

"Probably not long," he muttered, dropping his hand.

"Your accomplice is good at hiding himself, but, Fergus . . . "

He didn't reply. He didn't really know where he could lay low. He obviously couldn't stay here. He couldn't hide out at the old apartment either. There was no way he'd force himself on Raja and Evelyn, if they had even made it out okay, and he didn't know where Terry had gone, or if he'd return anytime soon. A weak curse escaped him. Ursula stood, going to scrounge through some clothes draped over a large chest. She pulled on a light blue sweater and hugged it tightly to her.

She said nothing for a long moment, peeking out the window, and Fergus realized that there really was sunlight coming in. He blinked, gaping in shock. She glanced back at him, read his expression, and replied, "The fire spread far. I was worried it would come here. I wouldn't have been able to move you alone. Your old apartment may be gone entirely. Who knows? Well, I suppose my view is improved a little . . . " She lowered the curtain.

Fergus wanted to stand and have a look at the devastation, but his head was pounding and even moving it from side to side caused him acute pangs of nausea. A realization dawned on him. "Are they looking for us because of the fight, or because of the fire?"

"The fire."

He felt empty all of a sudden, like he might just evaporate, which would probably be good – better than being executed by humans, at least. He shook his head dumbly.

"The Knights don't need the publicity," she continued. "Everyone down here knows it was them, and that means everyone is that much more frightened now, doesn't it? That's all they want. They're aiming to pin it on you two with the authorities, so that they don't direct too much negative attention from above. They don't want the humans to grow sympathetic towards us. It's obvious two people couldn't have done this alone, but when has anyone ever looked at our side objectively?"

"Why do you know so much about them?"

"Why do you not? They're a threat to us. Besides, Dom's place is right on top of mine, and they're just as likely to come here saying that the 'evil ones' are hiding up in the parlor and burn it all to the ground. Of course, I know about them. I've been setting up wards against them. Haven't you wondered what I've really been doing all this time?"

He blinked at her. "I thought you were . . . up there with her."

"You have that sort of petty logic in common."

Fergus scowled, but felt too awful to bother responding.

"Remember how I told you that my aunt had a vineyard? It's the one that my cousin Leonidas owns. I think you should go there."

"What?"

"You can work for him. Perhaps for about a month? Though they're all too happy to pin it on you now, in a month's time, the upper officials won't care anymore one way or another. I'll talk to the

Count and see if he can smuggle you onto an airship. He probably knows someone who can, at least."

"Me. On a farm."

"Well, you are a kelpie, so don't you think you'd be good at it?"

"I've never been further than the docks."

"Won't they root you out down here? Even the Count wouldn't be able to hide you in his penthouse. If you stay here, they'll find you, and you know what they do to so-called hybrid murderers."

"Do it," he mumbled, pressing both hands against his eyes and trying not to feel too despairing about the trouble he'd landed himself in.

"We should be able to get you out of here within a couple of days. Until then, you must stay in this room. Don't let anyone in. If there's someone who needs to see you, I'll be the judge."

He didn't protest.

"I'll come and retrieve you when it's safe. I do visit once a year for my own health, so it won't be odd."

"Why are you doing all this?"

"Doing what?" Her hair was haloed by the strange light – no, the *natural* light – coming in through the top of the window.

"Taking me in . . . " he paused, willing her to fill in, *the night Flynn was killed.* "Keeping me here. Finding me that other job. Smuggling me out. Pretty sure you're not in love with me. So why?"

She said nothing for a very long moment, wrapping her arms tighter around herself. He could hear the staggered ticking of the grandfather clock in the shop. Something heavy creaked and then crashed outside the window.

"Maybe that's so," she agreed at length. "But don't you think I like you?"

"You usually wouldn't go so far for someone whose primary role in your life is providing temporary entertainment."

He could tell she was frowning, though her face was shadowed. She didn't argue his word choice, however. Instead she replied, "Because I promised Ainslee I would."

Fergus's hands fell away from his face, and despite the discomfort, he slowly sat up, staring at her in bewilderment. "Ainslee . . .? My . . . My mom?"

"Yes." Ursula looked away.

"Um, sorry, but since when were you close?"

"While you were still in grammar school. I probably know her better than you do. Before you get your hackles raised . . . We were 'business associates.' No, perhaps friends. Perhaps she was the only friend I have ever had. Maybe she was a little like a third aunt, too."

Fergus shook his head, struggling to take it in. "What the hell . . .?" he muttered.

"Your mother was a very intelligent woman. Not just clever, but magically gifted. A lot of people owe her. Well, for me, it's more than that. Perhaps . . . Perhaps I loved her as much as I have ever loved anyone."

"That's . . . Isn't that sick? You loved her, and you and I? Did you and she . . .?"

"Oh, no." She said nothing for a moment and then added, "No, it wasn't really like that. But she may be the reason you've been sheltered this much. A lot of people owe her," Ursula repeated.

"What does that mean?"

"She never went to the universities. You know that, I'm sure. She was born on one of the middle levels, but she was kicked out when they realized what she was. She came down here. My Auntie Beatrice took her in. She was doing something similar to the job you're doing now. You see, even before she knew she was a hybrid, Auntie Beatrice was good with magic. She saw that Ainslee had a gift, and she began to show her things. She never realized how innately powerful Ainslee was."

"I don't follow."

"You know why hybrids exist, don't you? The souls of the fairies killed in the Cataclysm didn't go anywhere, so they latched onto humans, creating hybrids. But those hybrids who have bonded most strongly with their fairy-soul are those who can use that fairy's abilities best, and those who have the greatest control can even take on their fairy's form. Ainslee could do that. She could do it without . . . help."

"Without help? What do you mean?"

"Have you heard about how one fairy can take another fairy's powers?"

"Yeah, a little," he said, thinking back to his conversation with Terry at the docks.

"It's done by magic, and for those who haven't bonded enough to transform, they can sometimes manage it by subsuming another soul's power. It's based on chance. There aren't many hybrids who can do it through those means, and even rarer are those who can do it without. Ainslee could do it without. She was able to teach a handful of people how to do it. No, less than a handful."

"You?"

Ursula nodded. "But someone who can do it is perhaps worth even more on the black market, so you mustn't ever tell anyone – you understand? A few people – *important* people – became indebted to her because of that and a few other things. They've all been protecting you, though you've never even met one of them. A lot of people have come to know about Ainslee's ability, and . . . well, a lot of people also know that you have the same kind of fairy-soul. Both kelpies – a rather big coincidence, of course."

"You mean . . . there are people who want to . . .?"

Ursula nodded. "As I said, you've been sheltered."

"So, where is she now? Where has she been for the last *four years*?"

"Dead."

His mouth twitched, and his brow furrowed. "You're lying."

Ursula shook her head, bangs falling into her face. "I saw her die." She turned from him completely. "This wasn't a last request. You should know she was losing herself. It had been happening for a long time, so when it first was getting bad, she asked me to watch over you." Ursula paused for a very long time and then finally walked over to pick up a book out of a pile in the corner. There were lots of piles all around the room. Most of the books pertained to the alchemy business, and he got enough of fish scales and cats' claws and all that while stocking shelves, so he hadn't poked around much. She walked over and sat down, opening it to reveal a photo album.

There was a picture of his mother on the first page with Ursula. She had her arm around Ursula, and she was smiling. Their black mops of hair matched, though Ursula's eyes were dark green, and his mother's were such a pale grey that they almost seemed white. Ursula's face was rounder and heart-shaped, whereas his mother's was long and slim like his own, punctuated by a strong, square chin. It couldn't have been more than six or seven years ago, but the Ursula in that picture looked younger than he was now. He wondered how old she really was, and if his mother's death had aged her.

"How?" he finally managed.

"She drowned."

Fergus didn't reply. He bowed over, pressing his hands to his face. She was gone. She wasn't going to just return to the apartment someday. She wasn't going to apologize for leaving. How could she drown? She was the one who taught him how to swim in the rough waves beyond the docks when he was a small child. How could she do that? How could she really be gone-gone? He was grateful that this time Ursula gave him his space. She got up and went into the tiny kitchen. He could hear water being poured into the teakettle and set upon the stove. She returned after a few minutes, still hugging herself. Her photo album was still sitting open next to him, though he couldn't bear to glance at it. He swallowed roughly.

She didn't sit down again. Leaning on the doorframe, she remarked, "You came by not so long after that. I had heard from Felix that you'd been poking around for jobs. He couldn't give you enough to feed you, so he also asked me to give you a chance. I didn't even ask you for references, did I? I just told you to be here by 10 sharp. Fergus . . . " she trailed off.

"What?" he asked hoarsely without looking up.

"It wasn't entirely for her. Some of it was for you, too. You were surprisingly uncomplaining. To be honest, the aunt who left me this store? Auntie Beatrice, that is . . . She died suddenly one day. Actually, it was when I was about 16, too. Your mother helped me run things at the shop until I could do it on my own. Despite the fact you were a small child, she did it free of charge, so that I wouldn't suffer. She just worked harder . . . "

"Please stop."

Ursula did, for a moment, but then she added, "So maybe it was me, too, because you reminded me of myself and because you were strong."

He didn't say anything. His throat was locked up and try as he might, tears still pooled in his hands, leaking through his fingers. He cursed and tried his best to wipe them away. His mind had become blank – a drifting, meaningless wash of white – but despite that horrible cold feeling, his eyes wouldn't dry up. He cursed over and over, tasting the salt as it dripped down into his mouth. Ursula went back into the kitchen. She stayed there for a long time – longer than the whistle of the kettle. She was there until he had half-fallen asleep again. She settled down on the bed beside him on the other side of the abandoned album and folded his fingers around a cup, holding her own between her thighs until she was certain he had properly gripped it.

He stared at it bleakly, but the tiny warmth radiating into his palm was soothing. He could have fallen asleep then, but instead, he sat up, feeling that he should be mindful of the cup and drink the tea. Probably she'd put sedatives in. He thought that might be all right. Idly, he looked down once more at the photo of his mother. He only had a few stashed in this room with the rest of his meager belongings. Most were from when he was a small child.

"There's one more thing."

"More bad news? Are you gonna tell me my mom did some horrible ritual thing on my dad or something?"

"No, she didn't lie about him. He did reject her when he found out and moved to another city. Do you think he was afraid she'd hunt him down?" Ursula chuckled darkly.

"Who knows?" Fergus muttered.

"Have you ever heard of Niamh or Bandersnatch?"

He nodded.

"Niamh searches for the gateway to the fairy realm – to cast off their humanity and live comfortably as fairies once more. Bandersnatch thinks that is foolishness, because if the Cataclysm had not sealed the gateway, it would have been found by now. But perhaps some from both are thinking that if they can turn into their fairy's form, they can leave this place and go to the forests where the real fairies – the ones stuck here – dwell.

"You may know that they sometimes allow humans and hybrids to visit, but never to stay and never for long. No doubt, they blame humans as much as hybrids do for the Cataclysm. More likely than not, they'll make a meal of trespassers before they're through. But there are those who are hopeful enough to think they can get past that if they can just discard their humanity. And then there are some that believe that the gateway simply cannot be found by anyone in human form.

"So when you are away, you'll have to be careful. There are hybrids who want to take your powers. Not just that, but my cousin's farm is near some of the forests. There are parts that are fine to go in. Probably you'll want to, since you've never seen a forest before. But you must be wary and look for the fairy rings before you enter. If you see them, you mustn't go in no matter what. Unless you want to die."

"Of course, I don't," Fergus muttered, leaning down to put his teacup on the floor. He flipped the page of the album. There were a few more pictures of his mother from about the same time, but before he could properly look at them, Ursula snatched it up and shut it.

He could have sworn Terry was in one of the pictures.

Chapter Nine.

Fergus would've liked to have a few visitors to keep him from thinking about everything Ursula had told him. However, he heard her turning people away. Emily had come by, and there had been a fantastic shouting match, which if he hadn't been sporting a migraine might have been somewhat funny. Raja and Evelyn came by, too, but Ursula also told them he was away. Evelyn didn't seem convinced. He could hear her talking about an invitation, but shortly thereafter, Ursula slammed the door on them. Terry didn't come, which made sense. He was wanted, too, and even if he wasn't, Fergus knew he would be careful not to lead anyone to the shop while he was convalescing.

She did let Felix in. Fergus was rather surprised that the hoary old bartender came at all, but he brought with him some of the Magpie's famous leek soup, which tasted as good as it sounded bad. He entertained Fergus with a few recent stories about drunks he'd had to deal with, mentioning that he missed having him around. It would've been nice to have someone with a strong arm, he'd said. This made Fergus laugh a little, but also feel a bit guilty, because he couldn't think of anyone to suggest.

He thought he would like to see that album again, but Ursula had put some kind of magic on it. Even though he managed to locate it, he couldn't pry it open. He gave up and didn't bother trying to hide his tracks, since she seemed to have assumed he was going to go snooping anyway. He wondered if he'd made a mistake. He knew he'd seen reddish hair, a straight nose, and a wide mouth, though that could describe a lot of people. Still, these features came together for Terry in a particularly flattering way, so he kept flip-flopping on what he thought he had seen.

There was plenty of time to second guess himself, because though Ursula had theorized it would only take a couple of days, it seemed it wasn't going to be that easy. A couple of days had gone by, and there weren't any certain plans, which was making Ursula irritable. Probably, Fergus thought, she was actually worried, but it wasn't in her nature to show it more than she already had, so she'd become snappish and petulant instead.

Fergus was bored out of his mind. Having nothing else to occupy himself with, he'd resumed reading the book Flynn had loaned him. He had to start over from the beginning, because he'd forgotten most of it, but it was a fictional account that relied heavily on philosophy to press the narrative. It was a little dry, despite being a story about a forbidden affair, but he was forcing himself to charge through to the end. Upon reaching the midway point, he found a page missing. He suspected it was one of the only juicy parts to the story, which was rather jarring. Feeling annoyed, he put the book down and started poking around in the piles of Ursula's books, hoping to find something interesting.

This was how he discovered the map, folded over and hidden between a couple of heavy almanacs. It was a hand drawn map, though not in Flynn's hand, but the notes in the margins matched the handwriting on the receipt in his wallet. He took the receipt out and placed it over the map. It seemed to have the same general shape, and he wondered if it was the map key. However, he still couldn't make heads or tails of Flynn's notes. He scrutinized the note and the map until his head started to hurt, and then he decided he should hide them in case Ursula realized he'd found the page and tried to make off with it again, as she must have that night he'd heard her rooting around in the dark. He stuck them both in his wallet.

He didn't know what he should do with this puzzle, but he did know that Flynn would have probably wanted him to have it. Or maybe he wouldn't, but he felt like he should anyway, so he kept the pieces and pondered them. He tried looking around for any books on magic in the stacks, but they were too complicated, and none resembled anything in Flynn's notes, so he gave up on that rather quickly.

Moving around made his stitches itch and sting, but he couldn't help it. He was going stir crazy, stuck in that room wondering what would happen next and what everyone outside was doing. Ursula was out again. Presumably, she'd gone up to the Count's to continue either negotiating or finalizing the plans to smuggle him out. It was late morning, drizzly, and Fergus was lying in bed feeling bored out of his mind when there was a knock at the shop door.

Despite common sense telling him to ignore it, he got up and crept out to see who it was. Under the cover of a large shelf, he spotted red hair and white skin reflected in the glass. It was Jane, and suddenly he recalled that he'd said he'd meet her days ago. He didn't exactly trust her, but guilt compelled him to at least go and apologize for standing her up, so he crept along the wall on the other side of the shelves to the door and then reached out to unlock it. She looked around in confusion before realization dawned, and she pushed the door open and stepped inside, locking it behind her.

"Hi," she said, and Fergus motioned for her to step away from the door and back behind the shelves.

"Hi," he repeated when he felt they were definitely out of sight from any of the shop's windows.

"This is . . . cozy?" she said, looking around the cramped space between the rows of jars and vials and the wall behind them.

"Sorry about the other day."

She smiled a little sadly and shrugged. "Well, I didn't wait too long. She was watching like a hawk. I was worried, though. I heard from some of your other friends that you'd gone missing."

"I just went for a long walk," he replied, shrugging.

"I suppose everyone needs to sometimes. Listen, speaking of your friends, I wanted to invite you somewhere."

"That's vague."

She ignored his remark and continued. "I know a few of them, as well, and we're meeting up today – actually in about twenty minutes. Do you want to come?"

"What are you meeting about?"

"The state of the city mainly," she replied, "but no one has been able to see you for days, so you don't even have to stay. I think that they just want to see that you're all right."

"Who are they?"

She blinked at him. "Oh, well, your friends Evelyn and Raja, of course. I suppose you didn't hear them come by."

Fergus frowned, saying nothing. Evelyn and Raja knew Jane? Since *when*, he wondered. That settled it. He wanted to know what was going on – why all these people seemed to know each other – and so he agreed. He nodded for her to follow. They climbed out the back window, which led into a street that used to be dark and winding, but was unsettlingly bright and bare now thanks to the fire. Were it not for the fact that their destination was close, he thought he might have an anxiety attack. Though his hood was pulled up, he was sure someone would recognize him at any minute and run off to collect whatever reward was being offered.

"You shouldn't look around. It makes you seem suspicious," Jane remarked and then linked her arm through his. "Just lean on me, and no one will really think anything of it. We can even kiss, if we need to deflect attention – like in the old spy novels!"

She sounded much too cheerful about it, but it didn't seem like a wholly awful idea, so he allowed her to hang onto him until they arrived at a very upbeat looking coffee house. The front was painted blue with red and white designs, and there were luminescent ferns in pots all around. Inside was just as quaint, with room for only two tables and the bar. None of the chairs matched – neither in color, nor in style. There was a chess board set up on one of the tables, and the walls were covered with what looked to be graffiti, except that there were little buckets nailed to them with crayons, chalk, and markers inside. It wasn't really his kind of place, but it suited Jane.

She gave a friendly nod to the barista and headed straight for a closet off to the side where she started drawing things all over the wall. She opened the door to reveal a very precarious looking set of stairs leading down. Fergus followed her through, though he was starting to feel uneasy. Jane flounced down the stairs as though they were no trouble at all, though he nearly slipped at least twice. He found her excitement utterly bewildering. It was kind of like a dog that had done something good and was hurrying off to be rewarded by its master. She cleared the bottom steps before he did and disappeared from sight.

"I brought him!"

He stepped down into a brightly lit room. It looked a lot like the upstairs area, except there was a couch and one large table rather than two. The walls were painted orange, and there were a few photographs of the city in bright blue frames. A china cabinet was smashed into one corner with tattered books inside, which gave off a faint leathery smell. It was a little claustrophobic, and though he wasn't usually put off by tight places, with no route of escape . . .

Five people sat around the table, including Evelyn and Raja. Evelyn immediately got up to inspect him, hands on his shoulders and fussing. She demanded to see the cut. Lifting his shirt to show her the stitches, he wondered how she had known about it. She sucked in her breath, making increasing sounds of worry. He looked over her head to the others and found his answer.

Terry sat in the corner next to Raja. Beside him was Audrey, and then there was a last guy that Fergus thought he might have met once or twice when he'd gone out with Flynn and his university friends, but he couldn't recall his name. He was a foreign looking man with a baby face, but keen eyes. Evelyn dragged him over to the couch to sit between her and the young man.

Fergus leaned over, offering a hand. "Sorry, I know we've met, but . . . "

"Gavin," the young man replied, giving it a brief shake.

"Fergus."

Jane had settled down into a chair at the table and was looking way too pleased with herself. He glanced at Audrey, who was giving him a worried look, and offered a brief smile, which smoothed out her expression a bit. He turned to Terry, who was giving him an inscrutable look, but just shrugged when their eyes met. He really wanted to talk to him, but there were too many people. Besides which, it seemed he was about to be a part of this meeting whether he wanted to or not, because Jane cleared her throat and sat up with an authoritative air.

"Welcome to Niamh, Fergus," she said, grinning brightly.

He blinked and parted his mouth in shock. ". . . Niamh?" He glanced at Terry, but got no response.

"Yes. In case you don't know our reputation, we're mainly a scholarly society. We're researching the location of the gateway to Tír na nÓg, so that the hybrids can leave the cities and go back home."

Fergus nodded slowly. "Was Flynn part of Niamh?"

It seemed this was the wrong thing to ask, because everyone except Terry suddenly went silent and had somewhere else to look. Terry just gave a very tiny nod.

"Well, he helped us with some research," Jane said, clearing her throat. "He was terribly clever." Her mouth formed a tremulous line.

"Is this why you've been missing practice?" he asked Evelyn and Raja.

Raja smiled apologetically. "We wanted to tell you, but we're a republic, and a big decision like that has to be okayed by everyone."

Jane nodded. "We weren't really sure until recently, but now it's decided!"

"And is this everyone?"

"Oh, heaven's no. There are many more, but we're the ones who meet the most often. It all started at the university, you see. That's how most of us met. Mostly just discussions back then, but then people started bringing friends, and we started to think there might really be a way if we all put our minds to it. So here's Niamh. We're a bit more exclusive now, because of the times."

"Niamh is led by Fand, right? Are you Fand?" he asked Jane.

She blinked in surprise. "Why, no. But I'm flattered you think so. No, she rarely comes to gatherings like this. Before we start, why don't I go up and get some drinks. Anything in particular?" Jane asked, taking orders and then rushing off to take them upstairs.

Fergus looked between the others. He wasn't sure what to say. He knew most of them, but there was an uncomfortable tension, and mostly, they just kept exchanging polite smiles without trying to make conversation. Terry was giving him a meaningful look, but he didn't know what the meaning was, since it wasn't followed up by anything. It only made the knots in his stomach tighten. He was rather relieved when Jane returned. She put out a pot and tea cups, pouring out a carefully measured amount into each one before pressing it in its target's direction. He stared at his own without drinking and settled into the couch to listen.

At least maybe he'd learn something useful about Flynn if he stuck around, because he was pretty sure that none of the people who knew him would nominate him for a "scholarly" society of all things, and he knew he wasn't going to be able to contribute even if he had wanted to. Terry also seemed to be strangely silent, even sullen, though Audrey and Raja were surprisingly animated as the members began to discuss the things they'd read and heard, pulling out notes and books and charts and spreading them across the table. Fergus tried to look over it all, but it gave him a headache, and none of it seemed to resemble Flynn's notes.

Audrey had smuggled a rather large tome out of the penthouse, which she seemed a little uneasy about presenting with Fergus there, but as the meeting went on, she became more excited and seemed to forget about him entirely, pulling it out and producing notes. She pointed to various pages she'd earmarked in the tome.

"That *is* a very lucky find," Jane said to Audrey who seemed to glow under her praise. "Good work. So those are the coordinates for Lios, Ddu Yr, Lochasi, and," she said, drawing out the word as she jotted down a few things from Audrey's notes, "hmm, and Lyndcarney."

She glanced up at Fergus and smiled. "You probably know that a lot of books and maps were destroyed in the Cataclysm. Well, all that old technology was impossible to sustain with the changes, and a lot of information was lost. So we're chasing fairy tales and trying to guess at where these places might have been. Most are probably underwater now, but . . . " She paused considering him and smiling. "Well, that's why it's good there are those like you and me amongst us – good swimmers, that is. You can swim, right?"

Fergus nodded.

"How long can you hold your breath?" She was giving him a peculiar look.

He shifted uncomfortably. "Longer than average, probably."

She continued staring at him, nodding slowly. It wasn't hard to guess what she wanted to ask: *Can you transform?* She licked her lips, weighing whether to be so bold or not, but she kept hesitating, possibly because Terry was openly scowling at her. The look in his eyes was admittedly pretty scary. He was the only one not watching Fergus now, though luckily, only Jane's interest seemed to be pointed. He fidgeted with his teacup, staring down into the untouched liquid to escape the attention.

"We should go swimming sometime," she finally said.

He nodded blandly, not looking up. The others resumed poring over the maps and notes on the table.

"So that means we generally have an idea of the locations of the Circle Glen, Glastor, Fren-fa, Shreeve Cave, Fan Fach, and Castle Hau were – along with the locations Audrey found – and we know where the Feahrlin Falls, Goblin Nook, and Dusk Hill are," Raja said, writing furiously on a hand drawn map.

"Yes, well, there are still many more sites out there," Jane replied. "It's possible that the locations we're looking for are more obscure." She was frowning, twisting a lock of hair round and round her pointer finger. "If it wasn't so terribly dangerous, I'd suggest we make an expedition to the forests. Perhaps the fairies might know something."

Audrey's eyes went wide as she exclaimed, "But we'd be killed!"

"I know, I know. That's why I said I *would* suggest it. Not that I am." Jane sighed and picked up her teacup in both hands. "This would have been easier with Flynn," she added softly, gloomily staring into her cup. "I still can't believe he killed himself."

"He didn't," Fergus suddenly interjected.

Everyone turned to stare at him.

"He *didn't*," he insisted.

"Why do you say that?" Jane asked slowly.

"Because I know him. I know he wouldn't have."

"It would take a very strong person to hang him," she replied, eyes narrowing. She allowed a pregnant pause before remarking, "I wonder if a kelpie would be strong enough."

"What does that mean?" Fergus snapped.

"Where were you that night?"

"With us," Evelyn and Terry said at the same time.

"We had a gig," Raja supplied.

"Are you accusing me of . . .?" Fergus snarled, getting to his feet, but Raja tugged him back down.

"Of course not," Jane replied, her expression turning bittersweet and pleasant again. "You have an alibi. Besides, he always said you were like a brother to him." She opened up a book, apparently dismissing the accusation and leaving Fergus seething. "I just remembered – I think those coordinates do come up somewhere else . . . "

The meeting resumed its previous pace. No one seemed one bit concerned about what had just been implied as they once again became engrossed in maps and notes and books and discussion. Fergus glared at Jane for a little while longer, but it did no good, so he reluctantly gave up his outrage and turned his attention to Evelyn and Raja. Raja's map showed the world's surface as it presently looked. Evelyn, though, had an old map – so old it was barely legible – of the old world.

There was a better map in the history museum on the top level. It even sold copies, but they were enormously expensive. He'd always figured it was to keep hybrids from being able to buy anything in the shop; perhaps even a hopeful bid to deter them from coming in at all. He was surprised, though, that Jane hadn't supplied one, as Ursula had claimed she was an heiress.

He stood and loomed over Evelyn's shoulder to get a better look. There were things missing in places he would hardly have expected. It was difficult to even say where New Peiling might have been on the old map. Somewhere in the northern hemisphere. He tried for a few minutes to place it, but eventually gave up and sat down on the couch again. They began discussing old poetry – some of it memorized, the rest read aloud from books and notes – dissecting the lines to try to and eke out any clues. Fergus stifled a yawn. He wondered how much time had passed and how angry Ursula was right now, or if she was even back yet. That's when he noticed Terry trying to catch his eye. He gave a little nod towards the stairs, but Fergus wasn't sure what he wanted him to do.

"Anyone want more tea?" Terry murmured and was mostly ignored. He'd managed to switch places with Audrey, who had been scooting ever closer in her zeal, and was now creeping towards the edge of the sofa. "Gonna get some more."

"I'll help," Fergus said, catching on, and stood.

He practically ran at the stairs, so relieved to be free. Terry followed up behind him. As they arrived at the first floor, Terry directed him towards a table past the front window, giving the barista a chilly look until the man turned away.

"I didn't know you were part of this," Fergus whispered. He figured that they were already ridiculously conspicuous, so he didn't bother with trying to look casual.

"I'm not – not really. I've been to meetings a few times, but I ran into Evelyn after the mess with the fire, and she demanded I come with her. I've been 'sheltered' here ever since."

"'Sheltered'?" Fergus parroted and then went, "Oh."

"Yeah. I've got to get out of here. If someone does tip them off, I'm screwed down in that hole."

"Ursula is arranging for me to leave the city and work on her cousin's farm or something. Maybe she can sneak you out, too."

"That's an idea. It's better than sticking around here, but we gotta be careful, or they're going to stick us both down there for safe keeping."

"Should we leave now?"

"No, there's something I need."

"What is it?"

"That book Audrey brought."

"You want to steal it from her?"

"She stole it from the Count, and no doubt, he stole it, too."

"But why? Why not just write notes like everyone else?"

"Because they don't even know how to look at it. In a way, it'd be doing them a favor, because I do have an idea of what to look for, or rather, *how* to look for it, and if I did find something, they'd benefit, too."

Fergus sighed. At the moment, he didn't particularly care what happened to Niamh or some moldy old book; he didn't care about a lot of things. Probably, he'd be toiling in the country in a few days, and who knew if Ursula would actually come back for him? She might forget once he was out of sight. He probably *would* be safer out there, so she would have very tidily carried out his mother's request whilst leaving him in the middle of nowhere for all time. He suddenly didn't want to go, but as someone passed by the window, causing him to nearly jump out of his skin, he recalled that there was no way around it now. He felt like breaking something.

"What do you want me to do?"

•   •   •

Fergus went first down the stairs, carrying the pot of tea. It was pretty hot, but that was the point. He made sure to fumble the last step and slipped, falling to his knees. The pot crashed and shattering into a thousand little shards on the floor, hot tea spilling out. He let out a very real hiss of pain as the liquid burned his fingers, and he held them to his mouth, cursing around them.

"Oh my god, Fergus, are you okay?" Evelyn cried, jumping up and hurrying over.

"It still hurts a little," he muttered, leaning back and gingerly pressing his fingers to his stitches.

"Did you reopen it?" Audrey asked, joining them.

"Dunno," he said, pulling up his shirt to let the girls inspect.

"We need a rag. Careful, don't put your hand down," Raja instructed.

"I'll get one," Terry said, slipping around them back up the stairs.

The girls fussed over him a few minutes more, Jane also gravitating over to add her thoughts on the mild burns swelling up on the pads of his fingers, but it wasn't long before they noticed that Terry had not come right back with a towel.

"Maybe he just used the toilet," Fergus suggested, getting to his feet. "I'll go and check. I wanna get some ice anyway."

They let him go, though he noticed Gavin and Jane were both giving him dubious looks out of the corner of his eye. He didn't care. He went straight up, and when he didn't see Terry on the top floor, headed outside. He wasn't sure where to go, so he just started back towards Beathag's. Sure enough, after a block, Terry slipped out of an alley, joining him. The book was outlined against the fabric of his sweater.

"Thanks," he said, giving Fergus a rare hint of a smile.

"God, they're probably gonna be out here any minute."

"I doubt it, but it won't be too long. If we can get to her place, we'll be okay. Jane's not gonna tangle with Ursula."

"I can't believe she accused me of killing Flynn," Fergus muttered darkly.

"I can. She probably only invited you to test you – to see if he'd told you anything and if you'd be gullible enough to share. When you didn't have anything to offer . . . "

"She's a cow, isn't she?"

"Yeah, that's putting it lightly. She's just as bad as Ursula."

"Then why's she afraid of Ursula?"

"Because she isn't stupid. If it came down to an application of magical skill, she couldn't win. And if it was otherwise . . . Ursula seems like the type who'd go straight for the eyes."

"She kinda is," Fergus agreed. "Hey, Terry, um, this is kind of a weird question, but did you know my mom?"

"I've heard of her. Can't say I knew her personally."

Fergus tried to study his face, but his expression gave nothing away, so he nodded. "Yeah, right?

139

You'd have to have been up there still," he said, jerking his chin towards the plate above them.

"Why do you ask?"

"No reason," Fergus replied, shaking his head.

As they arrived at Beathag's, Ursula was standing in the doorway, arms crossed. She looked furious.

Chapter Ten.

Ursula was white-faced with anger, but as the two slipped into the shop, she held her tongue. Fergus wasn't sure if he was thankful, or even more worried. There was a brittle moment as she stared at him – he cringing and she glaring – but then she looked at Terry and shook her head, storming off into the back room. Fergus followed after her to get away from the front windows. He thought about redirecting into the kitchen to avoid her potentially delayed rage, but after a moment, followed her into the tiny back room that was the setting of their last big fight. She had her back to him, looking through some old books.

He cleared his throat softly, intending to apologize for worrying her, but she sharply cut him off with, "I don't care."

"Well, fine then," he replied and was about to herd Terry into the kitchen after all, but she shoved the book back into the shelf and turned.

She frowned at them both for a very long moment, perhaps counting back from ten, before speaking. "You should pack your things. You'll be leaving in less than two hours."

"What? Why so sudden?"

"Because Trevor Fennis turned up in pieces by the docks, and half this level was burnt to the ground, so the Air Guard suspects that the culprits will be trying to flee the city."

Fergus cringed a little.

"I thought so," she muttered. "I thought that might have been the purpose of that gala in the first place. I'm surprised you were careless enough to go along with him, though," she said, glancing at Terry before returning her attention to Fergus. "He's probably set this up in such a vexing way because he's irritated, and if you get caught and it turns out they charge you with both crimes, I imagine the authorities would simply burst from joy to find out the arsonists they're looking for were involved in Fennis's murder, too. Probably all traces of his involvement will be overlooked as they go about using you two to scare the rest of the bad little monsters straight."

"What's he annoyed at me for?" Fergus demanded.

"Most likely because you didn't move right in with him."

"Like I would have."

"That's one of the conditions."

"Wait, what? What conditions?"

"He's only doing this much because he wants you to move in as a full-time servant on your return."

"No way."

"Do you think arguing about it with me will help? Worry about it when you return. Right now, you should be focusing on how we're going to even get you out of here without being caught." She turned to Terry again. "I suppose this means you'll be going with him?"

Terry nodded. "Don't own much anyway, so packing's not a problem."

She pursed her mouth and nodded. "Well, I'll give you the details, then, while he gets ready," she said, effectively dismissing Fergus.

Fergus shrugged and went into the bedroom to sort through his things. He thought he could at least count on her to not throw anything out, even if it was likely she'd forget to come collect him. He fished his satchel out from under the bed, threw in some clothes, a couple of books to read, and a few other personal effects. It didn't take long, which was good since they didn't have a lot of time if they were going to catch the ferry from the docks to the airship base on the island adjacent to New Peiling. He was thankful they wouldn't have to take the lifts, because he couldn't imagine how they wouldn't be caught coming out of them. Maybe the ferry would be easier to get around.

He tried to open the album once more, thinking that he might borrow the photo of Ursula and his mother, but it was still bound tightly with magic he couldn't force with physical strength alone. He considered stealing it altogether and then maybe having Terry see if he could break the ward, since he seemed to know a little about magic, but thought that if he did, Ursula probably would throw out his things in retaliation. He grabbed his guitar and went into the other room.

Terry and Ursula were bent over an enormous book with a number of little jars and boxes around them. In the center of it all, they'd drawn a circle in chalk. When Ursula saw him, she immediately frowned.

"No. No guitar. If anyone has sold you out, they'll recognize you in an instant. We'll be lucky if they haven't hired any hybrids to see through this glamour."

"But it might take months."

"I'll send it if it does. Don't give them any clues. This is going to be hard enough."

Fergus glared, but Terry looked up and added, "It sucks, but we can't afford the risk."

"Fine," he grumbled, going to hide it under Ursula's bed, so that at least it would be safe in case Dominique visited.

He returned, ruffled and touchy, and stood off to the side to watch them. This time, neither paid him any mind. Like the Niamh meeting, he had little idea of what they were talking about. It involved runes and circles and fairy magic and various ingredients, which he was, at least, familiar with from having stocked them for years, but the actual properties and uses evaded him. Besides, he was feeling too angry about being stuck out on a farm for ages with no guitar to bother taking an interest. He was relieved when they finally stopped and called him over.

"Okay, put your hand in the circle," Ursula instructed him.

He did so, placing his beside Terry's.

"Since you probably don't know how to use your own magic, and because this way may make it just a tiny bit harder to see through, we're using a rune circle to produce the glamour. It won't last long – just a couple of days – but that's more than enough time to get you to the farm. I wrote in advance to introduce you, so you don't have to worry about that. Just make yourselves useful, keep your heads down, and everything should be fine. Are you ready?"

"Yes," said Terry.

Fergus nodded uncertainly.

Ursula tossed reddish powder over their hands. It had a sour smell like vegetables that had been rotting for some time, and Fergus forced back the reflex to wipe it off or cover his nose. She chanted softly, and he could feel a kind of pleasant heat radiating up from his hand until his entire body was tingling with that relaxing, bubbly warmth. He glanced away from the ceremony and caught a glimpse of himself in a glass case over Terry's shoulder.

"What the hell? You made me look . . . "

"Just wait a damn minute," Ursula snapped, tying a little piece of string onto his pinky finger and then another onto Terry's. "There. What? You have a complaint?"

Fergus pulled at his face, which felt like his face, except the one looking back from his reflection was entirely different. He looked unpleasantly similar to the Count: curly wheat-colored hair, pale green eyes, a sharp nose, and generally boyish and pretty. He wrinkled his nose. Terry seemed unchanged.

"Sometimes, I wonder if you're really a hybrid. Magical prowess must skip a generation in that family," Ursula scoffed, crossing her arms. "Or," she paused thoughtfully, "maybe I'm just that good."

"Shut up." Fergus scowled at her and then returned to squinting at his reflection until he thought he could sort of see himself through the mirage. "I can see through it," he declared, though not wholly true. "How come Terry didn't change?"

"Oh, I did," Terry replied, mouth twitching into something like a smile before he turned to Ursula. "See, he can see through others. Just . . . not his own." Fergus could tell Terry wasn't trying to placate her, but was making fun of him, so he glowered even more. Terry didn't seem to notice as he continued, "Your taste is a little funny. You really made us look like them?"

"Who would stop them from leaving? The Count is always flitting here and there, isn't he? Though . . . well, you may want to make up a story as to why *he's* back in the city, in case anyone asks."

"Who is 'he'?" Fergus asked.

"The Count's long lost lover," Ursula purred, "Rosslyn Weber."

Fergus's mouth twitched a little, but he abruptly decided not to ask in case Ursula decided to be free with her information and vowed to disavow all knowledge that they were masquerading as the Count and his boyfriend. Maybe ex-boyfriend if he was "long lost." He also muttered something about Ursula's tastes, but was generally ignored. He then grumbled about why he couldn't be this Weber guy instead of the Count, but this, too, was ignored.

"Are you ready?" Ursula asked. "I'll go with you as far as the ferry, but I'm afraid I can't send you off the usual way. Too many people would expect us together."

"Then what are you going to do?"

"Something that you two alone are going to be privy to, and you mustn't tell anyone." She flashed Terry an uncertain look.

"My lips are sealed, as always," he said, shrugging.

"Wait, are you gonna transform?" Fergus asked.

She gave a little nod.

Terry looked between the two of them and then said, "I'm going to put that book in your bag. I'll meet you by the front door."

"You aren't going to be . . . sentimental, are you?" Ursula asked cautiously as Terry disappeared through the door.

"In case you decide to never return for me, I think I deserve this much."

Her mouth formed a flat line, brows knitting. "I do go once a year. I'm sure you could remind me then, even if I forgot."

"Just shut up," he replied, taking her face in his hands and kissing her roughly. Her hands seized the front of his jacket, straining the fabric against his shoulders. He kissed her until he felt that he was thoroughly asphyxiated, and then he released her with a soft gasp. She looked a little strange, her eyes catching the light better than usual, her cheeks flushed, and her mouth moving in uncertain directions. She abruptly turned away from him, ducking her face and pressing her hair back into place.

"That should last you a few weeks, at least," she muttered.

He snorted softly. "Guess you'd be fine either way." He paused. She didn't reply. Her back was to him, and she was standing very still. "Hey . . . " he started.

"Don't make such a big deal about it again," she interrupted waspishly. She turned, wiping roughly at one eye and swept past him. "Someone like you doesn't get to say 'good-bye' like *that*."

He had no idea what she meant, but followed after her into the bedroom where Terry had picked up his pack and was shouldering it. Ursula was bathed in a soft distortion of air. It was like seeing lights out of the corner of his eye, or staring too intently at motes of dust in the sun. And then a small black cat was sitting on the bed, flapping its tail angrily. It had the same white spot on its chest as the birthmark on Ursula's and white toes on its front paws. Ursula-the-Cat hopped off the bed and slid into the other room.

"What will you do about your stuff?" Fergus asked as Terry began to follow.

"It'll be fine. Too risky to go for it. Ursula said she'll send it when we're settled in."

He scratched his head and nodded.

"We gotta talk. Weber and the Count usually bicker, so just follow my lead, okay?"

"As long as we don't have to hold hands."

Terry snorted. "They're not that . . . affectionate. Not that I've ever seen."

"So who is this Rosslyn guy?"

They stepped out of the shop and looked around. The street was mainly empty, but Fergus thought that such things didn't mean much. Curious eyes could find a place to hide anywhere. He felt uneasy and hastened his steps, thinking it probably would be weird to see them walking out when they hadn't been seen walking in.

"Take a deep breath. That guy never looks uneasy, you know."

Fergus sucked in a long breath through his nose, closing his eyes, and did his best to try to adopt the smug look the Count usually wore.

"Looks weird on your face, but better," Terry remarked. "Rosslyn Weber was the Count's . . . I guess you'd have to say 'lover,' because 'boyfriend' sounds too cute for them. The Count's background – not even I could tell you about that – but Weber came from a small town near where we're going. Not many people from the city can afford to go to the country, and it's doubly so the other way around, but his dad was a famous alchemist and potions specialist.

"He arranged for Weber to go to the Royal University in Clohaven to study potions where I hear he'd graduated with honors. Getting there was expensive, though. This is where the Count comes in. As usual, some kinda deal had to be struck with him to get him to agree. Said that Weber would have to come work for him for a few months as his private alchemist or something to that end.

"Most of this was before my time at the penthouse. I heard it from a guy named Olivier who used to work for the Count – the one who went off to Clohaven to model a few months after I moved in. Anyway, Weber was apparently a genius, but not friendly at all. He was good at keeping himself to himself. So good that not even his father knew he was really a hybrid. That's why that guy was the worst thing that ever happened to him. Probably he could have apprenticed himself to a top alchemist in Clohaven and earned enough that he could have bypassed the Count and lived wherever he wanted doing whatever he wanted. No doubt, the Count probably would have forgotten the deal by then, even.

"But Weber is the kind of guy who has his own little code of conduct, and he never breaks from it. His dad promised the Count, and so even though his father died of illness while he was away at university, he still went through with it to preserve his father's name. Seemed like he hated the Count at first. Olivier said he couldn't remember when it happened or how, but one day, he walked by, and they were . . . uh, well, busy in Weber's potions room. The Count started taking him all over. It was pretty scandalous, because everyone thought Weber was a full human."

Fergus nodded and then reminded himself to look haughty as a couple of people passed by. Terry put on a bored, but slightly annoyed expression until they were clear again.

"This story's longer than it will take to get to the docks, so you'll have to settle for the abridged version. Weber didn't just stay a few months, but their relationship was rocky, so they broke it off and got back together at least once a month. They were the number one topic for most of the society circles. By then, I'd been working there a little while. So basically, here's how it went down. The Count was angry about some ridiculous thing, so he took it out on Weber by getting with Olivier. Probably, he arranged for them to be found. Olivier really wanted to go to Clohaven, so most likely money was also involved.

"Weber *did* walk in on them. You can guess he's a pretty loyal person, and you can also guess that this wasn't the first time the Count was not. He said that was it and broke things off then and there. But imagine if somehow Ursula was scorned."

Fergus shuddered.

"Now times that by about five million and you've got the Count. He exposed the fact that Weber was a hybrid. He didn't stop there. At least, I don't think he did, because when the dust settled, Weber was completely disgraced. The Royal University sent word that they were stripping him of his honors and all the titles he'd earned. No one was willing to take him in here. He was forced to retreat back to his hometown where, at least, *probably* no one ever heard about what happened, but it's not like he can ever work here or in Clohaven again – not with what the Count did."

"That's sick. How the hell could he do that to someone he cared about?"

Terry shrugged. "Probably because he did care. That's how he is. He couldn't handle being left by Weber, and he just lost it."

"Well, why didn't he try to fix it?"

"Even if he had, he's not an idiot. He knew that Weber was never going to come back to him."

Fergus nodded. "So why are people gonna believe we're them?"

"Well, not all of them are. The hybrids are going to see us, so we're just going to have to hope we can get on that ferry before any of them get greedy. The humans will just believe whatever they see, and probably this is Ursula's way of getting back at him for demanding you come live with him. She doesn't seem to want to share. Guess she must like you."

"Hey . . . Can you tell the difference between a human and a hybrid?"

"Yeah, why?"

"Well, how can you tell?"

Terry blinked at him and then chuckled. "You could, too, if you paid attention." He tapped his nose. "Guess you don't know what kind I am, huh?"

Fergus shook his head.

"A *gytrash*. Most people know what they are because they ask Lady Gemini or one of the other dock fortunetellers. But I figured it out pretty easily, because I used to have a dog, and all the little things it heard and all the little things it smelled? I heard and smelled them, too, though my parents didn't. They were always surprised. They'd say the dog was barking for no reason, but I knew it was because it could smell the old guy from across the street going out. It hated that guy.

"Once, when I was little, I was trying to walk it, right? And it pulled free of me and went over to piss on the guy's steps. Old bastard came out and hit him with a broom. I hated that guy, too. He reeked. Even when he was halfway down the block, I could smell him. And sometimes I'd have dreams about running over moors and a big black dog. I always knew in the dreams that I was the dog. Stuff like that."

"That makes sense," Fergus agreed and then turned a little pink as he added, "Sometimes, I dream about being underwater at night. And well, my mom. Sometimes I would sit in the kitchen window and watch her cook. From the side her eyes were white. I thought maybe she was going blind or something at first, but then she explained . . . And all the stuff she craved and all the stuff she hated . . . " He paused, clearing his throat. "Well, anyway, so why does that mean you can tell?"

"I can smell the difference. Hybrids have a different scent from a normal human. Maybe it's the smell of magic, or maybe their fairy-souls just make 'em smell otherworldly or something. They don't smell the same, though."

"That's pretty handy."

Terry nodded. "You should train yourself to do it. Start taking notice. It can save your life, you know?"

They had arrived at the docks. The black cat stopped, sitting down and licking her back legs. Terry gave Fergus a nudge to keep him walking as they passed Ursula. He had to force himself to keep looking forward as they joined the queue for the ferry. It was a hulking black mountain of metal rising out of the waves, half-obscured by an early afternoon fog. Fergus craned his head back, looking for the top. Steam was pouring out of an enormous pipe, mixing with the clouds overhead. Fergus realized with a bit of a start just how overcast it was. He wondered if that would affect the airship.

Apparently, Ursula's magic was strong. He could only assume that most of the people in line were human, as few hybrids would have enough money to travel by airship. However, a few of the passengers were giving them second glances in confusion – seeing and then unseeing, perhaps. Fergus averted his face, trying not to draw attention. Probably it would be a bad idea to ask about the dynamics of airships when he was masquerading as the Count.

The line was shuffling forward at snail's pace, and his second thoughts on the whole matter only multiplied as they inched along, the drizzle becoming a light rain. He craned his head around, looking for Ursula, but she was long gone. Probably, she had no intention to see them off in the rain.

Fergus felt a little pinch in his chest. Sensing his discomfort with the entire thing, Terry suddenly put an arm around his back. He jumped, thrown off by the intimate gesture.

"We'll get there soon enough," Terry murmured. "Just keep your head and don't play with that string."

Fergus realized that he'd been fidgeting with the string Ursula had bound to his pinky the whole time, and the knot had grown a little loose.

"You'll need to keep that on until we're there, okay?"

He nodded. A big drop of rain hit him in the forehead. He shifted uneasily. Terry's arm grew tighter around him, which was comforting, despite also being distinctly strange. He closed his eyes. He could feel that a storm was blowing in, and there was nowhere he would like to be less than here in the open. He opened his eyes to see the thunderhead drawing closer on the horizon. The waves were rising higher, breaking against the docks and soaking his jeans from knee down with each burst of water.

The ship was strangely still, perhaps too big to be rocked by the smaller waves around the docks. He could see whitecaps on the horizon, though, and swallowed roughly. He turned his attention to the front of the line, now just wanting to be in the safe confines of the ferry, and saw what was holding things up.

A boy and a girl were arguing with the attendant checking papers. The girl had black hair with streaks of green and blue. She was particularly tall, and she was wearing a long, formless jacket, so for a moment, he thought she might be a man, as the actual man – or rather, boy – standing beside her was a good deal shorter. He had a thick accent – one that Fergus had never heard before – black eyes with matching shaggy black hair, and a very full, feminine mouth, which was open in rage as he and the girl went from arguing to outright shouting in tandem at the attendant.

Terry cursed. "If they keep on like this, they'll have the cops swarming down here in no time."

Fergus nervously looked over his shoulder for approaching officers, but for the moment they were clear. However, since it seemed like maybe it was in their best interest to intervene before the cops did, he stepped out of line, walking over to the bickering group. Some of the people at the front of the line glared at him, but then they blinked, recognizing him as the Count, and made way.

"What's going on?" he asked in a distinctly un-Count-like way, forgetting about the glamour.

The attendant looked up, also saw the Count, and then straightened immediately, face going bright red. "These people's documents are foreign."

"So?"

"So I can't read them! How can I tell they aren't forgeries?"

Fergus held out a hand, and the man handed him a stack of papers and IDs.

"Hey!" snapped the dark-haired boy.

"Those are ours!" the girl added angrily. Up close, she was very pretty. She had dark blue eyes in such a deep shade that they seemed nearly as black as the boy's.

"Yeah, I know. Calm down," he replied, flipping through the papers. They were, indeed, written in a strange, box-like script that looked more like pictures than letters. He squinted at it for a moment before handing them back to the angry owners.

"They have enough money for tickets?" Fergus asked.

The attendant nodded, mouth opening and closing like a fish out of water. "B-but," he stuttered.

"Well, that's good enough, isn't it? Let 'em through."

"But what if the Guard finds out that I let them through, and they turn out to be wanted criminals?"

"Are you criminals?"

The boy started yelling, even angrier, in a foreign language. Fergus could only assume he was being cursed at, but since he couldn't understand, he ignored it.

The girl's face had gone bright red as she spluttered, "How dare you!"

"I think they're too obvious to be criminals," Fergus replied. "At least around here, no one would be this loud if they did something illegal, right?" he said, his heart giving a little palpitation as he smiled to hide the flinch of guilt trying to escape into his expression.

The attendant didn't look convinced, but now the people in line were starting to back Fergus up, loudly complaining about the hold up.

"Fine," the man cried in exasperation, throwing his hands into the air. "It's a hundred each," he added, holding out his hand. Fergus was half-surprised that the two didn't complain, but just placed two notes in his palm. He hoped that Ursula had supplied them with enough to get through, because he had nothing in his wallet except Flynn's note and the page.

"And you, sir?" the attendant asked, apparently willing to let "the Count" through early.

He opened his mouth, at a loss of what to do, but quite suddenly, Terry was at his shoulder, putting two fifty notes in the man's hand.

"Very good. Please make yourselves comfortable," he said, ushering them in.

Fergus followed Terry into the ferry.

Chapter Eleven.

Terry seemed less certain once they entered the hallway. There were a number of doorways lining both sides and a set of stairs at the end of the corridor. The carpeting was red, perhaps rich once, but worn now and stained with age. There was a dank, moldy smell coming from somewhere. They stood idly for a moment before Terry started forward, looking into each of the rooms and then selecting one arbitrarily. There was no window, and the lighting came from a single, flickering candle jutting out of the wall. Fergus sat down on the built-in seat across from him. He couldn't smell the storm from inside the ship, but the air pressure was lower, and the way the ferry kept rocking was a keen reminder.

"You okay?" Terry asked. "You look kinda white. You aren't sea sick already, are you?"

He shook his head, closing his eyes tightly. "The weather," he muttered, pressing his temple against the wall.

"Will you be okay?"

"It's fine," Fergus replied quietly, wrapping his arms around himself and burying down closer against the hull.

"May we join you?" a soft, piping female voice asked from the door. Fergus glanced out of the corner of his eye to see the foreign couple from before.

Terry paused and then shrugged. "Suit yourselves."

The girl walked in and plopped herself down next to Terry, resting her hands on her bare thighs and smiling between the two of them. She was followed by the boy, who sat down next to Fergus, crossing his arms over his chest and not looking at anyone.

"Thank you for before," the girl said to Fergus.

He forced a thin smile, looking up as much as he could, because he could just *feel* the thunder rocking the ship. "No problem," he replied tightly.

"I'm Three," she offered cheerfully, looking between them.

"Three, huh?" Terry remarked, lifting an eyebrow. "Just Three?"

"Yup, that's right!"

"Why 'Three'?" Fergus muttered.

"Pray you never find out," the boy said with a dark smile, finally looking at him, though only for a moment.

"Whatever," he replied, going back to huddling.

"Pip! Be nice," Three chided. "This is Pip. We're a team. And who are you?"

Terry was laughing a little, silently. Fergus wondered how he could ignore the storm. "Terry," he said, holding out a hand to shake hers. She stared at it in confusion for a moment before hesitantly offering her own. Terry took it and gave it a shake, which did little to stem her bewilderment, but she smiled anyway. "And this is Fergus. We're also what you might call a team."

"Might call?" Three asked, cocking her head.

"Well, we're friends," Terry replied. "Right?"

Fergus lifted his head for a moment, blinking slowly, and then nodded. Smiling to himself, he added, "Yeah."

"We're friends, too! Right, Pip?"

"I guess," Pip replied. "Though if they're friends, and we're friends, we should sit on the same side."

"What?" she asked. She was quiet for a moment, trying to work out what he'd meant, and then she blinked. "Oh, *that's* what it is. Um, excuse me. Do you mind switching with him?" she asked Terry.

Terry looked a little confused, but he nodded and got up to change places. "You two are pretty close," he said.

Though he wasn't really looking, Fergus thought Terry must have been studying Pip, because the boy was scrunching down, as though trying to avoid attention. He felt a little sorry for him. It was pretty obvious he wasn't comfortable around strangers. However, his companion didn't seem too worried about this as she chattered on at Terry, asking him about what he did and where he was from and so forth. Terry was careful not to give away too much, piecing together a little about them and a little about the Count and Weber, in case anyone might walk past and overhear.

"And what do you do?" he asked her when at last he had a chance.

"We're bounty hunters. The best in the business!" she cheerfully exclaimed.

Fergus felt a little chill run down his spine. Luckily, no one seemed to be paying him any mind, because he was sure his eyes had widened and his face lost a little color. Terry, meanwhile, took it in stride, which was no less than what Fergus expected at this point.

"Really? How many have you collected?"

"Five so far this year."

"Not bad," Terry replied.

"We're hoping to beat last year's record, which was nine."

"Are you on the job now?"

"Not really. We were poking around in New Peiling, but the only decent looking bounty was really vague: a man with black hair and a man with red hair – arsonists. But there were a lot of people like that. For a reward that size, it just seemed like it would be a waste of time."

Fergus glanced at her, feeling a bit relieved that she apparently couldn't see through the glamour, and then realized that Pip was watching him with a narrowed gaze. He stared back until the boy turned red and looked away again. A hybrid, then. She was seemingly oblivious, however. He thought she must be human, but a human and a hybrid traveling together? Maybe she didn't realize. If the kid was hiding it, there probably was good enough reason for it. Besides, maybe if he kept it to himself, it would buy him some good karma, and Pip wouldn't remark on the fact that they were clearly a brunette and a redhead in a rush to leave the city.

"What did you say you do again?" Pip asked, staring at Fergus's knees.

"Airships."

"So I suppose this one we're off to must belong to you?"

Fergus paused and then asked, "Why?"

"Just wondering," Pip replied and returned to staring at the wall.

"Don't mind him," Three said, turning her attention to Fergus. "He's not used to strangers."

Fergus watched as Pip clenched his arms more tightly around himself. "How do you know each other?" he asked. "Are you from the same village or something?"

"Close," she replied with a smile. "I'm actually from a different island, but not so far away. We're both runaways, you see."

"Yeah?" Fergus replied, lifting an eyebrow and feeling another trill of unease in his stomach.

She nodded, leaning forward a little. "Actually, I'm the daughter of two – you call it 'hybrids' here, right?"

Fergus and Terry exchanged confused glances, but Terry nodded. "You mean, people with fairy powers?"

"Yes, people who have the spirits with them. Both of my parents are like that. Actually, everyone in my village."

"There were no humans?" Fergus asked.

"Well, none except for me."

"So . . . your parents chased you out . . .?"

"Oh no, not at all," she quickly replied, waving one hand.

"Then . . .?"

"See, they taught me magic from an early age. I think they were hoping that I would be visited, too. It seems that the spirits tend to gravitate towards other spirits, so most of the children in my village were 'hybrids.' Well, isn't it the same here?"

"Yeah, I guess so," Fergus replied, thinking that it did sort of make sense, given how many people born on the lower level wound up hybrids.

"So why did you run away?" Terry asked.

"I didn't want my parents to be shamed, because I was different. Even though I could do magic, it just wasn't the same, so I set out to seek my fortune, as you say."

"And that's how you met?" Fergus supplied.

"Yup! Actually, it was only a couple of years ago."

Fergus eyed Pip. He thought 18 might have been stretching it, which meant this kid was probably really young when they started out. However, Pip supplied no information about himself, and Three seemed disinclined to share what he didn't offer.

The ship was moving. Fergus wasn't entirely sure how he knew, because it was stable enough that the feeling was very faint, but he was certain that they had cast off. It wasn't long, though, before they hit the open water between the islands, and it became choppier. The ferry, despite its bulk, roiled with increasing violence.

"Are you sea sick?" Three asked, giving him a sympathetic look.

"No," he replied weakly.

"You look kind of bad."

Terry shifted a little closer to him, which he felt incredibly grateful for. "He's just getting over a cold."

"Oh, but he seems . . .?"

"Just a cold," Terry repeated firmly.

Fergus thought it would be good if he could sit up a bit, but even if he couldn't hear or smell the storm from within the ferry, he could still feel it, seeping into the air from outside. He clenched his eyes shut.

"Well, if you are feeling sick to your stomach, try pinching here and here," she said, demonstrating on her forearm.

"Thanks, I will," Fergus replied through clenched teeth.

"Here, give me your arm," Terry instructed.

Fergus glanced at him out of the corner of his eye, but Terry only shrugged. He took it to mean that if he didn't allow it, the girl was probably going to keep pestering him. He gave Terry his arm. The contact was comforting, even if the pressure didn't do anything. He closed his eyes again and tried not to think about how it was only going to get worse in the air. He tried to imagine being deep underwater.

If he was down past the waves where light didn't reach, the storm couldn't bother him. His ears would be filled with the roar of water, and his eyes with shadows that would blacken out the lightning. Though, he reasoned, he couldn't technically see or hear the storm right now, but he could smell it a little, which he wouldn't be able to in his watery utopia. Probably he would still be able to feel it, but it would seem safer down there. Between this and Terry's gentle pinching of his forearm, he drifted off.

•   •   •

Terry shook him awake. Pip and Three were already gone.

"So this airship belongs to 'you,'" Terry said as he stood. "We can probably pass you off as having a bug, so people won't bother you too much, but you should at least try to remember its name: The *Pulsatrix*. It's a kind of owl. Anyway, don't forget: The *Pulsatrix*. You ready?"

Fergus nodded. He knew without seeing that the storm was in full swing outside. They were nearly the last people out. He couldn't help it; he dragged his feet. However, Terry didn't seem terribly worried. He checked the string on Fergus's finger before they exited into the hell of pelting rain, bone rattling thunder, and lightning. That was perhaps the worst part, because it was flashing every few seconds. People were running from the ferry to the airship. A man in a heavy raincoat, holding the hood in place above his face, shouted at them to hurry on. Fergus flinched away as the runway was lit up from above, but Terry dragged him onwards.

They were greeted at the entrance by a lion. Well, not *really* a lion, Fergus thought, but as close to one as a human could be. The man before them was tall and athletic, with sharp brown eyes a few shades short of gold, and a wild, tawny head of hair that was dry, despite the fact everyone else around seemed to be entirely sodden. He was checking tickets and IDs. It seemed weird that someone with his bearing should be doing such a menial task. Then Fergus caught sight of the gallery of badges on his uniform, and his stomach flip-flopped.

The man recognized them, and his heart sank a little more.

"The Count Palatine," the man said, a hint of mockery in his voice. "You know, this journey would have been a lot safer on my *Wyrd*."

Terry elbowed him before Fergus could ask why they didn't do just that.

"You look a little under the weather."

"He is," Terry supplied.

The man turned to him, looking him up and down. "I didn't think we'd be seeing you in the city again, Weber. Isn't this a nice surprise?"

"Of course, Captain Guillory."

William Guillory. The Captain of the Air Guard. Not just the Air Guard, but he was also in charge of the militia that protected the city. He was supposedly the best pilot for several hundred miles, had never required more than four moves to win a game of chess, and could take a man's head off from a hundred yards. Of course, most of this was simply the drunken rambling overheard at the Magpie, but standing right there in front of him, Fergus thought that perhaps some of it could be true. He found he was so close to panicking that he couldn't control his expression. He desperately hoped that Terry would keep the Captain's attention.

"Well, this will be an overnight flight, so I hope you will not bother the other passengers with noise. It will be difficult enough with this storm."

Fergus wanted to ask if it was even safe in such a storm – maybe suggest that it might be better just to wait until it passed – but he didn't think the Count would, so he bit his tongue and wished that they could just go to some place where he could hide and wait until the horrible feeling of the storm ebbed.

"We'll keep it in mind," Terry said a little irritably. "Are you sure you're up to flying in this weather?"

"It'll take a few days for it to blow over, but if you'd like to wait, I wouldn't blame you."

"Can we just go in?" Fergus snapped, fumbling for the soaked papers that Ursula had conjured for them.

"Just don't cause any trouble," Guillory said, taking Fergus's and giving them a look over before taking Terry's. "You wouldn't have heard anything about the two men who burned down the lower city, would you? I hear you have an ear to many doors, *Count*."

Fergus shook his head. Lightning illuminated the entrance from behind them. He suppressed a shudder.

"I suppose you are feeling unwell. Why travel?" he asked, narrowing his eyes.

"We have something to deliver, and that, Captain, is our business alone. Why have you agreed to fly in such treacherous weather?"

Fergus wanted to kiss Terry. He wondered if that would seem "in character."

Guillory offered a "touché" smile. "We have something to pick up, which is our business alone. Besides, I've been doing much of the ferrying in the last few days. Between the weather and the arsonists, it's an unfortunate necessity. If you think of anything, please let me know. Go on and remember: no trouble."

Fergus was thankful that Terry seemed to have been on this airship before; once inside, he moved without a trace of hesitation. He was even more grateful for the little bit of support he offered, putting a hand between Fergus's shoulder blades. They remained quiet until they arrived at what must have been the Count's personal cabin. It was sumptuous to the point of gaudiness, but they were away from the storm, and there were blinds that they could secure over the windows to block out most of the lightning, so Fergus let out a shaky sigh of relief.

"Why don't you just lie down?" Terry suggested.

Fergus sat down on the bed and then flopped over sideways, pulling a layer of the velvety blankets over his head. It didn't drown out the boom of thunder, so he felt around until he found a nice heavy pillow and pulled that over, too.

"You really do hate it," Terry remarked from the armchair across from the bed. He sounded like he was laughing a little.

"That chair's probably gonna come loose," he mumbled.

"No, it looks like the runes are well done."

Fergus said nothing for a moment before asking, "What?"

"The rune circle. They're used for a lot of things, like holding objects in place. You know that's the only reason the upper plates don't collapse on us, right?"

"That's kinda creepy." He twitched as the thunder vibrated through the airship. "We really must be desperate."

"It'll be fine. Guillory's a legend, even if he is a pompous, self-righteous ass."

"Yeah, I know. I do know that much."

Terry chuckled softly.

The ship began to tremble, a low-level thrumming picking up through the mattress. Fergus's fingers tightened against the pillow.

"We're taking off. Just try to relax. I'll see if I can find you a drink."

"Passengers!" a tinny voice suddenly exclaimed from nowhere. Despite the screech of a poor intercom system, Fergus recognized it as Guillory's.

"Please remain seated and hold tight until we have lift off. This may be rocky. Please don't lose your lunch. You will be responsible for cleaning it up, if you do. Here we go!"

He sounded cheerful, and Fergus wanted to stuff the pillow down his throat, but he was paralyzed with fear as the airship began to ascend into the air, shuddering violently against the storm all the while.

"We're going to die," Fergus said in a matter-of-face tone. The room became a little lighter, and he peeked out to see Terry parting the curtains to have a look outside. "You're supposed to be sitting."

"I'll live," Terry said. "We'll be fine once we're up a little higher. Those waves look rough."

"I'd rather be down there than up here."

Terry lightly slapped him on the back. "Cheer up. Think of it as an adventure." He was also overly cheerful. Fergus wanted to hit him, too, but he was too terrified to move from his position.

"Looks like the icebox is empty. I'll poke around in the other compartments. Just count back from 100."

Fergus heard the door close. He lay still for a long time, as though the storm was a living thing, and if he just didn't move, it might pass him over. However, when it seemed this wasn't going to happen, he shifted, peeking out from under his pillow. At least, Terry had covered up the window again, but he could still see the highlight of lightning against the fabric every few minutes, and there was nothing for the gyrations of the ship itself. He pulled out his wallet and took out the note and the map, staring at them for a few minutes. They meant as little to him now as before.

Maybe, he thought, there was some clue in the book Terry had stolen, so he forced himself to ignore the storm's reckless hold on the airship and got up to retrieve it. It looked like a normal history book with a few notes of local lore tucked away in the margins. There were some maps and drawings. He flipped through the pages, looking for anything that might resemble runes. The words blurred together, and he gave up on trying to even skim, but just flipped at random, hoping luck might bring him to something.

He reached the appendices and found a few promising diagrams. There were more maps and drawings, but also a few strange circles made out of symbols. He sat up straighter, holding the book in his lap and flipping slowly now – page-by-page – with one hand, holding the note in the palm of the other. He found it, or part of it. It looked like there was more than one piece after all. Fergus knew he didn't have much time, and it would be too obvious if he ripped out the page, so he put it aside and started searching around the desk for a pen and paper. He began to copy it as carefully as he could, but unfortunately, there wasn't time to be precise, so it was more the look of it than the exact rendering. When he was done, he crammed the new note with the old into his wallet and shoved the book back into the bag.

He lay back down. His heart was thundering in his ears, his breath coming too quickly, and he was sure Terry would arrive any minute, demand what he had been doing, and then take the papers away from him, even though Fergus felt his claim was more than valid. They had been Flynn's, and he inherited everything Flynn owned. That *included* the notes. Still, he felt anxious, and the jerking of the airship and echo of thunder didn't help. However, being on the verge of panic was exhausting, and though his mind was still overwhelmed by uncertainties, he drifted off into a shallow sleep.

• • •

Toby was back. Fergus was standing in the doorway to his apartment. The fish tank alone illuminated the room. Silhouetted against its white-blue light was a long black tail. A cat was leaning into the tank, pursuing the poor clown fish, which was swimming desperately, but even when it tried to hide in its castle on the bottom of the tank, or in the reeds at the very back, the cat still could reach it. Fergus found he couldn't move, and when he tried to shout to chase the cat away, his voice came out so quietly that it just ignored him.

He knew that Toby was growing tired, though the fish wasn't showing it. Still, as dreams went, he just knew. The cat swiped it up out of the water. Its tiny body went sailing through the air, and he heard Flynn's voice cry out, "Fergus!" in despair.

He was jolted awake by Terry calling his name and shaking him violently.

"We're going down! Get up!"

"What?" he mumbled.

"We're gonna crash! Hurry!"

Chapter Twelve.

Terry grabbed him by the wrist, hauling him out of bed. Ink wells and letter openers were rattling off the desk, pens and cushions bouncing onto the floor, or just flying straight at them. An iron bookend clipped Fergus in the hip, and he let out a hiss of pain. At least, the airship didn't flip over. He supposed, in a moment of clarity amid the chaos, that it physically couldn't. Still, he could barely keep his feet, and they only escaped into the hallway by grabbing onto the items fastened to the walls and pulling themselves out of the room. The lights were flickering, and people were running and screaming every which way despite the crew's efforts to direct them. Terry, at least, seemed to have a reasonably good idea about where he was going and what he should be doing, and Fergus couldn't do anything but trust that. He doggedly attempted to keep up as frightened passengers pushed past him.

That was, until he realized that Terry was taking them outside to the deck. He dug his heels in, feeling he'd rather take his chances within than go out into the lightning and thunder. He shouted something to this effect, but the groan of the airship and the roar of the storm and the screaming drowned him out entirely. Terry held open the door, water spraying inside in sheets. He seemed to think Fergus would come, or maybe his survival instinct was overshadowing his concern, because he pressed his way out into the storm without looking back.

Fergus swore hopelessly, turning to the madness behind him. People were coming up the stairs, eyes rolling in panic, and he thought they probably were going to shove him out if he didn't go on his own, so taking a deep breath and shutting his eyes, he ran up the last steps and forced the door open.

As he feared, the lightning was striking very closely. He froze in terror, unable to look away from the dark clouds and flashes of light. His lack of attention cost him, and the force of the wind against the door threw him back. He heard a muffled cry of anger inside. Terry appeared again, grabbing him by the arm and pulling. He followed, too dumb with terror to protest.

"Don't fall off now! Grip the railing. We'll jump when we're closer!"

"We'll die!" Fergus replied.

"Maybe, but at least it'll be faster than suffocating in the hold."

The black waves were growing closer and closer. They looked huge, like they would swallow the ship the moment it struck the surface, but that was still more reassuring than being in the air in this storm, so Fergus readied himself, holding his breath, and waited for Terry to give the cue. His knuckles were white against the railing. Lightning flashed so closely it struck the side of the ship, sending sparks and a plume of smoke into the air. Both he and Terry were whipped about, barely managing to hang on.

"Go!" Terry shouted, hiking one leg up onto the railing and casting himself off.

He made it look easy, but Fergus felt a pinch of fear. Someone was shouting nearby, though he couldn't be sure if it was at him. He ignored it and took a deep breath, climbing up on the railing and kicking off, or he would have, except someone grabbed him last minute, and what might have been an easy dive turned into an awkward plummet. He didn't even have time to see who it was before they hit the water. He was knocked silly, pulled down by the tide, his waterlogged clothing, and whoever had grabbed him, because they had a death grip on him. He had enough sense not to try to breathe, but he'd expelled all the air in his lungs in the collision. The light of the surface was growing further away, but it didn't bother him. His lungs weren't straining yet.

He could remember long ago swimming around the docks with his mother, trying to see who could hold their breath longer. Together, they had made a full expedition of the murky waters around the city. He never had been able to beat her, and even she had found a way to drown. Recalling this, he was taken with a renewed sense of urgency. He could see bubbles. The force of the ship entering the water rocked him and his unfortunate companion. Bits of wood and metal spiraled off. He kicked what he could away, dodging the rest.

That's when he realized his passenger had let go and was starting to slowly descend into the dark waters towards the heart of the ocean. He reached out, catching the man by the wrist and jerked, kicking with all his might. The bubbles and light and froth from the storm were becoming clearer. His eyes were starting to burn, joined by his chest. However, the flashes of light were growing stronger and stronger. Blurry-eyed, he broke surface, hauling his hanger-on up with him. The man's hair was plastered to his face, but Fergus didn't have time to worry about identifying him.

Pieces of wood were floating to the surface, which he thought could be used as makeshift rafts, but where would they go? It was hard to see through his streaming eyes and the waves leaping up around them.

"Terry!" he shouted and then again, but he couldn't see anyone else, so he went with the waves.

The man coughed in his arms, coming back to life, and Fergus noted that his charge was no other than Guillory. Luckily, the Captain was too dazed to do more than breathe, which was fine by Fergus. They were closer to land than he'd expected, but it wasn't much of a relief, because he could see black rocks jutting up out of the waves, framed only by the whitecaps breaking against them. He did what he could to try to keep them from being pulverized or impaled upon the rocks, but the ocean was too strong, and he was thrust up against the spiky barrier of earth. Fergus grunted in pain, losing his grasp on Guillory. He made a grab for the Captain's jacket, but was caught up in another wave and tossed against the rocks. He felt his temple connect, and then nothing.

•   •   •

"Fergus."

He blinked. It was very cold and grey and his eyes were prickling. There was a stabbing pain in his head, and he could smell blood. He winced and squinted up at the voice.

"Terry," he mumbled.

"Glad you made it." Terry's face was still muddy, though his hair looked brighter than ever against the colorless sky.

"Anyone else?"

"A few."

Fergus nodded, closing his eyes.

"Stay awake if you can."

"Where are we?"

"God knows."

He forced his eyes open. Despite the sparks of pain bursting in his head, he slowly sat up and looked around. Bits of driftwood, rudders, and other fragments of the ship and cargo were lying in pieces on the rocky beach. Behind them, the rocks gradually turned to sand and then a thick line of trees – thicker than anything he had ever seen. Behind those, disappearing into the fog, were mountains or hills. He wasn't sure, as he hadn't seen either in person before. The hidden beach was sheltered on either side by great, round stones, which didn't look like they could possibly have come from nature, but Fergus couldn't guess where else they would've come from.

He pulled a piece of seaweed from his hair and allowed Terry to help him up. His vision swam for a moment, and his stomach lurched as dots filled his eyes, but he managed to blink away the vertigo and turned his sights on the forest before them, because it was most definitely a forest. The trees were bigger and taller than anything he'd ever seen. He opened his mouth, trying to think of how to express how amazing they were, but nothing came out, so he just stared up at them with his mouth agape.

"Now what? Where do we go now?" a familiar voice demanded. Fergus turned to Pip. As expected, Three was standing behind him, clasping one arm and looking worried. Nearby lay Guillory, who appeared to be unconscious.

"This is all?" Fergus asked.

Terry nodded grimly. "There may be others washed up in different places, but no one else here."

Fergus wondered where exactly "here" was.

"Probably if he wakes up," Terry said, jabbing a thumb in Guillory's direction, "he'll find some way to figure out where we are, but I'm gonna guess we'll have to go through there to get anywhere. No ships are gonna be able to pass through those rocks, and there's nowhere for an airship to land, either."

"That forest . . . " Fergus started, trailing closer to it.

Terry caught him by the arm. "I wouldn't wander in, if I were you. It's most likely what you're thinking."

At this point, Pip apparently forgot to be misanthropic and stomped over to them. He pointed up at Terry. "What do you mean? What is this forest?"

Terry did not look impressed, but though his mouth thinned for a moment, he nodded towards a ring of stones near the trees. "It's a fairy ring. There're real fairies in there, and I don't know what they're like where you come from, but they're usually not so friendly here."

Pip didn't reply. He looked a little pale as he reached out, clutching Three's arm.

"Are they going to attack us?" she asked softly.

"Depends on what we run into. Don't go off by yourselves, though."

It looked like they wanted to argue, but from somewhere in the woods came a queer, creaking noise that sent goose bumps running up Fergus's arms, and all of them went silent, staring into the shadows between the trees for a moment.

"We're going to die," Pip declared.

"Maybe," Terry replied.

"Damn," was all Fergus managed.

Three shook her head. "We won't die. You know how to fight?"

Fergus nodded uncertainly. He wasn't sure knowing how to punch someone was going to help with a fairy, but Terry looked more assured.

"And do either of you know magic?"

"A little," Terry replied.

"Well, that makes three of us who can fight, and three who can use magic, and maybe with the Captain, that will be one more for both."

"Oh, he can fight, but he wouldn't know magic if you hit him in the face with a lightning bolt," Terry said, mouth twitching.

"Still good enough for me," she replied and went over to check on him.

Fergus trailed after her, wondering what had become of the man he'd nearly succeeded in rescuing. Guillory did not look very lion-like now. At best, he was a half-drowned cat. Fergus leaned down, gently patting his cheek. Three caught one of his hands between her own, trying to rub some warmth back into it. The Captain groaned softly.

"Wake up," Fergus instructed.

Guillory cracked open one eye. "Where . . .?"

"No idea," Three cheerfully replied.

Guillory opened both his eyes and stared at Fergus. "Who are you?"

Fergus blinked and then realized he'd lost the red string somewhere along the way. "A passenger?"

"I don't remember you. Are you a stowaway?" he demanded.

"No, you just hit your head."

"No, that can't . . . "

"You lived after all."

"Weber," Guillory replied, raising his eyes to Terry. "Where are we?"

"Looks like the wilds. No idea which ones exactly. Get up and see if you can figure it out."

With a little help from Three and Fergus, Guillory managed to sit up, staring around him in befuddlement. He looked utterly lost, which Fergus thought was fair enough. There was no sun to tell direction by, after all, nor any landmark that he'd ever heard of. The Captain closed his eyes for a long moment, and Fergus wondered if he would concede defeat and if they would have to camp out here until they could get a handle on where they were when he finally asked, "Has the wind changed direction?"

"No," Terry replied. "Not that I know of."

"The storm came down from the north, so . . . looks like we've gone a bit west of it. I should think you would know this area. Your home village is supposedly on an island near here."

"How the hell would I know where anything is in some little cove like this?" Terry demanded.

"No matter. It looks like we won't be able to go up, and no ship will be able to come in, so we'll have to hope there's farmland on the other side of those trees."

"Yeah, obviously," Pip muttered under his breath.

Guillory slowly got to his feet, brushing off Three's attempts to help him. He turned towards the woods and peered for a long time, his frown growing deeper in his brow and the lines around his mouth. "Will they come out this far at night?"

"Probably," Terry replied.

"Well, are we better off waiting until morning to cross, or just heading straight in and praying that the way is short?"

This silenced Terry, who also frowned. Fergus followed their gaze into the trees. He could feel a buzzing in the air, which he guessed must have been magic – a little piece of the Otherworld that had been lost to the Cataclysm. Despite the threatening shadows, eerie sounds, and prickle of old, wild magic, he found that he wanted to go in. Maybe it was the novelty of the trees, or maybe he was being lured. He couldn't say, but the longer he looked into the forest, the more he yearned to enter it.

"It's hard to say," Terry finally replied, shaking his head. "We're not well protected here. There's nothing to even hide behind, but if we all took a turn at watch, maybe we'd be all right if nothing particularly hungry was around. Plus, there's no food or water, or any dry wood we could use for fire. We'll just be lying out in the dark and the cold all night. Even if we had a fire, it might attract them."

"What would keep them away?"

"Nothing that isn't going to annoy me, too," Terry replied. "What do you think?" he asked Fergus.

"Let's go through," he replied without even thinking.

"Well," Terry remarked with a little snort of laughter, "it seems you're decisive enough for all of us. Anyone disagree?"

No one replied for a moment. Three and Pip glanced at each other and shrugged, and Guillory frowned at the forest. However, no one said "no," either.

"That settles it. Let's get a move on. We probably only have a few hours before dark. Cross your fingers that we can get out of the forest by then. I'll go first. Guillory, you stick behind me. The kid can go after him, and you two can decide who's last."

"I'll go last," Fergus volunteered before Three could.

She opened her mouth, glanced at Pip who looked nothing short of relieved, and shrugged. Terry started off towards the forest, and everyone fell in line. Fergus was a little sorry he didn't get to go first, though he supposed with his sense of smell, it was only reasonable that Terry did. Fergus felt a twinge of regret that he'd never honed his abilities, but he never thought it'd be important. Still, he wished he had, so that he could be in the lead. He walked a couple of paces behind Three, so that he could at least look around a little. He'd never been in a forest before, and he wanted to go racing through the trees, but he soon discovered the impracticality of that whim.

This particular wood was very old, and everything was covered in moss and bracken. The trees were twisted and bent, probably shaped by shifts in the earth, though Fergus could only guess at the cause. Roots rose up like archways that either had to be crawled through or climbed over. Vines and branches hung low, smacking them in the heads when they weren't paying close enough attention. It seemed the trees were arranged somewhat like fruits shaken haphazardly out of a grocery bag, some growing nearly on top of each other, and none exhibiting any particular rhyme or reason in their spacing.

He wondered if that was how trees naturally grew. Certainly, the ones in Erstwyre Park demonstrated artistry in their placements. He'd seen the gardeners trimming back the branches and raking up the leaves. If they were left alone, would they eventually turn overgrown and mossy like these?

He craned his head back. There was something sweet and strange in the air. By turns, it smelled of honey and then of vomit, and sometimes a little of both. He wondered where it was coming from, because there weren't many animals or insects around. Certainly, no happily buzzing bees to produce honey. There were a few spiders hidden way up in the boughs of the trees, fat and lazy in their webs.

There were also other, even less pleasant crawling things that escaped under the bark or around the back of the trees as they passed. Three shuddered at these and complained several times under her breath, but like everyone else, she was being as quiet as she could. He noticed that now and then, she put her hands on Pip's shoulders, her head ducking down between her shoulders like a turtle shrinking into its shell.

As they progressed, he smelled the fresh scent of running water, though he couldn't hear where it was coming from. It struck him that there were bigger issues at hand, though. Looking back, he couldn't tell what path they had taken. It was as if the scenery was shifting around them. He figured Terry probably had noticed, too, as he always seemed to notice that kind of thing, but he wasn't mentioning it, so Fergus kept this fact to himself.

Soon, growths like those in the lower sector of the city began to appear amidst the vines and regular moss, illuminating the way a little, though these made Fergus even more certain that the path behind them was different from what they had traveled, because they had just passed two orange mushrooms and one pinkish blob-like one, and when he turned, all he saw was a patch of small green ones. He bit his lower lip. Well, they definitely couldn't go back, but could they trust that forward was any more certain?

The path became increasingly difficult. They were forced to make their way by grabbing handfuls of moss and hooking their legs up through the low hanging roots to haul themselves up, but it eased a little as they started winding up and around a ridge. The smell of water was now accompanied by the distant sound of trickling. At least, if there were any farms on this island, then maybe they might come out near one if they just followed the water. That or they might find some place they could rest a while, because it had grown too dark to see the sky through the trees, and only the insects glowing on and off just out of the corner of his eyes and the phosphorescent fungi provided anything like light. The trees thinned, and he found at last that he could look down through them.

As he suspected, they were climbing up a ridge, which abruptly dropped off at the side. He couldn't see the water below, but he could hear it, nor could he tell if it was deep or just a brook. It was peaceful, though. The smell of decay had been replaced by the smell of clean water, and the forest was quiet aside from the chirping of whippoorwills and frogs and crickets joining the chorus from below. Fireflies also came out as the evening deepened. Overall, he thought it was like stepping into the pages of a storybook. It was just as he let himself be lulled by these things that they heard something moving nearby.

It wasn't the same large sound as before. More like a clicking or buzzing sound. Something dark and amorphous was moving just outside the shadows cast by the lights of the mushrooms and fireflies and will-o-the-wisps, and Fergus felt the hairs on the back of his neck rise.

"Terry," he said, as quietly as he could manage, though he was pretty sure that if he knew that thing was over there, it knew they were over here. "*Terry.*"

"I know, Fergus."

"Terry?" Guillory demanded, and Fergus suddenly recalled that he wasn't seeing the tall redhead at the front of the line, but whatever Rosslyn Weber looked like. Guillory stopped in his tracks, causing Pip to run into him, who let out a string of unintelligible curses until Three clasped her hand over his mouth, turning wide, uncertain eyes on the dark.

"It's coming closer," she whispered. There was a thread of fear weaving through her voice.

"What is?" Fergus hissed.

"Dunno. Get ready," Terry said.

It seemed that even this wasn't going to derail Guillory, though, because he was reaching out to make a grab for Terry when the thing sprang out from the trees above. In an instant, a flurry of black wings was beating at their heads. Sharp claws gouged at their faces. Somewhere amidst this flock of feathers and talons was a funny sound like shrill laughter, though it was certainly not a sound any human throat had ever made.

A burst of fire went up into the air, driving their tormentors back. Bird-like cries of alarm and protest sounded as the flock lifted and then settled into the trees around them. They looked to be birds of every size, though all were black in color, and all had the look of raptors with sharp, strong beaks and talons, and thick, powerful wings. A few smelled distinctly of blood, though whether that was from the scrapes they'd just meted out, or something worse, Fergus couldn't say.

Three was breathing heavily, her hair obscuring her face and creating disturbing shadows over her eyes. For a moment, Fergus thought he would prefer the nasty birds. In her cupped hands, a small flicker of flame still flared, held to her stomach as though it was a living thing in need of protection. Beside her, Pip pulled out a slip of paper with strange writings all over the front. Fergus wiped his cheek, feeling fresh blood come away against the back of his hand. He glanced at Terry who looked less ruffled than the others, though blood was coursing from a cut on his forehead. He merely blinked it away and watched the birds with equal stillness and silence. Guillory extracted himself from the brush, nursing several deep scratches to the side of his face and brow. Fergus turned warily back to the birds.

"Now what?" he asked quietly.

"We move on, but don't take your eyes off them."

A rumble echoed though the forest – a deep, wild sound that shook Fergus's bones. He suddenly felt cold, numbed by a certain sense of dread. The birds all began shrieking again, taking off into the canopy.

"This just gets better and better," Pip grumbled, crouching a little, hand moving as though to throw his paper, though Fergus wondered what good that was going to do.

"It's inevitable. It's smelled our blood," Terry replied with token grimness.

"We should run," Fergus suggested just in time to be swept off his feet.

The creature seemed to have miscalculated, because its lunge took them both over the side of the ridge. He caught a glimpse of Terry's blood-framed eye widening, his mouth opening, and then they were falling and falling and falling – so much further than the drop looked from above. Fergus couldn't even tell what had grabbed him, except that it was furry, and it had very sharp teeth. If he didn't die from the fall, he was pretty sure that it was planning to finish the job. He tried to struggle, but it dug its claws in. He grunted in pain, making futile grabs at it.

They struck the water. It was so much colder than the sea, perhaps only a few degrees short of freezing. More than the fall, that took his breath away. It hurt everywhere the water touched him, which was soon enough his entire body. The cold, at least, also shocked his attacker, and he was able to regain his senses quickly enough to kick and squirm his way free. Even in the darkness, he found in the clear, unspoiled water that he could see rather well. For a moment, he and the creature stared at one another. It was an amorphous black beast with a broad head like a cow and claws.

In a rush of bubbles it shot forward, moving unbelievably quickly through the water. Fergus barely managed to dodge and turn in time to be clipped by its second charge. He cried out, losing valuable oxygen, and pain sprung up along his side. It was coming a third time. He felt a large rock under his foot. He waited until the beast was close, and then kicked off of the stone, cutting through the water, but not before lashing out with one foot with all his might. He wasn't sure where he connected, but the creature let out a muted cry, a rush of air bubbling out of it.

They'd disturbed the muddy bottom of the waterway, and it was nearly impossible to see. At least, he hoped that thing's visibility was as affected as his own. It appeared from behind a cloud of glittering silt and struck him head on, pressing Fergus down into the muck. He could see teeth flashing, eyes rolling. It bit down on his shoulder, and he let out another cry, the last of the air escaping his lungs. One shoulder was pinned by claws or talons – he wasn't sure which exactly – but the other was free. He felt around for anything to defend himself with, and his fingers passed over a stone the length of his hand. He latched onto it, swung it around, and jabbed as hard as he could at the creature's side. He felt it penetrate.

The water filled with something that tasted like blood. It prickled over his tongue unpleasantly. He ignored that and wrenched his weapon free, this time aiming for the front of the thing. It was a lesser blow, but it served its purpose. The beast kicked off of the bottom, sending mud everywhere, and broke surface over Fergus, clambering out of the water. It left a river of dark blood in its wake, mixing into the sparkling sediment.

Fergus kicked, surfaced, and gasped, his throat and chest tight with pain. He managed to grab onto a root, clinging to it like a half-drowned rat, and closed his eyes against a wave of dizziness. Besides his unhealed wound from the fight – besides the injuries from the rocks – his shoulder was bleeding, and it felt like every muscle in his body was bruised and torn, every cut reopened and throbbing. He tried to turn his thoughts away from the pain. Somehow, he needed to return to the group. If there were more things like that in this forest, then they definitely weren't going to do well split up; at least, he was going to be in serious trouble if he couldn't find them.

"Hello?" he called out quietly, looking up the face of the ridge to where he guessed he'd fallen.

No one answered. Despite his newfound fear of attracting the wrong attention, he tried again a little louder. His voice echoed, but met with no reply. Either he'd wound up further downstream than he'd thought, or they'd moved on. He hoped they were trying to find him. Maybe it would be okay if he just waited until they arrived. Letting go of the root, he floated on his back, listening for the sound of anything prowling around nearby.

The water began to feel less cold. He wondered if hypothermia was setting in and thought it might be better to climb onto the bank, but he felt safer in the water. His scent was cloaked, he probably could swim better than most of the things that might want to eat him, and he felt sheltered there – protected but sleepy, which he thought was very likely symptomatic of hypothermia, a mild concussion, or blood loss. Maybe some variation of all three. He wasn't really sure about the extent of his injuries, only that the cold water numbed them pleasantly, so they seemed less troubling.

He opened his eyes – not even realizing he'd shut them. It gave him a little jolt, and for a few minutes, he was alert, but soon the desire to sleep came creeping back. Worse, he was starting to wonder if he was awake or dreaming. He thought he might be dreaming, because it was a vision he'd had many times: a dream of being deep underwater and looking up at the light on the surface. He'd always assumed it was his fairy-soul's memories leaking into his own. Now, though, he wondered if it was actually a premonition. He moved one arm sluggishly, but managed little more than to stir the weeds around him.

The light became a tinier and tinier smear overhead. Maybe, he thought, this was what it was like when his mother drowned. Had she been looking up at the light reflected through the water's shadows? It was very pretty. If he was about to die as his mother had, at least he would see something nice in the end. He would rather see Ursula, though, which came as a mild surprise to him. He thought about her sitting in her big arm chair, perusing those dusty old books that took up her entire lap; lying in bed, stretched out like a cat, with the candlelight catching the hints of red in her hair; watching the tea kettle with annoyance as she waited for it to boil; and then of the last kiss they'd shared. That was only earlier that day, he realized, though it felt like weeks had passed.

His thoughts trailed from there onto when she had actually turned into a cat. He wondered what it had looked like when his mother had turned into a kelpie. From what he understood, she would have looked like a wet black horse or a pony. He thought a horse would suit her better. What would it be like to turn into a fairy? Would the world look different? Smell different? Feel different? He couldn't see the light on the surface anymore. He must have floated beyond the pool, because it hadn't seemed so deep before. He slowly let out a train of bubbles. They were swallowed up in the gloom, and he wondered if he'd reached some truly deep part of the water. He felt too tired to swim back up. He felt too tired to even hold the remaining oxygen in his lungs. He let it expel in a flurry of bubbles.

He'd heard that drowning was either very painful, or very peaceful. He couldn't remember which it was supposed to be, though despite the burning in his lungs, he felt very serene. Calm, but sad. He didn't want to disappear here. He didn't want to die. He still had songs to sing, to find out who killed Flynn, and he wanted to see Ursula again. He *couldn't* die now. A rush of adrenaline hit him, and he thrust his legs as hard as he could, reaching for the promise of light. He struggled, kicking against the loamy bottom and swimming with all his might, and yet it seemed he wasn't drawing any closer. The bottom was still just below his feet and the light far above. His throat burned, freckles of light jumped around in the corners of his eyes.

He had to reach the surface. Somehow, no matter what, he had to reach the surface. He swam and swam, feeling sicker and dizzier, and still making no progress. He let out a silent cry, and water filled his mouth. He choked, faltering. Despair pressed in as tightly as the water. He could see a glimmer of light just above, and then he started to black out. Water went up his nose, stinging violently, offering a last shred of consciousness. He grasped at his throat with one hand, reaching towards the surface with the other.

He started to sink again and realized he wasn't just sinking. The plants around him seemed to be growing longer, stretching up to encase his arms and legs. He tried to tear them off, but for every one he ripped away, another took its place. He couldn't concentrate; panic was being replaced by a detached feeling.

I don't want to die, he kept thinking, trying to pierce the sluggishness with the will to survive alone.

That's when it happened.

The bruises on his head, the ripped stitches in his stomach, the gouges in his cheek and shoulder, the agonizing call for air – these were nothing compared to the pain that hit him. He screamed, but no sound came out. He writhed violently. It felt like someone was trying to rip his arms and legs off. The pain didn't end with the horrible stretching sensation, though. He simultaneously felt like he was being crushed, compressed as in a vice. Every nerve in his body seemed to be going off. There was a freckle of light glinting above, dancing on the still surface as though laughing. He reached for it as he passed out.

• • •

When he came to, the plants had released him, and he was floating on the surface once more. He sucked in a deep breath of air. His tangled brain began to unwind from the shock. The rotting fruit and honey smell was back and extremely strong, but he didn't mind it as much as before, because with it came the scent of the water, the soil, the leaves, the crushed moss and grass from his attacker's escape, and things that he had no idea how to describe, save they were very distinct. He even thought he could smell the faintest trace of human blood, though it was steadily becoming weaker.

His hearing, too, was so sharp that at first he thought his ears were ringing. He could hear a frog slip into the water from further down the stream, the snap as a beetle burrowed under a piece of bark and broke it from the tree, and the whispers and murmurs of odd things in a language he couldn't understand, but the meaning crept through. *Something strange in the forest tonight. Some fun to be had.*

He couldn't hear Terry and the others, and their smell was drifting away. He didn't pursue them, because one thing was different in the wrong way. He couldn't seem to see directly ahead of him. Everything was coming to him from his periphery, and he had to twist his head to the side to see in front of him. Though the shadows were easier to decipher, the method of seeing was unfamiliar, and it made his head hurt. He tried to reach up to rub his eyes, but he found this impossible. His arms wouldn't lift higher than his chest. He started to panic, kicking, and found the bottom easily. He launched himself onto the bank in a single motion that sent water spraying everywhere.

He was black – black and *furry*. Soggy weeds stuck to his furry knees, because he did not have elbows anymore. He jerked back and nearly fell into the water again. Instead, he fell onto his side. He lashed out, but getting back up was not instinctive.

His body was difficult to move, and it took several tries before he could roll himself enough to sort of sit up. Very slowly and unsteadily, he put out his front legs and then managed to get his back legs under him enough to heave himself upright. He stood there for a long moment, dripping into the moss, feeling woozy.

"Overwhelmed" was an understatement; every sense was trying to take in several dozen things at once. It made his head swim, but in a good way, he realized. In fact, he felt very good. It was a little like that perfect state of tipsiness when he felt warm and effervescent and just disconnected enough that nothing could easily get to him. No, it was far better than that. Better than being with Ursula. Better than being on stage. It was so indescribably good that it made him want to run through the forest until he couldn't move. He wanted to let the new scents burn through his nostrils with the racing wind. But above all, he felt voraciously hungry. He stamped a foot, flicked his tail, tossed his head, and tried to jump into a gallop, except that he had not mastered his legs yet, and he was sent sprawling into the bushes.

Croaking laughter emitted from the other side of the leaves. Fergus stiffened and turned to see an ancient, saggy face. An old woman was looking down at him. Her eyes were hidden in the folds of skin - shadowed slits, if they existed at all. She smelled old. It was a very strange smell, and he wondered why "old" was the word he came up with. However, that was the only thing to describe it. She smiled at him, and he saw that she had all her teeth still, though they were more like fangs behind her thin, weathered lips.

"Pretty pony," she crooned, pushing away the leaves with a wooden staff. "Pretty pony, you want to dance, but perhaps you don't know how." She laughed again. It sounded like the croaking of bullfrogs, except with something unnamable and exceedingly grating just underneath.

She grabbed somewhere around his shoulders and hauled. He was shocked to find that she was incredibly strong. With her help, he was back on his feet.

"Come with me. I will give you something good to eat," she beckoned.

Fergus watched her, feeling that he shouldn't go anywhere with her. He especially thought he shouldn't eat anything she gave him. After all, he'd heard plenty of stories about how humans who ate the food of fairies became trapped in the Otherworld for decades, or worse, never escaped but became the fairies' slaves. At the same time, he was nearly out of his head with hunger. In fact, despite her show of strength, he was wondering what *she* would taste like.

Though common sense told him he should figure out how to work these legs and get away from her immediately, his stomach won out, and he slowly put one foot in front of the other and began to follow her. She led the way nimbly, moving up the river until they came to what he could only assume was her home, though it was not a house, but more a strange assortment of fallen branches and glowing things and strips of moss in the shape of a dome. She clambered inside, but Fergus could not fit.

"Sit down," she instructed.

Slowly, he maneuvered himself onto his side. He could see that the interior of her home was much more house-like. It was filled with little sparkling things – shells and rocks and pieces of gold and metal. She also seemed to have already acquired pieces of the newly wrecked *Pulsatrix*. She sat on a pile of clothes and began rooting around in various boxes before producing something brown, withered, and slimy. He snorted uncertainly as she held it out. It smelled good. It smelled really good.

"You don't know how to speak, I think," she mused, "because you are not really one of us, but aren't you close? Oh, you seem very close, my lovely."

He flicked an ear, hearing something pass near the hut. It didn't draw closer, but only paused before slipping away. He turned back to the old woman and sniffed the thing again. It smelled a little like everything he had ever loved eating: steak and meat pies and sausage and chips and fried fish and even some things he had only smelled from afar, but had never had the luxury of tasting. His vision momentarily swam, hunger canceling out thought, and he took it from her none too gently. She did not seem troubled by this, but rather wiped her hand on the pile of clothes, humming to herself.

"Did the tide sweep you here, my pony?"

He was busy trying to figure out exactly how to eat like this. It came easier than walking, at least, but it was still considerably different from eating with his hands. He swallowed down the lump and felt somewhat satisfied, but not full. He craned his head into the tent, sniffing around in hopes of another. She reached out with crooked, knobby fingers to put a hand on his forehead. He threw his head in surprise. However, she held her hand out coaxingly, and he could still smell the residue of the food she'd just given him on it, so he licked it, trying to eke out one last bit of that wonderful taste. She reached up, scrubbing the top of his skull, knocking dark, heavy hair into his eyes. He snorted in annoyance and shook his head, to throw it out of the way. This earned another croaking chuckle.

"If you can stay like this, you can stay, but oh, I think you do not want to. You just don't know how to turn back, do you? Oh, where was that? Where was it?" she asked, putting her fingers into her mouth and leaning over to stare at the assortment of boxes and bottles that lined the wall. At length, she pulled out a jar of what looked like fireflies. She popped off the lid, fished one out, and then jammed it into his face. "Eat it. Be a good pony."

He started to grunt in protest, but she shoved the thing into his mouth. It went down his throat much like swallowing a gnat. He coughed, and then the same pain as before struck, only far, far worse. He fell to his side, shaking and kicking, unable to even pass out as his limbs jerked out of his control, shifted and reshaped themselves and finally left him lying soaked, unable to even move his fingers, and entirely human once more. He was fairly certain he was dying. He couldn't shake that sense of dread. A soft sound of despair escaped him, and she reached out to brush his forehead with her rough knuckles.

"Poor, pretty baby," she murmured. "You look very tasty."

She cackled, and he thought maybe this had been her plan all along. She'd poisoned him. He let out a choked sound, managed to flex one hand, but was unable to force anything else into movement.

"Oh, no, I won't eat you. Not today. But only if you find some way to buy your life from me. I think you may owe me."

She chuckled, dragging him by the shoulders from the threshold into her house, and began to drape clothes over him. They smelled moldy and sour, but he was in no condition to protest. He was pretty sure that he wouldn't live to see morning. Helplessly, he watched her move around, starting a fire and rearranging her jars. Despite the uncertainty and the persistent sense of doom, he found himself lulled into sleep.

Chapter Thirteen.

It was still dark when he woke again, and yet he felt like he'd been asleep for a long time. He could move again, and the horrible feeling of imminent doom had passed, though his limbs still tingled uncomfortably. Slowly, he sat up. The old woman was sitting across from him, the fire casting odd shadows across her face. It was smoky inside the hut, and his eyes burned. He rubbed at them, looking around. He was starting to feel hungry again, but he didn't dare eat anything else she might offer. He turned back to the old woman. For a moment, he wondered if she was asleep. Her chin was nestled into her throat, eyes hidden in her wrinkles, and her wiry hair frizzing everywhere. Fergus wondered if he should take this as a stroke of luck and make a run for it.

He shifted and started to climb to his knees to shuffle out of the hut when she raised her face. For a moment, they just stared at each other, and then he settled back down. She smiled, revealing sharp teeth again.

"Is my pony feeling better?" she crooned.

"Fine," Fergus replied uncertainly. "Just fine."

"Is there pain anywhere?"

There wasn't pain exactly, but there was an aching feeling in every part of his body. Fergus stared at her for a moment before shaking his head "no."

"Do you hunger still?"

He was starving, but again he shook his head.

"Then I should have a reward," she said, clapping her hands together and bouncing.

"What sort of reward would you like?" he asked and a new kind of dread leaked into the pit of his stomach.

"You must make me a gift of something. Something that is worth much to you."

He frowned. Judging from the old tales, she might want his firstborn, or she might be hoping for a literal piece of him, so that she could control him for the rest of his life. At least, he doubted a fairy would want anything carnal from him, because he was pretty sure that would not happen, even if his life depended on it. Maybe she wanted his riches, though he definitely didn't have any of those. He thought about what was important to him: friends, family, music. He had no family now, though, and he wouldn't offer a friend. Maybe he could sing her a song, he thought, but he worried that she might steal his voice if she liked it too much. There were fairy tales about that kind of thing, too. He didn't think he could live without that, so he hesitated. Then he thought of something.

He pulled out his wallet. Inside were his and Flynn's notes. These were all he had of Flynn right now, and they were his only clue about what Flynn might have been involved in before he was killed. However, they weren't doing him any good presently. He had no idea what they meant, and if he got out of this alive, maybe he'd find other ways to get to the bottom of things, like asking the Niamh members. Probably they'd be angry that their book was stolen and lost, but they seemed likely to know the things Fergus wanted to know. Maybe he could find a way to barter with them.

So he took out the original note and stared at it a moment, second-guessing himself. Should he really give it to her? His little scrap of evidence – the only thing he knew that no one else did. But he wouldn't be able to do *anything* if he didn't get out of this forest. He had to get out of there, so taking a deep breath, he handed it over.

She took the note and looked at it for a moment, and then her brows drew back enough that he could see her watery eyes for the first time. "Oh, this is curious," she said.

"Will you accept it?" he asked through gritted teeth.

"Oh, no. It's of no use to me," she laughed. "But it is a rare thing, indeed. Very rare."

"What is it? Some kind of spell?"

"No."

"But it has runes on it," Fergus protested.

"If they are runes, I can't read them, but then, I can't read," she cackled. "It is a map, don't you see?" She handed it back to him.

Fergus unfolded the page he'd torn from Flynn's book and pointed at it. "*This* is a map," he said, shaking his head in frustration.

"They are both maps, but this one will guide you when you need it to," she said, tending her fire with a vacant smile. "That is not a gift I want," she continued. "Give me something else."

"What else do you want?"

She eyed him for a moment before repeating, "A gift you think is important."

He definitely couldn't give her any part of him, because he knew she would use it against him later. It seemed the only thing he could offer was his voice. He hoped she wasn't going to steal it and that she wouldn't hate it. It was his last bargaining chip, so he nodded slowly, taking a deep breath and trying to let his uneasiness out with the exhalation. He began to sing. It was a song he had written when he'd first gotten it into his head that he wanted to be in a band. Back then, he'd just saved up enough to buy a used guitar, and it was the first song he'd composed on it. He'd never shared it with any of his band mates. The original version had been bad. He'd gone over it a few times since. It was, in fact, taped to the inside of his lyric book – the permanent first page.

"Deep, deep into the dense quiet, a cycle of ephemeral things. Things that should end stretch into infinity, deep, deep into the dusky cold. Skimming the surface, ghostly flickering, soundless, faceless, called, calling . . . "

The melody was based on a lullaby his mother had sung to him when he was little, except his version was about wanting to leave the city. It seemed a little ironic that he should be singing about such a thing when right now there was nothing he wanted more than to be back in New Peiling.

"Above the muted rumble, sunless spaces under trees and brook. Still, very still, tumbling into boundless days. Still phantom fingers dip and beckon, far, far above the blackness."

The song wasn't very long, and he wondered if she would be annoyed as he finished the final lines. He cleared his throat a little and stared at the fire. The old woman did not move for a long time, though he could tell she was looking at him. He focused on the flames to try and escape the sharpness of her gaze.

"Funny pony," she muttered at last. "Strange pony. Why do you know that song? I have not heard it in many, many years. Sing me the song that made that song."

Fergus blinked. "Um, okay . . . " he trailed off, trying to recall the words to the lullaby.

His mother had sung it to him nearly every night when he was a child, but a good many years had passed since then. It was a song about a changeling child, who'd been tossed out when the human parents realized it was a fake. It lay by the roadside – a grotesque, miserable thing – but the crows came to it and gave it things to eat and took care of it, so it was able to grow a little. But as was often the nature of changelings, it soon became sickly again. The crows watched it every day, teaching it to speak their language. In the end, all it learned to say was "thank you" before passing away.

"The crows will cry tomorrow, the sun will warm their wings, but oh, oh, the little changeling will never see such things. Under the dying mulberry, he spoke his very last: 'Thank you, of you I was blessed.'"

He found it wasn't too hard to fill in the words he'd forgotten. Even as a child, he'd felt it was a very bitter song and singing it now made his throat feel tight and chest constricted. He swallowed, trying to banish his sudden melancholy.

The old woman let out a long, low sound and rocked herself. "Yes, that is it. That is it. Just the way it should be, too. I accept it. I will even give you a gift in return." She cackled. "This one will be free, perhaps. We will see."

Fergus watched her uneasily. He didn't know how to decline this offer without earning her wrath, but he didn't think he wanted to risk that "perhaps" either. She ignored his discomfort and began to sort through her belongings again.

"You want to learn how to turn back again, don't you? I will show you. Perhaps you might be able to cross this place if you can. But you should be careful. You have a human mind. Oh, you dislike hearing it? But you do. Too much of our magic will strain it beyond what it can take, I think. Yes, it will break if you are careless." She rubbed her hands together over the fire. "Maybe you know someone who has met this fate? Your face says you do. Will you accept it?"

Fergus turned red, embarrassed that he'd let down his guard, but his thoughts had immediately jumped to his mother. Probably that *was* what happened to her. Recalling the thrill of being more than alive, feeling the ache of mortality still with him, he couldn't help it. He wanted to return to that form, to feel the rush of power once more, so he nodded "yes."

"Very well. Go and fetch me some frogs for breakfast, and after that, we will begin."

"Frogs," Fergus parroted.

"The ones with the golden eyes, if you can manage it."

His mouth twitched, a refusal trying to form, but he immediately thought better of it.

•　　•　　•

Fog was settling between the trees as he slipped back outside. Standing on his own two feet again, he began to think a little more sensibly. He started towards the sound of the water, but hesitated. Perhaps the best thing to do would be to make a break for it now and hope he could get out of here by himself as he was, but he didn't feel particularly confident about his chances. Though his head had stopped hurting, and all the normal injuries he'd sustained before entering the forest were either half-healed or wholly gone, he wasn't sure where to go or how to even tell which way he should start.

He tried to do as Terry recommended, but though he sniffed and sniffed, he couldn't smell anything that seemed "human." He did find his way down to the stream. It was shallow, flanked by thick reeds filled with fireflies. It looked nothing like the body of water he'd dragged himself out of before.

In fact, nothing looked at all similar to anything he'd passed on his way to the hut, and as he crouched by the water, listening for the sounds of these so called golden-eyed frogs, he noticed that things were shifting out of the corner of his eye. He would look away, and something would ripple in his periphery. The minute he turned his head, whatever had been there before had changed in some way – a big tree replaced by two smaller ones, pinkish moss turning to blue toadstools. Even if he could figure out which direction to go, he didn't think he'd be able to stay on the path long.

At least, the water seemed constant, but it was going the opposite direction from earlier. It cut the forest into two, but it was across rather than through, and he wouldn't be able to follow it out. He would have to go back to the old woman's home (provided he could even find that). The forest was filling with the gentle sounds of crickets, night birds, and frogs. He couldn't hear anything large moving around, and so he relaxed a little and tried to think more clearly about his situation. It seemed his best bet was to try to learn what he could from the woman. At least, in that form, his senses might be good enough that he could navigate back to Terry.

Of course, no golden-eyed frogs came out. His feet were starting to go numb, as he continued to search. He'd seen some normal looking frogs around, but nothing with brilliant metal-like eyes. He could hear lots of frogs in the reeds, but they all scattered when he parted the plants to search for them. His efforts took him further and further up the river until he was thoroughly lost and extremely annoyed. The croaking was beginning to sound distorted to him. It was more like the thin clashing of a tambourine or a cymbal than the earlier trill, and more and more frogs kept joining the chorus, so that soon, the din became a high-pitched buzzing that made his head hurt.

He cursed under his breath, stamped straight into the water, and grabbed at the first frog he saw. It had bright red eyes, but it slipped out of his grasp before he could even lift it up above his knees. He rubbed the slime onto his jeans, hoping it wasn't poisonous and grabbed at another and another until he was dripping with pond scum, his head was pounding, and he was at the end of his patience. He cursed loudly, punching the surface of the water, and then realized that his hands were covered in what looked like gold dust.

He stared at the thick, greasy coating. It reminded him a little of the glittery lotion that Emily used. Whatever it was, he was fairly sure it wasn't a good thing, because it was making his skin tingle and itch, so he decided that he'd just grab a couple of regular frogs and hope for the best. Light was coming through the trees when he finally managed to snatch some small green-eyed ones. He stood with the frogs trying to struggle through his fingers and mud dripping down his face and realized he was hopelessly lost. Lost, exhausted, and cold.

Fergus slowly turned, trying to get a feel for direction, but around the bank were six old oaks all of the same width, height, and even sporting the same notches and boles. He laughed weakly and then climbed out anyway, his trainers squishing with every step. With no better idea of where to go, he started to walk forward.

Perhaps the old woman had realized that he might have such a problem, because as soon as he managed to clamber onto the bank, he realized that every step he took elicited a miniature light show. He experimented, slowly lifting one foot and putting it back down. The ground under it glowed white, spider webs of light stretching ahead several inches and then slowly fading away as he lifted the other. He considered this for a moment and then took a step back to make sure, and though veins of light did creep into the moss to either side of him, the illumination didn't spread out behind him, so it must be directing him, he thought. He followed it back to the old woman's hut.

She took the frogs from him without comment. In fact, she didn't even look into their eyes before she plopped them into her pot. Having done that, she grabbed him by the wrists and surveyed the golden slime coating his palms.

"Perfect," she declared, releasing one hand so that she could pick up a knife and scrape the residue into a jar.

The skin beneath the goo was irritated and red, but she gave him some herbs and told him to rub them between his hands and soon the stinging went away. He realized that she'd sent him on a wild goose chase for just that, and he was more than a little chagrined, but he was also hungry, and the frog stew she was preparing smelled even better than the weird blob she had given him before.

His previous trepidation about eating her food was overshadowed by hunger logic, which told him that since he'd already eaten the blob, he was probably screwed anyway. He crouched eagerly on the balls of his feet, looming near the pot in anticipation of breakfast. She did not speak to him, but hummed the song he had sung to her rather cheerfully as she threw in dried things and crushed things and some slightly fresher bits of vegetation. He hoped this wasn't going to poison him.

When at last the food was prepared and eaten, she said, "Go outside and wait."

She didn't make him wait long, which was good, because Fergus could hear larger things prowling around just outside his vision. The old woman crawled out after him on all fours and then plopped down on her bottom, staring up at him expectantly. He wasn't sure whether this meant he should also sit or not, but decided to remain standing in case whatever it was that was snuffling about nearby decided to descend upon them. She eyed him with a moony expression and then finally nodded.

"If you were true kith, this would be little trouble, wouldn't it, my pony? But you are only an imitation." She nodded to herself. "But you must have some ability. Yes, tell me what you were thinking of before."

"That I didn't want to die."

"Is that all?" she asked, gnawing on a shell.

"I don't know. I was about to drown. There was dark water everywhere, and I didn't want to die, so suddenly it happened."

She scratched under a fold in her cheek. "You need to be frightened."

Fergus hardly had time to feel apprehensive about the remark before she stood up, walked over, and jammed the shell into his shoulder. He grunted in pain, grabbing for his arm as she pulled her makeshift knife free and then went to sit like she hadn't just stabbed him. Blood leaked out through his clenched fingers. There was a sudden silence from the thing nearby, and Fergus realized what was about to happen only a moment before it did. The creature, which turned out to be a very large black dog, leaped down from the crest of trees just above them. Fergus stumbled backward, shielding his face with his arms.

The fairy-dog was on him in a flash, jumping up with such force that he first stumbled and then was knocked to the ground. Specks of saliva hit his face. He pushed as hard as he could against its chest, just barely keeping out of reach of its teeth.

He could see the old woman from beyond the fairy-dog's thrashing form. She was chuckling, holding up her little shell to the light, and he could have sworn she licked it. However, his attention could not stray for more than a fraction of a second, because the fairy-dog was only slightly weaker than the thing that had attacked him last night. He managed to gather his legs under it, and with concentrated effort, shoved it off with hands and feet. He rolled back to his feet, panting.

At least it hadn't bitten him, but it wasn't stunned, and as quickly as he righted himself, it did, too, lunging again. This time, he just managed to dodge, but it corrected itself faster than he could and hit him in the back, knocking him forward. He stumbled, struggled to keep his feet, and it latched onto his left wrist.

"You don't want to die, right?" the old woman asked, chewing on her shell lazily.

He grunted as the fairy-dog attempted to shake him, teeth tearing into his skin. He kicked at it, but it wouldn't let go. He could feel blood dripping down from its jaws, spilling between his fingers, and he had little hope that other things wouldn't also gather at the smell. He really didn't want to die. He didn't want to be eaten by this stupid mutt, nor by anything else here. Panic and the will to survive coiled together in his brain. He struggled even harder, though it did little to shake his attacker. It was dragging him, trying to pull him low enough to get at his throat.

He twisted violently, kicking at it, and then he felt the incapacitating pain. His senses blipped out. He forgot where he was or what he was doing. He wasn't even clear on *who* he was for several minutes.

He must have fallen over, because as his senses returned to him, he was on his side. The fairy-dog had backed away, not so certain anymore. He hoisted himself to his feet, though the injury from the fairy-dog made it difficult to support his own weight. Gingerly, he held that foot up, trying not to strain it, and let out a squeal of anger. The fairy-dog was not retreating, and he couldn't charge it, so he snapped at it. The sound of his teeth clacking together was loud even to him. It jumped, lowered its head, the hair of its ruff rising, and glanced at the woman before looking back at Fergus.

"Don't like, don't like," it growled, and then, tucking its tails between its legs, spun around and dashed off into the brush. Fergus snorted, throwing his head, and reared up.

Not so tough now, he thought, coming back down slowly.

The old woman got to her feet, coming over to scoop the blood splashed moss and dirt into a little jar, climbing under him when necessary, though she didn't bother with the blood seeping from his wound. He was hoping she might help him, but she didn't seem particularly inclined to do anything but gather the soiled moss and leaves and then go back into her hut, leaving him standing there. With his leg stinging and little choice otherwise, he stood still and waited, hoping the wound might scab over, at least.

The sun moved higher into the sky, though it seemed to take twice as long as usual to do so. He stood and stood, feeling the blood ebb and then turn sticky and tight. By then, he was getting hungry and tired, and his other legs were starting to feel strained.

The old woman came back out. She blinked at him, obviously surprised that he was still there, and then toddled past him. She stopped for a moment, putting a hand on his shoulder, before instructing, "Don't forget the feeling," and then she wandered off into the brush.

•   •   •

She didn't return for hours, but by that time, Fergus had given up on any hope of further aid from her. He limped towards the water. The sun was starting to set, and he could hear things coming alive around him. He sniffed for any hint of humans and managed to find an old trail of scent. He now could see the trees changing; they moved slowly, switching places and shifting their shapes. He paused to watch for a while. Even seeing it happen, it was hard to believe he wasn't dreaming. He continued on until he found the ridge they'd been crossing last night. The smell was old, but it was a little clearer here.

He lowered his head, looking down into the water for a long moment, ears flicking, and found that he'd forgotten what he was doing. All he could think of was that he should go to the water. He wasn't sure how long he stood there before the breeze picked up, and he thought he could smell Terry. Reluctantly, he tore himself away and continued on. It seemed that even wounded, this body could travel faster, for the smells began to become stronger and fresher as he progressed. The other creatures left him alone, which probably made sense. He wondered if there even was a fairy or beast larger than he was in this forest. He saw others pass by, but none approached him.

He realized that the forest was brimming with life. Frogs croaked, deer peeked out at him from messy canopies, and dark birds took to roost wherever there was space. However, watching small glowing things gliding along together and hearing their chittering laughter, or seeing a pair of foxes curled up together in the roots of a tree, made him feel very lonely. Despite the pain in his leg, he hastened his steps.

Though the smells were growing stronger and stronger, and he even found a fresh splash of blood on the leaves, it seemed he never was able to come within earshot of the others. He didn't run – he didn't think he could bear it – but as the night wore on, he knew he would have to stop and rest. He didn't want to sleep out in the open, but it seemed he had no choice.

He could hear the stream somewhere behind him, though he knew he'd been walking away from it for hours. Surely it couldn't be so close, and yet when he turned, it was loud and the smell strong, as though it was just beyond the last rise. He shook his head, pawing the ground. He must have walked several miles since he crossed it, so there was no way it was that close, but then, he also had been smelling his friends for the last few hours, and yet he never seemed to get any closer.

Was he caught up in the old woman's spell? Was it because he ate her food? Thinking of food made his stomach growl, and he was too hungry for true panic. He wanted to eat, though he wanted to eat meat, and for a moment, the smell of humans became so enticing that he didn't realize he'd begun trotting in the direction of his companions again until he nearly stumbled over a root. He stopped, suddenly realizing what he was doing, and shook his head violently. No eating those people, and no going to the water, he told himself, but it was hard to ignore these instincts. He was too tired to will himself to think properly, and though he didn't like the idea of it, he gave in and curled up in the roots of an old tree, quickly falling asleep.

•   •   •

The leaves printed patterns of shadow over the forest floor. The sun was high in the sky, and it was warm. It was perhaps the first time Fergus could recall feeling truly warm for some time. He lifted his head sleepily. The trees around him were unfamiliar again. Even the one he had curled up next to had changed, becoming a half-circle of saplings in the night. He got to his feet, shaking himself off and taking note of his situation. He was starving and thirsty, but he told himself that one way or another, he would get out of the forest today, and then there would be plenty to eat and drink.

He paused for just a moment to chew at an itch in his flank before he started on his way. His leg was hurting a little less, and so he was able to quicken his pace. The trees began to thin, and he thought he might even reach the edge of the forest by the time the sun crawled to the other side of the sky. It wasn't long before he could smell humans on the wind: humans and the rich, exquisite smell of fresh blood. His stomach growled, and he began to trot in the direction of the scent.

But as he neared a break in the trees, he hesitated, twitching his ears and sniffing the air, because he could smell something musky and unclean with the humans. He snorted, throwing his head irritably, as he recognized the scent. It was the smell of the thing that had attacked him before, and now it was trying to steal *his* breakfast. He turned his head. His vision wasn't as good in the daylight, and it was hard to see from the periphery anyway, but he was able to discern the scene after a few minutes' observation.

Terry looked to be in decent shape, but he was breathing heavily, clasping one arm to stem the flow of blood. Maybe Pip was okay, but he couldn't see him around Three, who looked ragged and bruised and smelled delicious, gasping for breath and wiping blood from the corner of her mouth. Guillory was perhaps the worst of the lot. He was crouched on the ground behind Terry, cradling his arm to his stomach.

The thing attacking them was definitely the same as the other night, though now Fergus could see it a little better. It generally looked like a great black bull, except that its back was a hulking mishmash of feathers and fur and skin that ought never to have been grafted together in such a way. It wore these things like a shell – unwieldy, weird, and intrinsically vile. Though it was feathered, it had no wings. It also had no tail. All four legs ended in paws with sharp, heavy claws that were no doubt responsible for the rents in the ground, Three, and Terry's arm. It had long, drooping ears, curling horns like misshapen conch shells stuck to its head, and saliva dripped from its jaws in thick, silvery lines.

It let out a roar and charged. Terry reached out, trying desperately to make a grab for its horns. He was shouting something at Guillory, but his words sounded like nonsense to Fergus. A burst of fire struck the side of the beast, fraying feathers and fur. The smell was terrible. Fergus could see that Three was already preparing a second round, and Pip had joined her, moving his hands in an elaborate fashion. The wind began to pick up, as though drawn from the trees behind him, pulled by those strange hand gestures and thrust towards the beast. Only, it was not simply wind, but fire inflated by this breeze, and the creature spun away from Terry, sending him sprawling, and turned on Three. She didn't seem afraid, but instead was starting a strange pattern of runes in the air with a dot of fire at her fingertip.

The creature turned away from her, and Fergus realized that the beast was sniffing the air: it'd caught Fergus's scent on Pip's conjured wind. His lips drew back, baring fangs, and he snorted, throwing his head. For a moment, the creature looked straight at him, holding his gaze in a silent battle for who would be enjoying this breakfast buffet. Fergus stamped his good foot, shaking his head more violently. The creature lowered its head, snapping its jaws. He did not let loose any wild war cries, no outraged stallion's roar, but rather dug his hind legs into the moss and burst forth out of the trees, pounding towards the creature.

He drew up just in time to avoid being gored by its horns, its lower fangs just grazing his shoulder. He lunged again, this time snapping at its neck, but it was too bulky to get his teeth around. It moved especially quickly for something of that size, and Fergus felt a horn catch in his side. He let out a squeal of pain and whipped around, this time coming down on the beast with his front hooves. It was knocked to the ground. He didn't stop, rearing back up and stomping again. It kicked out with all four legs, trying to find purchase. Fergus felt something give – heard a loud snap – the third time. A horrible, piercing cry escaped the struggling fairy monster.

It scratched at him, turned its head to snap at him, threatened him with its horns, but with his full weight bearing down on the injury, it was trapped. Cornered, but not incapacitated. Fergus attempted to remedy this, trying to get around its jaws and horns to its throat, but it was too well defended. He backed off, shaking his head warningly. It stumbled to its feet, though nearly went down again.

Menacing it might have been good enough if he just wanted to escape, but the blood was thundering in Fergus's ears. This beast had infringed on his territory, and instinct told him that he must be rid of it entirely. He reared up, jabbing at it with hooves. It lowered its head, horns fending him off. He moved to its side. It gingerly turned, trying to keep its horns between Fergus and the soft skin of its throat. He snapped at its legs, and it kicked out. He was quicker and more agile, but it was built like a tank, and its horns kept him at bay. Maybe, he thought, he could knock it over again, and if he was quick about it, make his move.

He barreled into it, feeling a horn catch and rip his skin. Blood dripped down his leg. It wasn't enough to hinder him, though, and he turned, kicking as hard as he could. The creature was sent rolling through the dirt. Fergus whirled around and descended on it, trying to find an opening between the swirl of leathery skin and claws and teeth and horns. He snapped several times without catching more than fur or feathers, but as the creature's momentum slowed, he saw his opening. He latched on and gave a violent shake. Blood gushed into his mouth, tingling like electricity over his tongue. It tasted like silt or sand, and it burned.

Fergus released the creature, shaking his head and spitting out flecks of black blood. Gasping for breath, he searched for signs of life. He waited until he was certain it wasn't going to move anymore before backing away from its limp form. Now, he thought, he could have breakfast in peace. He turned to the four humans.

Pip and Three were trying to help Guillory up. Terry was standing before them, looking wary. Fergus bared his teeth, taking a step forward and snorting. The redhead's expression was inscrutable, but Fergus could smell fear, and he felt sick with hunger. He began advancing with greater purpose, but Terry began to move forward, too, holding both hands up. His mouth was moving, but the sounds coming out were unintelligible. Fergus stopped, stamping a foot angrily.

Yet Terry continued progressing until he was too close to easily escape, and Fergus gave a half-rear, growling at this show of audacity. Terry kept speaking. His words still made no sense, but his tone was gentle, and Fergus found himself bewildered. He took a step back, pinning his ears and letting out another grumbling sound of warning.

"Fergus."

He heard the word, and for a moment, he didn't know what it meant, but he knew it. He stood entirely still.

Terry reached out slowly, repeating, "Fergus."

What was "Fergus"? That was not his name. He knew his name. It was older than the riverbeds lying under the ocean. It was not "Fergus."

"Fergus."

He felt like this word was a part of him, but what part? He snorted uneasily. His tongue was coated in tingling, black fairy blood, and he longed to wash away the taste with the delicious promise of human flesh. Terry smelled of blood. It was all over him. It didn't smell as good as Three's or Guillory's, but he could make a meal of all four of them. He was hungry enough, and it truly was a terrible, delirious feeling. It twisted his stomach. He ached with it.

But Terry kept calling to him, hands outstretched and beckoning, and something at the edge of Fergus's mind was tugging him away, telling him he mustn't hurt this human. He took a few steps back, now thinking he should retreat and find less troubling prey. However, Terry reached out, taking his head in both hands. He leaned very close.

"*Fergus.*"

He felt a gut wrenching pain come over him and let out a gurgling cry. Things were compressing, reforming, changing in ways that they should not have been. He could hear screams. He wondered who they were coming from. He flailed disjointedly. The trees were growing further away. Smells were becoming fainter, as were noises. His vision, though, was growing more focused, the colors dimmer, but the outlines sharp and crisp in ways that made his eyes hurt and his head throb. His throat was on fire. He realized he was the one screaming.

Arms wrapped around him. He could see a shock of ginger hair. Terry's hand pressed to his forehead.

His voice was soothing. Fergus's arms and legs and fingers twitched out of control. Drool dripped down his chin. He couldn't seem to make anything move except his eyes. He was seized upon by the horrible feeling from before, which his mind supplied as "dying," and the strange part of his mind that had not yet receded called "mortal."

His body was human once more.

"It's okay," Terry whispered into his ear, rocking him.

Fergus stared bleakly up at the clear blue sky.

Chapter Fourteen.

They left the woods: Guillory aided by Three and Pip, and Fergus slung over Terry's shoulders, piggyback style. Unlike the night before, he remained conscious the entire time. He thought that probably in some way this must have meant that he was recovering faster, but it also was its own kind of torture. He was ill twice within the hour, only barely able to warn Terry in time to be dropped off into the bushes where he had to hold Fergus up to keep him from lying on his face and vomiting. Having not even eaten anything for 24 hours didn't help, and when he was able to move around a little and stand on his own, he felt so dizzy that he still couldn't walk. He felt awful enough that even the drying blood on Terry's arm didn't entice him, which was, he thought, a good thing.

Terry's nose led the way out of the trees into what would have been the most beautiful scene he'd ever witnessed had Fergus not felt like puking again. He tapped Terry's chest to let him know to let him down, and though he swayed violently, he managed to stay on his feet. Stretched out before them was a wide, rolling meadow filled with red flowers as far as the eye could see. The mountains petered out to the sides, framing the right edge of the field with a picturesque waterfall. A warm breeze sifted through the flowers, turning them gently this way and that and making the field seem to shimmer. Bees buzzed between the blooms, birds chirped merrily, and a rabbit – spooked by their sudden appearance – darted out in front of them, disappearing into the wildflowers.

"Amazing," Three murmured, closing her eyes and raising her face to the sun.

Guillory freed himself from her shoulder, giving a thankful nod to Pip, who did not look magnanimous in the least, and began to shuffle forward. In silent agreement, they headed towards the falls. After traversing the enchanted forest, the walk across the meadow was nothing at all. All five collapsed by the water, drinking handfuls in great gulps. Fergus had to stumble back, losing his water in the flowers a few feet away. Still, he was thirsty, so he returned and drank with less urgency, testing to see how much he could keep down.

"Well, as long as we're here, let's bathe and redress our injuries," Three suggested.

Fergus stared at her.

She blinked at him and then turned pink. "Well, I can go after everyone else."

"No, you should go first," Guillory quickly piped up. "Besides, you seem to have the greatest medical knowledge of all of us."

"I'll watch for you," Pip declared, giving the others a frosty glare.

Fergus just shrugged and went over to lie down near Terry in the sun, closing his eyes. He felt a little less like he was about to die, which was a vast improvement. The wind ran over them, bringing with it the faint smell of smoke. He felt a shadow pass over and opened his eyes to Terry's scrutiny. He put a hand on Fergus's forehead and hummed.

"Think you might want to skip the bath. You're pretty feverish. Your cuts are probably infected . . . "

"Shouldn't I clean 'em?" he slurred, closing his eyes again.

"I can smell something human nearby, but we might not make it before nightfall. Maybe that Three girl knows some tricks to patch you up, but . . . "

Fergus laughed weakly.

"Don't do that. Gives me the chills."

He didn't answer, but fell into a restless doze.

•　　•　　•

"Okay, we've made a fire. Everyone but you and me has gone, so get up."

Fergus opened his eyes and struggled to his feet, feeling lightheaded and nauseated again. Terry helped strip him out of his clothes, and the two slipped into the icy water. For a moment, Fergus felt a little better. Terry let him bob near the reeds for a few minutes as he scrubbed himself before returning.

"I can do it," Fergus protested.

"Well, you haven't yet."

He carefully began rubbing at his skin, avoiding the cuts and bruises. Terry sighed and began scrubbing those, despite the angry hiss of breath

Fergus let out. He thought about fleeing, but it appeared that he didn't have the strength to climb onto the bank, so he clung to the long blades of grass and cast reproachful looks at Terry over his shoulder, who was trying not to smile.

"What's so funny?"

"Nothing. You know, you really are a little like a human-sized filter. It's a lot clearer near you."

Fergus looked down and then turned red. "Are you looking?!"

Terry chuckled. "No. Hold still. This is gonna hurt."

They crawled out a few minutes later, pulling their shorts back on and going over to where the others were tending a small campfire. Guillory's arm was set, though it looked like part of Three's top had been sacrificed for the cause. She was bruised and scratched, and the cuts on her arms looked deep, but they were scabbed over, and she was talking animatedly, pausing only to glance up for a moment when Terry and Fergus came over.

"Who first?" she asked.

"I can handle myself," Terry said, preparing to rip up his shirt to bind the gash in his arm.

"I wish we had real bandages," she sighed, watching him. "Okay, Fergus, right? Stay right there," she said, getting up to crawl over on hands and knees and plop herself down beside him. She considered him for a moment, inspecting his right arm before climbing on her knees to his other side to inspect that arm, too, and making humming sounds that gave Fergus an uneasy feeling. "This one on your shoulder needs stitches. It's probably already infected. I don't have anything to put on it. I don't know the plants around here well enough to guess, and it'd be too risky."

She chewed on a lock of hair, eyes cast skyward. "Well, you aren't going to die before we get past this field or anything, but you'll be in trouble if we don't make it before tonight," she said, picking up the rest of her undershirt and ripping it up to try to make a few bandages. "That was pretty cool back there. I've never seen anything like it. No one in my village could do that."

Fergus grunted weakly, glancing at the others out of the corner of his eye. Terry was fastidiously looking away. Pip, for once, was looking almost interested, and Guillory was looking between him and Terry with a frown.

"Though I thought you were dying when you changed back. Right, Pip?"

The boy gave a little nod, hair falling into his face. He pushed it away with the back of his hand. "How did you do it?"

He shook his head. "I thought I was gonna die, and it just happened."

"So this was your first time?"

He nodded, wincing as Three tightened the bandage.

Guillory cleared his throat. Terry didn't look at him, though the rest did. "A redhead and a brunette."

Fergus tensed.

"Oh," Terry muttered, "did you just notice?"

"No. Your hair's been getting redder since this morning."

Terry sighed, pulling the string off of his finger. "Well, now what?"

"You stowed away on my vessel in disguise. You match the descriptions of two suspected arsonists. What do you think I should do . . .?" Guillory paused, mouth tightening. "I think we've met before a time or two, Bridges."

"Have we?"

"I believe we're well past the stage of playing stupid."

"We didn't start any fires," Fergus interjected. "It was the humans trying to burn down that building."

Guillory raised an eyebrow. "The humans?"

"Fergus," Terry warned.

"The Knights of Evalach. They were trying to trap everyone in that building like they did before!"

"What are the Knights?" Three asked, but was ignored.

"*Fergus*," Terry snapped.

Guillory looked thoughtful. "Could it be retaliation for Trevor Fennis?"

"Get up," Terry suddenly said. "We're going."

Fergus blinked, but seeing the stony look on his face got to his feet, searching out his clothing. Three and Pip shrugged and got up, too.

"I'm going to take you in as soon as we get back," Guillory declared, getting to his feet.

"You need someone to blame, after all," Terry replied, starting to walk.

"No," Guillory replied, annoyance seeping into his voice. "If these 'Knights' burned down the first level, then they need to be found and arrested."

"Like you care what happens to a bunch of poor hybrids," Terry spat, stopping and whirling around. Fergus had never seen him angry before.

He took a step back, bumping into Pip. Goosebumps ran down the nape of his neck. He cleared his throat softly, but was ignored.

"A lot of innocent *people* were killed in that fire, not to mention the property damages," Guillory replied.

"Which is only a problem because we're holding you up."

"Wrong again," Guillory said, face coloring. "We must seek out justice, or the violence will only perpetuate."

"*We* don't need your help."

"What's your problem?"

"Humans who get all high and mighty when it suits them. If you're so concerned about justice and fairness and the welfare of the little monsters, then why are you only getting upset about it now?"

Guillory stopped, opening his mouth and then shutting it. Wind rustled through the flowers. Pip fiddled with the buttons of his jacket. A strange call came from the direction of the forest, and birds scattered into the sky, casting their shadows over the party.

At last, Guillory spoke, "I don't know, but better late than never, isn't it?"

Terry snorted, resuming his usual detached expression as he slid his hands into his jeans and turned. "Just don't forget we've both saved your life several times over."

•   •   •

Guillory managed to walk without aid for the rest of their journey across the fields, over the hills, and down to the squat farmhouse below. His features were pinched and white, but he was able to keep a few paces behind Terry, who walked ahead of them all without speaking, leaving Fergus to Three's mercy. At her insistence, Pip begrudgingly lent a hand. Though Terry and Guillory were silent and tense, Three made up for it, happily chattering about how pretty the field was, how nice the weather was, how lucky they were to have escaped, what she wanted to eat . . .

She made them stop at the foot of the last hills to check him again. "You're healing better than I'd expected . . . " she noted, pulling off the bandages. "You looked pretty bad earlier. Guess you're back to good spirits! That always helps a little."

"You know a lot about healing," he remarked.

"I . . . well, I've taken a certain interest in it," she replied, surprising him with her hesitancy. Pip gave her a worried look, and she smiled again. "We're in a dangerous line of work. You have to expect sometimes you'll be on your own. Kind of like we are now, you know?" She looked away from him.

Fergus cleared his throat softly. "You know, the police are probably offering some kinda bounty for us . . . "

"What?" She turned back, blinking owlishly.

"Well, you're bounty hunters, right? So I guess after this . . . "

"Do you think we're the kind of people who would turn on someone who saved us?" she asked, cheeks going red. "Where we come from, that's unforgivable."

Pip gave a wistful nod. His expression didn't really match the offense on her face.

"Sorry," Fergus mumbled.

"That thing was stalking us for days. I thought it had gotten you. We searched down at the stream, but we couldn't find you anywhere. Terry said he could smell your blood, so we looked all night, but you were nowhere to be found. "

"Days?"

"Yeah, we spent four days in that stupid forest."

"I thought it was just two nights."

"You probably were unconscious," Pip offered, pointedly looking away.

"We thought we'd killed it the second night, but by the third, it was back. It didn't like fire, but it didn't seem to take much damage from it either, which kind of made me useless. Fire magic is my specialty, you see, and when the airship went down, I lost my weapon. I couldn't really go hand-to-hand with it. Well, I tried, but that's how I got all these," she said, nodding to the cuts going up her arms. "Pip summoned something that scared it off, but that was his last charm. The next day, it was back again. I kind of thought it was our last stand, and then you came out. Well, actually, I thought it was one of those 'out of the frying pan, into the fryer' things. If it didn't eat us . . . "

Fergus cringed a little.

"But then you saved us!" she quickly amended. "It was amazing." Pip glared daggers, and Three immediately schooled her expression. "So, of course we wouldn't turn you in. Probably the reward wouldn't be worth going back anyway, and you said you didn't do it, right?"

"So where are you headed next?"

"We'd heard there's some guy hiding out in the farmlands around here who has a really big bounty on his head back in Clohaven. That's why we're out here."

"What did he do?" Fergus ventured.

"Murdered and ate three people."

"Jeez."

"We're hoping he didn't go into one of these forests, thinking he's a real fairy. He's probably a goner if he did. He might be preying on the local farmers, though. Guess we'll find out when we find people again."

"Can he change?"

"I'm not sure."

"He'd be the first for us, if he could," Pip chipped in. "There are a lot of . . . 'hybrids' who lose it. Many end up doing terrible things like that, but it's rare to see one of us who can change. Anywhere." He stared at Fergus.

Fergus's mouth twitched in annoyance, but he didn't dignify the unspoken accusation with a response. Instead, he turned back to Three. "I hope you catch him, then."

"Thanks. If he's alive and nearby, we definitely won't let him get away," she replied, grinning.

"We really didn't start that fire. We didn't kill anyone," he suddenly said. "We were at a concert, and those guys showed up, and we got into a fight. There were a lot of them, so we couldn't stop them all." He paused, lowering his voice enough that he hoped Terry wouldn't hear. "Guess the Knights really hate us, but . . . Okay, I get if some guys were pissed about a freak like the guy you're after, but then, shouldn't they go after him instead of just attacking people randomly? Do the Knights exist anywhere else?"

Three shook her head. "If they do, I've never heard of them. Pip?"

He shook his head, too. "There are other groups, though. Humans are weak compared to us. It's natural that they would be afraid. It's not rare that hybrids commit crimes either."

"Yeah, but usually not violent ones," Fergus argued.

Pip shrugged without replying.

"I'm sure most only do it because of their circumstances," Three added, smiling tremulously. "Most live like you do in New Peiling. At least, in this part of the world. There are places even worse than New Peiling, though, where they kick hybrids out and make them live in colonies outside the human cities. They're not very . . . nice places, either."

"What about where you live?"

"Depends on the city. In some, they're revered. In some, humans are under them. Then there are places like here, where they're oppressed."

"How many cities have you been to?" Fergus asked, voice pinched in longing.

"Seven so far. We usually go where there are lots of bounties, so we don't do much sightseeing."

"Guess you've seen a lot of the world, though, right?"

"More than most, I guess?"

"Can I show you something?"

Three glanced at Pip and then nodded.

"Later, though, okay?"

Her brow puckered, and she started to open her mouth to ask, but then she shrugged and said, "Okay."

Smoke snaked into the sky beyond the hills. As they crossed over, they could see a small cottage nestled in between an expanse of fenced off fields. More of the brilliant red flowers grew from the edge of the fields to the house. The flowers were so thick it looked like the cottage was welling out of a fresh wound. Fergus shivered a little at the thought. He wouldn't be surprised to find that some old witch lived there, and he'd had enough of witches. Terry was already headed down towards it, though, so they tromped after him. Fergus could see lines of smoke from the neighboring houses further down the horizon.

A man came out to stand amongst the flowers as they drew nearer. He was tall and thin – that much was obvious from even a distance – and wan. He looked especially pale against the rich sea of flowers.

"I don't believe it," Guillory muttered.

Terry raised a hand in welcome, and the man did not move. He had a grave, sour expression carved into his features. His blonde hair hung lank and long around his face. His eyes were so brown they were nearly black. They were presently narrowed on Terry. However, as the others caught up with him, the man let out a sigh and finally nodded to the redhead.

"Your hospitality is still one of a kind," Terry called out to him.

The man looked past him, mouth twitching in obvious irritation when he saw Guillory.

"Relax, Rosslyn, I've got him in the palm of my hand."

Guillory stopped, bristling. "Watch it, Bridges," he muttered, though only Pip, Three, and Fergus heard him.

It took a moment to click, and then Fergus stopped, too, shocked that this was *the* Rosslyn Weber. He'd been expecting something a lot different from Terry's impersonation. Maybe cleaner and less angry looking. He was exuding irritation in waves, so much so that Fergus wasn't sure they should be trying to call upon his hospitality at all.

Rosslyn finally stopped glaring at Terry to stare at Fergus. His expression became a little more pleasant. "Is that Ainslee's son?"

Terry nodded.

"He looks like a dullard."

"What the hell?" Fergus spat, feeling suddenly a lot more vigorous. Three gave his shirt a little tug.

Rosslyn snorted, though no smirk followed. Instead, he issued a long-suffering sigh. "Fine. Bring them all inside. Don't touch anything. Especially not the cat."

They timidly followed Terry into the house. It was a moment before Rosslyn followed. The interior of the cottage was far less quaint than the exterior. It was a little like Ursula's shop, though dustier and more spacious, which made it feel barren. Two young boys peeked out shyly at them from around a large old bookcase. In fact, they had to go through a number of shelves before they entered the actual home, which was sparse. It was like he'd taken a section from a library and plopped it down inside the shell of a cute country cottage. All Fergus could see was shelves of potions ingredients, books, more books, and a reading chair and table in the back. There really wasn't anywhere else to sit, so they stood.

"So this is Peygham," Terry mused.

"That or Hell."

Terry chuckled and took a seat in the armchair. Fergus stared at him for a moment, because something was tugging at the edge of his memory. Terry was very familiar with Rosslyn, yet he thought that Terry had said they hadn't met, or at least that he hadn't been working for the Count long before Rosslyn left. He wasn't sure what to think, so he chewed on his lower lip and tried not to. At least, not until he could get Terry alone. There was a rather lovely picture window looking out towards the next farmhouse. It seemed rather surreal that a forest full of man-eating fairies and crazy witch women lived less than a day's walk away.

"It's . . . cute. Where's the rest of it?"

"Just look for the old sign by the only road that goes from here to the coast. There's really no way to get lost. But you came from the field, so I'm guessing you didn't come into the port, and I think you didn't arrive by airship," he remarked, frowning at Guillory.

"We came from the forest."

"*That* forest?"

Terry nodded.

Rosslyn laughed. "No wonder you look half-dead. I wonder how long you got caught up in there."

"Mister . . .?" Three started.

"Rosslyn Weber."

"Um, Mr. Weber, you're pretty close to that forest."

"Are you afraid the bogeymen will come out after you? They won't. They hate these flowers. All of them."

Everyone in the small, tattered party relaxed just a little.

"Proves how unpleasantly close to human we are, though, that we aren't bothered."

"Optimistic as always," Terry remarked under his breath, scrunching down in the chair.

"Caelyn, Jamey, go make tea," he snapped at the two boys, who nearly fell over, jumping from their hiding spot. They disappeared down a corridor between the shelves, whispering excitedly. Rosslyn rounded on Terry. "I'd like to see your optimism out here in the sticks."

"I *was* thinking of becoming a farmer."

This time, Rosslyn smirked. "You wouldn't last a day. How long should I expect to be entertaining you lot?"

"Give us a couple of days. Dunno where these two were headed, but Fergus and I have a date with a farm."

"You weren't joking?"

"Don't even think about it," Guillory cut in. "If we're going to capture the real arsonists, then you both have to return to the city with me to testify. We'll need you at hand."

"I'm not testifying," Terry bluntly replied. "So go screw yourself, Guillory."

Three put a hand on the bristling Captain's arm. Rosslyn looked genuinely amused for the first time. Fergus cleared his throat, which he immediately regretted, because it brought the angry blonde closer to him. He leaned down and peered into his face for a moment in which Fergus tried to look anywhere else.

"You've had a bit of fairy blood," he remarked reaching out with a long, bony finger to press at Fergus's temple, stretching the skin away from his eye. He took him by the arm, pulling back at the tears in the sleeve. "Amazing what it will do, isn't it?"

"What do you mean?" Three asked. She had seated herself on the floor, which meant her head was craned nearly all the way back to look at him.

"That's a lot of blood, isn't it?" Rosslyn remarked, jerking at the torn fabric. "It's all over him, but he's hardly scratched at all. Plus, his eyes. I've seen that look before."

Now everyone was staring at him, and Fergus wanted to hide behind the armchair, except that he spotted the angry looking cat there. It flipped its tail, as though sensing his desire to infringe on its territory, and opened one eye. Fergus could see a scar over the other, sealing it shut. It growled, and he coughed lightly, staring out the window until he could feel their gazes dropping away.

"Be careful," Rosslyn said, but didn't expound. "Well," he continued, crossing his arms over his chest. "I have nothing for you to wear, probably little to eat, and only three rooms for sleeping. I can put some of you up elsewhere, if you like, but if that's good enough for you, I can offer you a hot bath and porridge."

"Good enough for me," Terry shrugged. Fergus glanced at him and then nodded, which cued Three and Pip to do the same. Guillory hadn't quite stopped looking at Fergus. He nodded slowly as well.

"I'll have my apprentices take care of you. I've work to do. Rest if you like. They'll show you the other rooms, if you need privacy, or if you want to wash, have one of them draw a bath." He paused, staring at them all blankly before settling on, "They'll bring you tea, at least." And then, rather abruptly, he turned and disappeared through the shelves.

"Well, you heard him," Terry replied, picking up a paper from the table and drawing it closer. "Roam if you like, but don't touch anything. You never know what *he'll* have." He paused, holding up the paper, and then blinked, brows climbing towards his forehead. "Two months."

"Two months?" Guillory asked. "Wait, we were in there for *two* months?"

"Seems so. Well, that's how those places are, I've always heard. Four days could easily have wound up four years. We're lucky."

"It was only three for me," Fergus muttered, but only Three glanced at him and having heard this before, didn't remark.

"They probably think we're all dead," Guillory said, sinking down to the floor, and Fergus had to feel a little sorry for him, because his head was so bent, and his eyes were so empty. Then he felt annoyed, because probably nobody was worried if he was dead or not. Well, perhaps Ursula would have worried at first, but with two months gone by, she probably was over it. This made Fergus feel as depressed as Guillory looked.

"You've got a strong back. You could always start over as a farmer," Terry remarked rather snidely.

Guillory looked up, life coming back into his face with the heat of anger, but he didn't rise to the bait. "I'm going to ask one of those boys about a place to lie down," he said, getting to his feet and waving off Three's efforts to help him. He skulked off down the hallway.

Terry let out a sigh of relief, the nastiness sliding out of his features to reveal exhaustion. He rubbed his forehead.

"May I see that?" Three asked, and Terry passed her the paper, which she and Pip began to pore over, pointing and talking rapidly in a foreign language. Fergus wondered if they could read the print, then decided they must be able to, since they had spoken to him with little trouble so far.

Fergus wandered over to Terry. He wanted to ask why he'd lied about Rosslyn, but it wasn't quite private enough. Instead, he just leaned against the armchair and tried to ignore the growling of the cat.

"Remind you of your girlfriend?" Terry muttered, his face softening just a fraction behind his hand.

"Maybe."

"We might have to leave during the night," he continued, growing serious again. "Guillory may think he's got the best intentions for us, but I doubt he can actually protect us. Maybe they won't care – it has been two months – but his ridiculous . . . " His face twitched. "He's not going to let it go, so don't get too comfortable."

Fergus nodded, leaning his forehead against his knee and closing his eyes. He was exhausted enough that he thought he could sleep there, though he did note he was feeling a lot better than he had that morning. Maybe there was something to that fairy blood theory. He felt a weight on his head, and then Terry ruffled his hair. Fergus turned around, but Terry had his eyes closed, trying to find a spot to rest his head.

"It'll be okay," he slurred.

The boys returned with a plate bearing a teapot and several mismatched, chipped cups. Both were tall and scraggly, much like Rosslyn, though tidier. They tried not to stare at the guests, but they kept glancing at them, especially at Three and Pip, elbowing each other in wordless communication.

"Hi," Fergus offered.

They both froze, staring at him. Then the taller cleared his throat and mumbled, "Hello."

Fergus tried not to be obvious about studying them, but he was noticing some things more clearly now, such as the fact that they did smell differently from Terry and Pip and Rosslyn. They didn't quite smell like Three either, though she was decidedly human, but a human with beyond average magical ability, which probably explained it. They smelled more like Guillory. Or rather, perhaps it wasn't smell exactly, but a feeling he got – a lack of tingling in his nose that he'd begun to associate with magic. He realized with a start that they probably didn't know that Rosslyn wasn't a human, and that they thought they were seeing hybrids for the first time.

"I'm going to get some fresh air," he suddenly announced. Terry was already asleep, Pip didn't care, but Three gave a little nod.

"No tea?" the shorter boy asked uncertainly.

""I'll come back for it," he said, trying to smile, but being looked upon like a caged animal was a little much for his already frayed nerves.

He went back out the way they'd come in. He didn't realize how musty it was inside the cottage until he stepped back out into the warm breeze, which was drawing the smells of flowers and trees and grass to him. He had to admit it really was astounding. Erstwyre Park was like one of the old dock ladies' potted garden collections in comparison. He wanted to run around, or maybe roll in the grass and flowers, except that he was still very hungry and fighting off waves of dizziness.

Rosslyn was standing off to the side, throwing crumbs. Fergus looked up and realized that there were at least half a dozen nests assembled on the edge of the roof. Their occupants were presently on the ground, cooing and pecking at the bread. He wandered closer, and Rosslyn glanced over his shoulder at him. He tried to give him a smile, but earned a blank stare in return. Fergus wasn't entirely sure how to approach the blonde, though he did seem to have the good fortune of being "Ainslee's son" on his side. After a moment, Rosslyn silently turned and went back to feeding the birds.

"I'm surprised they can live so close to the cat," Fergus remarked.

"He knows better than to trouble them."

Fergus nodded and then began to fidget with a tear in his jeans. The line of Rosslyn's shoulders tightened. He continued to persist in not making conversation, and Fergus wondered if he should just meander elsewhere, but instead, he pulled himself together and asked, "You knew my mother?"

Rosslyn gave a curt nod. "All of us did."

"You and Ursula?"

"And Terry."

Fergus stared at the birds, swallowing. "Oh."

"I see that comes as a surprise to you."

"I don't understand. He's younger than I am, so how could he have known her?"

"Younger? Did he say that? He does have a very young face, but he's only a little younger than Ursula and I. He's got a good four years on you."

Fergus said nothing, trying to digest this second lie.

"He never says anything without a reason, so if he led you to believe otherwise, I imagine he thought it was for the best."

He tried to nod, but he couldn't quite force himself to look convinced. "So . . . did she teach all of you to transform?" he asked.

Rosslyn nodded. "She had a few other students, but they weren't very good."

"How did you learn?"

"It was somewhat like learning regular magic. All of us were versed in that, so translating it to how to feel for our fairies' forms wasn't too problematic, but it took a while. Let me guess, you've inherited her ability to do it without training?"

"Not exactly. It happened cuz I thought I was gonna die, and I don't really know how to control it."

"You should learn. Or rather, you should have Terry tell you about how to do it, but I would avoid doing it too much."

"Why?"

"I think you know why. It's like nothing else to turn into a fairy, but it will make your mind unstable."

"Because of the pain of turning back."

"Somewhat. That becomes more bearable over time, but the feeling . . . of being mortal? That never quite goes away, and that's worse than the pain. It'll make you want to do it more and more to escape, but we aren't really fairies. Certainly, the fairy-soul attached to us as children, and we are as much like them as we are like humans, but we spent enough years growing as humans that the strain is simply too overwhelming."

"Is that why my mom . . . " He paused, swallowing. ". . . killed herself?" It felt very weird to say it so bluntly, and it wasn't much of a relief, but rather it gave him a lost feeling, like he'd just put a heavy part of himself down on the table, but without it, he was empty.

"Yes," Rosslyn said quietly. "There are as many hybrids who lose their minds as end their own lives, but you rarely have one that does both. The ones who lose themselves prefer to take the lives of others, generally speaking. But she hadn't lost herself completely, I suppose. I wasn't there. I didn't find out until several days later. Only Ursula really knew what had happened, and she was in shock. I actually hadn't seen Ainslee much in months. I was embarking on a long series of . . . personal issues."

Fergus nodded.

"She wasn't well, though. She'd lost weight, and her eyes were always verging on desperation. You've seen Fairy Dust addicts? It's basically the same when a hybrid – whether they can change or not – begins to feel that yearning to be a fairy. Most of the time, the spirit itself is to blame, but in her case, it was probably the ecstasy of being a kelpie: the power, the immortality." He paused, before adding, "Though perhaps the spirit that bonded with her was unbalanced, too. There are theories about it, since that soul won't die when the human body does, but I don't want to bore you."

Fergus's eye twitched a little.

"It could have been a lot of things, but probably that was the main thing, so I'd avoid making a habit of changing."

He nodded and sighed. "You know, you explain a lot more than they do."

"I have little to lose."

"Well, what about if those psycho cannibal fairies come and try to do some weird magic on you cuz they want to absorb your powers?"

Rosslyn blinked, pieces of bread dropping from his long fingers. "Has that become common?"

"Dunno, but Ursula's pretty scared of people knowing about her, and Terry lied altogether . . . " Fergus trailed off.

"Interesting," Rosslyn mused and then lapsed into silence.

Fergus watched him feed the birds for a few minutes more and then went back inside, deciding that he probably could stand to lie down - at least until there was something to eat. He caught one of the apprentices, and the boy directed him to a room that he might have mistaken for the attic, if it weren't for the bed stuffed into the corner. Guillory was already there, seemingly asleep on the floor. The boy hurried to prepare some quilts beside him, as Fergus slipped out of his shoes and jacket and thanked him. He settled down, pulling a sheet over himself. There was a small, round window over Guillory's shoulder, which was cracked open. It creaked when the wind blew. The room was peaceful and still despite the sound; warm, too. He was starting to drift off when Guillory rolled onto his back.

"Sorry, did I wake you up?" he asked without feeling, as his happy thread of relaxation abruptly snapped.

"No," the Captain replied. "What's your last name, Fergus?"

He wanted to lie, but he was too tired to think quickly. Besides, it probably was only a matter of time before Guillory found out that the famous

Ainslee's surname was Irvine and applied it to him, so he sighed and replied, "Irvine."

"Bridges is probably going to have you slipping off tonight or tomorrow. I know his type well enough. They say a dog kicked too many times can't trust men." He sighed, going quiet a moment, and Fergus hoped that he'd gone back to sleep, but he continued just as Fergus was dozing off again. "It's not that he's missing valid points, but he is missing the bigger picture."

"How's that?"

"You can't just get angry and break things when something goes wrong. Imagine, for instance, if all the angry people like Bridges got together and attacked the Governor's office. Maybe they'd chase out all the bad politicians and overthrow the humans, but would it help in the long run? Then humans would be at the bottom . . . "

"What's so bad about that?"

Guillory held up a finger, motioning for him to wait. "The humans are just going to be angry, too. Over time, they'll plan their own rebellion and take power back again. It'll happen over and over. Violence doesn't help; *thinking* helps. Doing things the correct way is what helps. What do you think would save more lives? Biding your time and then retaliating against these Knight people, or trying to bring them to justice through the system, ensuring that they aren't going to retaliate against you?"

"The 'justice system' seems to favor their type."

Guillory raised an eyebrow.

"Humans. The system favors humans. In the end, we'll be painted as the criminals, and we'll be the ones punished. Probably executed."

"If you come forward of your own volition, your innocence will be more obvious. Besides which, I am prepared to protect you. Think about it, at least. If you want to change things, it may seem like working from the outside – making a loud statement – will do more, but it's temporary. The system itself must change if you want permanent results."

Fergus considered rolling the other way and ignoring him, but before he could, Guillory said one last thing.

"You saved my life twice, though it would have been easier to let me die either time. I know you're innocent. Rather, looking at you, I think you're the sort of man who has it in him to make things better for others. I won't say anything more about it, but think about it at least."

He wished that he'd put his pillow over his head.

Chapter Fifteen.

Two days passed in quiet recovery. Three and Pip helped around the house, which earned them some favor with Rosslyn. Guillory and Terry skulked about, mainly avoiding each other. Fergus drifted, feeling disconnected with no music, no girlfriend, and no job. He watched Terry wandering around restlessly, and when he wasn't doing that, he watched Pip and Three brewing potions with Rosslyn, trying to learn by watching, but he soon realized he didn't even know the basics to follow their art.

No one was very talkative as the sun set, setting the red flowers aglow. Once again, Fergus was reminded of blood. Staring out the window, he felt like they were floating on a sea of it. The windows in the house were all cracked open, and the scents that wafted in were unfamiliar, but comforting: smoke from nearby homes, animals and manure, flowers, trees, and the ocean. Perhaps the smells were what flavored the tasteless porridge, or maybe it was because by this point, Fergus was ravenous, but he was pretty sure he could have eaten four or five bowls. He settled for two, for although Rosslyn's apprentices returned to their respective homes for dinner about an hour before sundown, Rosslyn was obviously living very modestly.

Afterward, they were treated to warmed cider, which had an actual flavor, and which caused Three's cheeks to go pink. Terry and Rosslyn began to speak lightly of affairs in the city, and Guillory went outside with Pip to have a walk, though it was more like laps around the house. Three and Fergus were left to their own devices, playing with a shabby old set of cards on the floor. She was terrible at anything that required dissembling, staring with open dismay when her hand was poor. It was charming in a way, though bluffing her was a little too easy to enjoy.

She reminded Fergus a little of Emily, except with a broader outlook. Perhaps if Emily had been a bit less uptight – a bit more like Three – he might have been able to get on with her better. But though she did remind him a little of his ex, Three was conversely so unlike Ursula that it made him keep comparing them, too, and then wondering what she might be doing and missing her all the more.

"Hey, Fergus," Three said, finally putting down another bad hand. "You said you wanted to show me something before, right?"

Fergus cringed a little and glanced over his shoulder, but Terry and Rosslyn were wrapped up in conversation. He turned back to her, putting a finger to his lips briefly, which earned a stout and overly earnest nod from her, and then pulled out his wallet. The paper was still safely tucked inside, but it was stuck together in places, and he had to hand it over to her, conceding to the nimbleness of her fingers. With her tongue sticking out of the corner of her mouth and more concentration than he thought necessary, she managed to pry it free with minimal rips. She smoothed it out on the floor, studying it silently for several minutes.

"It's a map," she said, repeating the old woman's theory. "It . . . *seems* familiar, but I just can't place it. Do you mind if I borrow it for a little while? I want to make a copy of it, so I can think on it."

He nodded. "I know you're gonna be busy soon and all . . . "

"No, sadly," she sighed. "They found our bounty knifed in the back just west of this island. Seems whoever did it didn't realize how much he was worth alive. You can barely get anything if you bring them in dead. We've had some of them even try to hold us on murder charges." She rolled her eyes, shaking her head.

Fergus snorted, too, trying to make it look like he agreed that the thought was ridiculous, but he felt a little disconcerted that she and Pip had apparently killed – even if accidentally – their targets on more than one occasion. "Anything to save some cash, I guess."

She sighed again, nodding. "Well, it's been two months, so we were thinking we'd go back to New Peiling and see if anything new turned up there, and if not, take an airship to Clohaven. There's always something in Clohaven. Well, that's what the saying is in our business."

Fergus flopped onto his back, watching from the window as the stars came out over the distant trees. "This is like where you grew up, right?"

"Sort of. It's softer and brighter here. All the mountains where we're from are kind of craggy and dark. It's like someone trying to draw a straight line on a shaky airship." With one finger, she pushed a card around in a circle on the floor. "I miss it."

"Why don't you go back?"

Three looked away, twisting her hair in her fingers. "I could. I'm just busy. There's someone Pip and I are looking for. Not a bounty." She pursed her lips. "If we could meet with that man, then I think I could finally feel it was right to go home."

"Why? What did that man do?"

She glanced at him and then at Terry and Rosslyn before shaking her head. "Not right now. Someday." She started gathering up the cards, neatly fashioning them into a stack again. Fergus could hear someone stepping lightly over the wooden floor. Though it seemed they were trying to be extra quiet, the boards were so old that even soft steps creaked. Figuring it was Pip, he closed his eyes. The steps drew nearer, and he heard a sharp "ahem" from a female voice. He cracked one eye.

Ursula was standing between the rows, dressed in a knee-length jacket that was as red as the flowers. He thought it accented her hair perfectly, though it made her face look wan, or perhaps she simply was that pale. Her cheekbones were sharper, the shadows around her eyes deeper, and she looked upset about something. Fergus realized it must have been him, because that's who she was staring at. His stomach gave a little twist of excitement, and he felt his face warming. He opened his mouth to say her name, but was cut off.

"That was fast," Rosslyn remarked, swirling the cider around in his glass without looking at her.

"Your bird died on my doorstep. It had a sense of urgency."

He looked annoyed, putting down the glass. "I liked that one."

"I buried it at sea. You could say it was a hero's funeral. Well, I see you've both survived the crash and the fairies." She paused, her eyes falling on Three and immediately narrowing. "And with new friends, too."

Three blinked and smiled pleasantly. Fergus wondered if she could really be as unaware of the souring atmosphere as she looked. "Is she your friend?" she whispered to Fergus, who gave a tense nod. "Oh, I bet you've missed her," she said, patting him on the shoulder excitedly. She cleared her throat, standing. "I'm going to go find Pip and Mr. Guillory. It's getting dark out." She passed Ursula with a jaunty stride, leaving her utterly baffled.

Ursula shook her head, turning back to the men, and shrugged out of her jacket. "You live in a hovel, Rosslyn. He didn't even give you severance pay?"

"I threw it into the ocean. I didn't want his charity."

She snorted and came to hover near Fergus, who took this as his cue to sit up.

"Guess you all know each other," he carefully said, looking at Terry. He thought he saw some emotion flash in eyes, but it was gone before Fergus could give it a name.

"Well, we are her chosen students," Ursula replied, folding up her jacket and putting it on the floor beside him.

She walked over to the table where Rosslyn sat and Terry leaned against the window. He, too, put down his drink as she neared, clearing his expression. She crossed her arms, looking between Terry and Fergus.

"You didn't tell him yet? Looks like he already knows. Rosslyn, did you let the cat out of the bag?"

"In more ways than I might have liked," he muttered in reply.

"Well, I'm glad that you're both all right after all this time. That may be the last of the good news for tonight, though."

"Black cats are always bad luck," Rosslyn said quietly, staring out the window.

"It may concern you, too."

This earned a hint of a functional backbone as Rosslyn sat up a little, brows rising in dubious expectation.

Ursula paused, taking a deep breath, and then her expression fell. "The Knights took Audrey – the Count's maid."

"What? We gotta get her back!" Fergus said, quickly trying to get to his feet, but the look Ursula gave him made him sit back down. "What is it . . .?"

"She's been exorcised."

Exorcism. Not only would the fairy-soul be permanently destroyed, but the human soul, too. Fergus swallowed roughly. Rosslyn had gone even paler, and Terry's mouth was set in a grim line.

"No way," Fergus finally managed.

"Deirdre found her body outside the penthouse."

"Weren't they . . .?" Terry trailed off.

Ursula nodded. "No one's seen her since, which is a bit of a problem. She may be looking for them on her own, and if so, that's the Count's problem." She paused, glancing at Rosslyn for a moment before continuing. "Or she might have lost her head, and if that's the case . . . "

"Right," Terry replied.

"Wait, what does 'right' mean?" Fergus demanded.

"She knows a little too much to be allowed to go around raving in the streets."

"You can't."

"It may be unavoidable. The Count is looking for her. His estate is a wreck. There's no one around to tidy up for him, and I imagine . . . well, he does rather poorly on his own. He arranged for a rather lovely memorial for Audrey, hoping to lure Deirdre out, but it didn't work."

"I'm gonna go back and find her. You can't just kill her."

"She killed Flynn."

Fergus stared at her, his mouth gaping. "What? How . . .?"

The other three exchanged glances.

"Well, if you are going to tell him, say it before the girl gets back with the others," Ursula said.

"Fergus, we *are* the inner circle of Bandersnatch."

His jaw fell open a few centimeters more as he looked between them. He slowly drew it back in, gulping. "Wait, *you're* the evil hedonistic cannibals?"

"Terry, what have you told him about us?" Rosslyn demanded.

"Well, some are more evil and others more hedonistic, but very few are *cannibals*," Terry said with a shrug. "That part may have been a hyperbole."

Ursula took over. "Your mother founded Bandersnatch. It was all her idea. She came up with it about two months before she died. You probably don't remember, but it was the beginning of what we have now in New Peiling."

"Uh, hate to correct you, but I can't remember things ever being different in the lower level."

"It hasn't become really bad yet. It won't be long now before it does. You are so very unlike her. I could swear you've never read a paper in your life."

"Guess that means you aren't planning to ask me to take her place."

Terry gave him a lop-sided smile. "You're missing a few qualifications."

Fergus ignored the remark, his expression sharpening. "So basically, both of you have been lying to me for years. You've lied about my mom, you've lied about who you are, and you lied about Flynn, too."

"It's not a lie. Deirdre did kill him," Ursula replied tartly.

"Shut up," Fergus snarled at her, on his feet now. He could feel a funny tingling just under his skin.

"Whoa there, let's just calm down," Terry said, pushing away from the window and holding up both hands. "It's not as simple as she's making it sound."

"Tell me."

Terry and Ursula glanced at each other nervously.

"It was a little like Deirdre's situation now," Terry said.

"Flynn wasn't crazy."

"Fergus, listen. Evalach has been active since at least last summer. They weren't attacking or exorcising anyone then, but it wasn't long until they started to. The Senate began to change with Paige Harriet at its head, and like I said before: Governor Whitehurst is a sympathizer compared to her, and you probably don't remember this, but he's the one who made it so that first offense hybrids can be permanently banned from the upper levels. We think she has some kind of in with the Knights. Remember how I said they don't know about Bandersnatch? Well, they do know about Niamh."

"What does this have to do with Flynn?"

Ursula cleared her throat. "He actually disappeared the night before your concert. *Niamh* heard that the Knights had him." She stopped, nodding at Terry to continue.

"Jane's not Fand, but she is close to Fand, so pretty much everyone in Niamh has to listen to her. Flynn knew a lot about Niamh and maybe even a little about Bandersnatch. I think he knew something about how to find the entrance to Tír na nÓg. I dunno why the humans would want that information, but according to Niamh, they did. Guess she felt like she didn't have a choice. She asked us to deal with her boyfriend for her."

"At least, she should have done it herself . . . "

"I agree, but she's not very strong. Probably they would've gotten her, too. That's not really Bandersnatch's concern, but . . . well, the Count decided to act as substitute Macha and sent Deirdre out. Probably, he wanted Niamh to owe us one."

"Misguided as always," Rosslyn muttered, brows lowering darkly.

"What the hell is 'Macha'?"

"Rosslyn, or his alias, at least. Mine's Badb Catha, and she's Morrígan," Terry explained. "We're

Bandersnatch's leaders, though the rest only know us by those names. They don't know who Macha, Badb Catha, or Morrígan really are. We'd probably have to go into hiding, like Fand did, if people found out."

"Okay, fine. Go on."

Terry picked up the rest of his cider, downing it. He stared at the light reflected in the glass for a moment before he spoke again. "They hadn't killed him yet, so Niamh assumed they must have been questioning him. Their messenger went to the Count. Probably, they figured he knew our true identities, which he does, but rather than ask us, he jumped the gun and sent Deirdre and Audrey. Far as I know, Deirdre did the dirty work, and Audrey helped get him back to your apartment."

"How could they . . .?" Fergus asked, staring at the floor between his socks. It blurred dangerously.

"They always do what he asks. They believe in him, the way the humans believe in Harriet, the way Niamh believes in Jane, and the way we believed in your mother. I don't know the rest. I doubt even the Count knows exactly what happened. But as soon as it was done, Jane turned around and said that she had wanted him rescued, not killed, and things have been pretty tense between Niamh and Bandersnatch since."

Fergus dropped to the ground, cradling his head in his hands. "Dominique was right. You *were* in on it."

"I wasn't," Ursula said, shaking her head, her voice catching.

He didn't look up. "That's why you waylaid me that night."

"I didn't know what was going to happen. I was asked to keep you from going home, so I did. I'm sorry, Fergus. I really didn't know."

"I worked for that guy. I worked with *them*. All along, they were the ones . . . "

"It wasn't personal," Terry said.

"Does that even matter? Do you really think that matters? Flynn was like my brother! He was the only family I had left when Mom went and offed herself. You think this is okay because it wasn't personal?"

Terry looked away, cowed for the first time in Fergus's memory.

"We wanted to protect you," Ursula said softly, clutching her arms tighter to her chest.

"Because I'm Ainslee's son? You can shove that."

"No," she spat back, hesitated, and then softly added, "No, because you are . . . because I like you, and he likes you."

"Don't continue," Fergus replied, looking up. "If you say what I think you're gonna say . . . "

Terry put a hand on Ursula's shoulder. She looked out over the shadows stretching across the fields.

"I can't believe this."

Ursula and Terry were silent. Rosslyn slowly shifted and stood.

"I understand," he said quietly. "When someone betrays you to such an extent, how could they ever be forgiven?" He picked up his glass, examining it. "But sometimes, they're all you have, and you end up being your own biggest traitor, because it's the only way to survive."

"Rosslyn . . . " Ursula mumbled.

"I think I see the others, and it looks like they've brought a friend. Say, Ursula, you wouldn't have happened to have stowed aboard one of the Air Guards' airships, would you?"

She shook her head. "As if I would be so stupid."

"Well, it looks like Vice-Captain Ashton Harriet is here to pick up Captain Guillory. I suggest, Terry, that you two make yourselves scarce," he instructed Ursula and Terry.

They both nodded. The air around them began to distort, turning hazier and receding, until all that was left was a great black dog and a cat with a white spot on its chest. Fergus wasn't sure what they were so worried about, except the guy had the same surname as this Paige Harriet woman, and he thought perhaps it would be best to vacate for a little while until his own temper was burning lower.

Without explanation, he went outside, managing to just round the corner as the others' voices came into hearing range. He stopped there, slumping down against the wall. He wasn't sure what he wanted to do – scream, hit something, run away, turn into a kelpie and never return – but all he could seem to do was sit there, shaking, and stare at the ground. Presently, something silky slipped under his fingers, and he glanced at Ursula, who sat down beside him, wrapping her tail around herself. He retracted his fingers, clutching his arms around his stomach.

She sat quietly for a moment before speaking. The sound seemed more like variations in purring than words, which made her hard to understand. It was also very disorienting to be spoken to by a cat, so he had to stop pretending to ignore her to focus.

"I'm sorry. I didn't think this would happen."

He paused, parsing the words, before replying, "This is obviously what would happen. And what's the point of saying sorry for something that you knew would turn out badly when you did it?" He wanted to believe she was just sorry she'd been caught, because her remorse was grating in its honesty.

"Even we don't know everything. If I had known, I wouldn't have allowed it. I'm sure he wouldn't have, either."

"Not sure how you can expect me to believe you."

She said nothing, scrunching down and tucking her legs under her. He resisted the urge to scratch her. It would have been comforting, he thought, if she'd been a real cat. However, he wasn't going to give her that satisfaction. They watched the stars as the sky darkened. It seemed like new batches appeared every few minutes. He'd never seen so many stars. He'd rarely seen the open night sky. It was a bit terrifying. He felt like he was going to be swallowed up, or crushed in the vastness. He found himself huddling a bit against the wall of the cottage.

"They're arguing inside," Ursula mused.

"They are?"

"Rosslyn has had run-ins with Harriet and Guillory before. He's usually okay with Guillory, but the only person who can get to him more than Harriet is the Count."

"He seems like he wants to go back."

"He does," Ursula agreed. "Though I hope he doesn't."

"Why?"

"Because the Count just doesn't learn, and Rosslyn will get caught up in that again when we need his attention with us."

"I can kind of understand how he feels."

She made a rumbling sound in her throat.

"You know, the only reason I survived that forest was cuz I wanted to get back to you. I thought about if we could really be together."

"As in . . .?"

"As in just me and just you and no one else. A real couple, Ursula."

Her tail flipped. "It's not possible."

Somehow, the horribleness of being lied to by the only two people he had left to rely on padded this moment. He was surprised at how he didn't feel as bad about the rejection as he might have. He didn't feel angry either. Still, he didn't want to give in with just that.

"Not now. Maybe someday."

She sat up. "It's not in my nature, Fergus. You're going to end up as miserable as Rosslyn."

That time it did sting, and he didn't reply. He plucked a blade of grass, wrapping it around his finger and unwrapping it again.

"Why can't what was be good enough?"

"Because it isn't."

She peered at him, unblinking. "Then maybe it's better that there's nothing between us."

A tendril of anger slipped up his chest through his throat. He clenched his jaw. The blade of grass snapped in his fingers. "Yeah, maybe so," he replied, getting to his feet.

"Where are you going?" she mewed.

He didn't reply.

•　　•　　•

He dreamed that he was standing naked under the clear night sky. There was nothing around him except the flowers. There was nowhere to hide, and the weight of the heavens was coming down, down, down - crushing him. He awoke to the smell of bacon. After days of porridge and stew, it smelled so good, it brought tears to his eyes. He got up and threw on his clothing quickly, heading for the narrow kitchen where the two apprentices were busy preparing breakfast.

The taller one (the one Fergus now recognized as Jamey) smiled at him. "It'll be ready soon, Mr. Irvine. Go and have a seat."

He went into the sitting room. Three was already awake. She perked up until she saw it was only Fergus and then flopped back, deflated, against the armchair where Pip sat. Ursula-the-Cat was glaring at the one-eyed-cat from across the room, and perhaps as a show of disdain, the one-eyed-cat was letting Three pet it. She turned from the raggedy old beast and began to clean her paws, tail flapping angrily.

Outside, he could see Guillory and Harriet standing near the road talking. Harriet was waving his hands, and Guillory kept shaking his head, which caused Harriet to move his hands with even greater agitation. Fergus wished he could hear them, though he did notice that a black dog was lying in the flowers not far from them.

It seemed Guillory was entirely unaware of Terry's canine identity. Fergus hadn't been around to catch his reaction to Terry's mysterious disappearance, but he could guess that's what the arguing, which had continued long after he'd gone upstairs, had been about.

Rosslyn was nowhere to be seen, but that wasn't rare. He didn't seem to appear until about thirty minutes after his apprentices had arrived and begun their morning's work. Fergus wondered where the bacon had come from. He sat near Three, also staring hopefully towards the kitchen. She smiled at him, though her attention was only waylaid for a moment.

"They said they've got the *Wyrd* docked at the port. We can leave this morning, even."

Fergus nodded slowly, feeling less excited about the bacon. On one hand, if he went back, probably Guillory would make him testify about the Knights, and then he'd be risking the chance that Guillory wouldn't be able to protect him, and he'd be executed. On the other hand, he needed to find Deirdre. He wasn't sure what he was going to do when he found her, but he knew he had to. He didn't think anything would make what happened okay, but he might be able to move on if he at least had an explanation. He wondered if he could just give a testimony and leave, or if Guillory was going to insist on keeping him in custody. He shifted nervously and changed the subject.

"Where'd the bacon come from?"

"The boys brought it. Apparently, their families got really excited about seeing the airship and Mr. Harriet, so they gave them some food to bring along. Great, huh?"

He nodded, though he didn't feel particularly grateful to have two Air Guard higher-ups looming over him. If they wanted to detain him, he was going to have a hard time getting away. Then again, Guillory hadn't pressed him too hard yet. He'd said it was up to Fergus. Maybe he wasn't lying, or maybe he was just biding his time. Given how hard it was to trust his friends, trusting strangers seemed out of the question.

The smell of bacon drew nearer, and the apprentices entered the room, holding a bowl of eggs and a plate of bacon and toast. Fergus and Three jumped to their feet. Caelyn brought out a plate of fish for Ursula, which she sniffed and then daintily began to eat, casting smug looks at the one-eyed-cat.

Fergus and Three were in the process of stuffing themselves with a second plate when heavy boots sounded across the old wooden boards, and Guillory and Harriet appeared. If Guillory was a lion, Harriet was a panther. He stared at them without expression from weathered features. Dark curls would have fallen over his face, save for the bandana holding them back. He looked a bit more like a pirate than Vice-Captain of the Air Guard, which was not helped by the scar over his temple. However, when he spoke, he had a particularly polished accent.

"Will this be everyone returning?"

"Where's Bridges?" Guillory asked.

The black dog slipped through his legs, coming over to try to nose at Fergus's plate. He shrugged, handing Terry-the-Dog a piece of bacon and bread.

"Figures. Well, if he wants to be a farmer, all the better. He can be the local constables' responsibility."

The dog wagged his tail.

"So, just the three of you," Harriet asked.

"Four," Rosslyn said, appearing behind them looking rumpled and groggy. He rubbed sleep from his eyes and glared at the assembled. "Guests are supposed to be quiet."

"Are you sure?" Guillory asked, raising a tawny eyebrow.

"I have errands to do, and I suspect you owe me a free ride, at least."

"What do you need to do?"

"Buy books – those things with words. I know you've never opened one."

Guillory rolled his eyes and came over to get some breakfast. "Fine, anyone else? Your apprentices?"

"No, they'll be taking care of things here, but I will need my dog."

"Why?"

"Because it's the city, and it's dangerous. You are a terrible guest."

"You are a terrible host."

•   •   •

An hour after the plates had been cleared away, they set off for the *Wyrd*. Rosslyn's home truly was at the outskirts of the village. Someone had put up a sign there, perhaps for when his fields had been a public landing strip, but it was in a state of disrepair. The pink paint had chipped off from the letters "a" and "m," and it was starting to tilt as the base rotted away, but since Rosslyn had closed the field off, no one had bothered to fix the sign or replace it. They wound their way down the dirt path, past the other farms, to Peygham proper.

It was a small village – a forgotten relic of the Cataclysm – protected by the mountains, which started up again three or four farmhouses down the road, and made up of two rows of about twenty shops. Beyond the shops, the land sprawled into hills and forests down into the sea. Nestled in these inhabitable plots of land were the houses of the Peygham residents. There were few people to be seen, but those who were up were calmly going about their daily business. They waved to Rosslyn, gazed with awe at Guillory and Harriet, and then stared in open bewilderment at the rest of the motley group.

Fergus stared at them, too. They didn't look like the humans in the city. It wasn't that their features were different, but their expressions were. They didn't seem suspicious or busy or tense in any way. Rather, they looked a little dopey to him, but in a nice way. He nodded to some of them and was very surprised when he received a nod *and* a wave in return. For a moment, he thought about staying. Maybe he could become a farmhand. People didn't have to know he was a hybrid. He could live like a human, and people would probably treat him decently.

As long as they didn't see his eyes in the dark.

He sighed, scrapping that, because inevitably they would learn about him, and if Rosslyn felt it necessary to hide his background from these people, then it probably meant they were no better than those in New Peiling, and at least in the city, there were others like him to commiserate with and lean on in hard times.

At the center of the village stood a fountain with a statue of a saint facing the sea. Her eyes were a little sad, but her lips looked like they were about to twitch into a smile. From the fountain, they could easily see down to the port. Just before it was a field where a large, black airship with splendid blue and silver trappings hovered. Two smaller airships lingered over the water nearby. That made three ships full of Air Guard crewmen waiting for them. Fergus thought of just running the other way.

"That's quite the entourage," Rosslyn observed, pausing for just a moment before steadily continuing down the road.

"If you'll excuse me for saying so, Captain," Harriet politely said to Guillory before addressing Rosslyn. "The men insisted on looking for the Captain. It was only by allowing this many that I could keep the rest in the city."

"Seems the Air Guard's grown since I last visited."

"And why shouldn't it? We are the city's elite, led by the city's hero."

"No need for that, Ashton," Guillory replied, shaking his head.

"But it's true!" the younger man insisted.

"Our city is safe, at least from the outside. Now we must see what we can do within. Can you imagine? New Peiling as the safest city in the world, both inside and out . . . "

"It sounds nice," Three agreed.

Fergus glanced at Guillory, who was busy smiling and nodding and explaining to Three about how it would be more than nice. It seemed like he hadn't said anything to Harriet about who Fergus was. He also, if he *had* realized it by now, hadn't mentioned anything about Terry, who was walking a few paces behind. Ursula was slinking along the side of the road. Stowing away wouldn't be a problem for her, Fergus guessed. He wondered if that's how she visited her cousin every year. It would cut down on the cost. He idly wished that he was a cait sìth, too. Maybe he should go into bounty hunting, like Pip and Three. That might also get him out of the city.

Presently, he wanted to be anything but a displaced rock singer with an infamous mother searching out his best friend's murderer. No, he thought, he didn't like that much at all. However, his feet moved forward, and he followed the others down the path to the airship below.

At least, Guillory hadn't ratted him out.

He paused and then amended that with, *yet.*

Chapter Sixteen.

It was nearing evening, and every level of New Peiling was lit up, giving it the look of a misshapen Christmas tree plopped down in the middle of the ocean. The white buildings of the upper level glowed against the cloudy sky like a halo. The lower levels were obscure smudges of lamplight and shadow smashed together. It was absurd to think of the upper city as a halo, because the plates below it looked more like a hulking, crippled beast than an angel. Airships slowly cut through the surrounding skies, heading towards the port and away towards Lancaster and Clohaven. He remained by the window as they made the descent into New Peiling.

The ferry docked late in the evening. Guillory and a couple of his men disembarked, including Harriet. The docks were dark and empty, save for a singular, bent form. The soldier with Guillory and Harriet let out a little gasp, drawing back. Guillory,

Harriet, and Rosslyn nearly ran into him, and Rosslyn started to curse when he saw the cause of the pile up. He abruptly went silent. Three and Pip were nearly to the old fortuneteller before realizing that no one was following and stopped, turning to the others in confusion. Fergus walked past them.

At this point, Lady Gemini was not particularly frightening. In fact, he felt very calm about walking up to her, which prompted Three and Pip to follow, though a step behind, whispering to one another uncertainly. Fergus wondered if she was about to tell him that Deirdre would kill him when he found her. Yet, he was not afraid of dying. After all he'd been through, it was difficult to believe it could really happen, and besides, there were worse things than dying. He drew up in front of her. For a moment, she watched him with clear eyes. Then they rolled back, and she reached out and clutched his arm.

"Green."

"Green," he repeated.

She released him and turned, toddling off into the dark maze of boardwalk.

""What's green?" Three asked, leaning around him to look up at his face.

"No idea," he said, shaking his head, and continued into the city.

When they reached the lifts, he waved briefly to Guillory and Rosslyn and kept going. He could hear Guillory's question catch and then fade into disappointment. Harriet asked what was wrong, but he didn't hear the answer. They didn't come after him, though he held his breath until they reached Beathag's, and he felt certain that neither Guillory, nor Harriet, nor the other officer had followed them.

He didn't hear Ursula go, but somehow, he knew that she'd taken the detour into the alleyway beside the shop. His things were still there, but he felt certain this time, at least, she would hold them until he returned. Pip and Three followed him, in part because they had no where else to go. It seemed the abandoned garage where Everyday Resources practiced was as good a place as any to stow them until they did, so that's where he led them.

It was deserted except for a note in Raja's handwriting that read: *Evelyn, if you read this, just stay here. I'll check back in a couple of hours, so wait for me.*

Fergus stared at it for a moment and then put it back down.

"Is something wrong?" Three asked, finding a place to sit.

He shook his head. "I'll worry about it later, but if a curly-haired girl comes in, don't let her leave, okay?"

They looked at each other and then nodded.

Fergus went back out into the night, Terry trotting behind him. He wondered how long Terry planned on following him, and if this was part of his mother's screwed up plan to take care of him after she drowned herself. Probably it was. After all, despite the fact that his mother was very familiar with these people, he'd never seen them until she died, and then Terry had joined his band, and Ursula had become his livelihood. They'd become daily fixtures in his life. The worst part was how miserable he felt when the bitterness bubbled up, because he didn't want to hate them, and he didn't want to think that all this time, he was their charge rather than their friend. He stopped, and Terry-the-Dog sat down.

"Terry," he said without turning around. "If you're just here cuz she told you to be, then go. Don't follow me."

He could hear claws scrape against the concrete. Something was welling in his chest that just wouldn't stop; something that had come unhinged by the absoluteness of Ursula's rejection.

"It's nice you did what she asked for all this time, but I'm not a kid anymore, and I don't want it. So just go away. Your obligation to . . . " he paused, feeling choked by resentment. He lowered his face, hair falling over his eyes. "Your obligation to *Ainslee* is over. Good-bye, Terry."

He heard the dog get up, the clatter of nails against the street, and then Terry pressed his cold, wet nose against his hand and whined softly. Fergus looked down. He was pretty sure that since Ursula could talk as a cait sìth, Terry could speak as a gytrash, but he didn't say anything, just looked up dolefully.

For a moment, Fergus felt angry. He jerked his hand away, drawing it back, and thought about just hitting Terry, so that he'd go away, but he couldn't. Terry wagged his tail uncertainly, and Fergus slowly lowered his hand to the dog's head. He stared at the black fairy-dog who was perhaps the closest thing to a friend he had left and thought about Rosslyn's words. Would he betray himself just to survive? Did he really need these people so badly? Terry whined and nosed his hand again. Fergus sighed, giving him a pat.

"Don't get in the way," he grumbled without feeling.

He had to admit, there was something a little reassuring about hearing the click-clack of Terry's paws over the pavement. He remained out of the way as Fergus drifted in and out of shops and bars, asking about Deirdre. Someone had seen a tall, pretty woman with her hair pulled back in a severe ponytail wandering near the docks. Another had seen her in the Magpie three days ago, juggling for beers. One man recognized her as his ex-wife who'd stolen his dog and threatened to punch Fergus. Stories ranged from believable to beer-soaked ridiculousness. Fergus tried to glean what he could, but in the end, even the ones that seemed reasonable varied too much to even tell if she was actually on this level. She could just as easily be roaming one of the upper levels, or floating by the docks, waiting to be found.

He gave up on sleuthing and decided that though he rather wanted to push the Count out of a high window, the Count probably had the best idea about where Deirdre might have gone. He might have more than just an idea, though Fergus imagined he'd demand payment for it. He wondered if a threat would do, though the Count had killed Fennis. He probably didn't scare easily. Or *had* he? Fergus considered and recalled that he hadn't seen Deirdre much that night. The Count had been bloody when they'd come up to his room, but the body had already been out back, which was probably Deirdre's work.

Now he was without Deirdre, but he wasn't without Rosslyn, who could potentially turn into a very large, hungry fairy monster, depending on what kind of soul he shared. Would he protect the Count? Fergus glanced at Terry and thought he probably would, just as Fergus would still have Terry's back if needed. But maybe with Rosslyn there, the Count would be so busy with other things that he wouldn't make any wild demands. It was worth a try, he decided.

He set out for the penthouse, Terry just behind him. As they stepped out of the lift, he noticed the street was empty, but despite that, it was not quiet. There was an amazing shouting match drifting down from the upper floor of the penthouse. He heard something break and wondered if maybe now was a bad time, but steadied himself and pulled the bell. The fighting abruptly stopped. Fergus waited. The cook would have gone home by now, and unless the Count had found some temporary staff, he probably was alone, so he'd have to answer the door himself. Sure enough, a few minutes later, he opened the door. Fergus could see Rosslyn in the shadows behind him.

"Fergus," the Count said, face still red and looking generally unkempt.

"Where is Deirdre?"

"I don't know. I've been looking for her for ages."

"Well, where does she usually go when she's not here?"

"What will you do if you find her?" For the first time in their acquaintanceship, Fergus heard anxiety in the Count's voice.

He gathered himself, straightening. "I'm gonna ask her what happened that night."

The Count's brow puckered, and he blinked uncomprehending.

"The night you told her to kill Flynn," Fergus supplied.

"That's what we were told to do – by that girl . . . by *Fand*, even."

Fergus said nothing.

"It was nothing personal," the Count insisted, voice speeding up. "They said he had secrets that would endanger us all and paid us to handle things. The Knights are a very persistent lot. Unless he'd left the city, they would have found him again, so Niamh told us to make sure they didn't."

"Where does Deirdre usually go?" he calmly asked once more.

The Count glared. "If she was in her normal mind, she'd deal with you in a second. I suppose you think you'll take care of her while she's weak?" He whirled around to Rosslyn. "Did you and the others decide it? Tit for tat to make *her* kid happy?"

Rosslyn snorted. "When were you privy to our decisions?"

The Count cursed, and Rosslyn smirked before disappearing around the corner. He turned his fury on Fergus. "Just leave her alone!"

"I want to hear the truth from her."

"I won't tell you where she is," the Count snapped and slammed the door shut.

Fergus tried knocking again, but there was no answer this time. He sighed and turned. Terry was nowhere to be seen, but he could hear snuffling sounds near the rubbish and whistled. Terry emerged, wagging his tail. He gave a little woof and then put his nose to the ground, sniffing some more.

"Why didn't I think of that before?" Fergus muttered, smacking his forehead.

Terry took over, leading him back to the lift. They paused for a few minutes back on the lower level as Terry-the-Dog tried to get his bearings. He led Fergus to the docks and then past them, around the outskirts of the city where his mother had taken him as a child for swimming lessons. It was rockier here and more perilous, but after the fairy forest, even the slippery, jutting slabs of stone seemed tame. They walked nearly halfway around the city before they saw the lone, thin figure standing on a dilapidated pier, watching the waves crashing against the rotting wood. Terry stopped, letting Fergus lead now as they both carefully climbed over the slimy rocks to the little path that led to the abandoned pier.

Deirdre's hair had come out of its usual twist. She had her back to him, hands in the pockets of a dark grey jacket. She slowly turned when he was about ten feet away, and he stopped.

"I didn't think it would be you," she said without expression. Even in the shadows, her eyes looked swollen and bruised. Her mouth lifted in the impersonation of a smile.

"I'm sorry about Audrey," he said without thinking and then kicked himself.

"It will be very hard for you to kill me if you're thinking like that."

He said nothing. He wasn't sure where Terry was anymore, but he couldn't hear him whuffling around. "Tell me about Flynn."

"The Count was told by one of Fand's messengers that someone who 'knew too much' had been taken by the Knights. I think he and the redhead were close, and she's close to Fand, or at least they say she is. I don't really know. Audrey didn't either. She pleaded with me not to do it. I didn't want to, for her sake, but we had to at least find him."

"And?" Fergus asked, nails cutting into his palms as he waited for the full story.

"We killed him."

"You're lying."

She laughed weakly. "I'm not. It's not a lie. It's all the truth there needs to be."

"You're lying, Deirdre."

"Then come and make me tell the truth."

"I don't want to fight," he said, shaking his head.

"Then that's all you need to know," she replied.

He barely caught the flash of the blade as she took her hands from her pockets and lunged at him. The knife cut through his shirt, and he fell backwards to avoid being sliced open. She moved incredibly fast. Her hand arched through the air again with the discipline and grace of a dancer. He kicked, managing to catch her in the hip and throw her off balance. The knife sunk into the decaying wood of one of the supporting beams. The entire structure wobbled perilously, and Fergus dug his fingers into the wet wood, afraid that it would give out at any minute and send them crashing into the waves.

"Stop it, Deirdre," he pleaded.

"No."

She wrenched her weapon free, and Fergus scrambled to his feet. He didn't have Terry's training; all he could do was dodge, shoes slipping on the wet planks. He could feel an army of little scrapes amassing, but he managed to stay just ahead of being gutted.

She was herding him to the end of the pier. Most of the boards had already given away into the ocean, and what was left didn't look like it would hold him. He tried to dart to the left, but she was right there, jabbing the blade at him. He tried for the right, but again, her speed was uncanny. He froze, and she pressed the tip of her knife to his throat. He could feel the prick of skin breaking.

"This won't bring Audrey back."

"I know."

"And it's not what she'd want either. Deirdre, listen. Maybe . . . Maybe if it was just me, I *would* wanna kill you and the Count, too. Flynn was like a brother to me. He was the only person I could trust. But because he was like a brother, I knew him better than anyone, and I know that he wouldn't want it. You should already know, too."

She swallowed, her eyes gleaming. The tip pressed deeper, and he could feel a trickle of blood begin to drip down his throat.

"I know, but I can't do what she would want me to, and I can't fight those monsters alone. I can't do anything."

He very slowly and carefully reached out and placed his hand over hers. His heart was drumming in his ears. It took all his willpower not to swallow. Slowly, he tightened his fingers over her hand. She didn't lower it. She didn't even blink.

"You can't take revenge against someone you don't even know, and if you did, it wouldn't make her happy. If you really love her, you'll do what you know she would want, no matter how hard."

He held her gaze. He felt a shiver run down her arm. The ocean sounded very loud. The brine smelled very rich. The wood quaked under their feet. He could see Terry sitting at the end of the pier over her shoulder. She glanced in that direction, too, though without a hint of recognition. She turned back to him and relented. Her arms dropped to her sides, the knife held loosely in her fingertips. She stared at the ground. Most of her hair had come free and was covering her face. He rubbed at his throat, wiping away blood.

"He wasn't dead, so Audrey begged me to spare him. They were going to exorcise him and then he would be gone . . . " She pressed one hand to her forehead. "Gone forever, like Audrey. We got rid of most of them, but there were more coming. I told her that he would die if we moved him, but it was that or exorcism, so we did anyway. We tried to take him to your home, but he was dead before we got there. We didn't know what to do. The police will never be on our side, and the Knights thrive on fear. That's why we tried to make it look like a suicide. We hoped the cops would leave us alone, and maybe the Knights wouldn't have their way. Not entirely."

"That's a lame plan."

"I *know*. There just wasn't enough time to think, and Audrey was in hysterics. It was all I could come up with. And now look at them picking Niamh off. The redhead's probably next."

"I doubt it."

She ignored him. "They're weak. They aren't like us. The only ones who can stop the Knights are Bandersnatch, but who knows if they will? They probably don't want to draw attention." Her voice caught. She slowly sat down and hugged herself.

"What will you do?"

"I don't know."

"The Count's pretty much all alone up there."

"He'll be fine."

Fergus crouched down in front of her, careful to stay out of her knife's range. "He's worried about you. Listen, there aren't that many people who are gonna worry about you. Not here. So if there is someone who wants to help you, it's a rare opportunity."

She said nothing, huddling further, and he sighed.

"Maybe she's not around anymore, but you still think of her, and if that's all she's got, at least she has that." He stood and ran a hand through his hair, staring up at the starless sky. "Well, that's all I'm gonna say," he said with a sigh and gingerly stepped around her to head back down the pier to Terry. He stopped for a moment to let the dog nose his hand and then scratched behind one shaggy black ear before they began picking their way back around the city. Terry returned to human form just before the docks.

"She's probably going to jump."

"I don't think so," Fergus replied.

Terry gave him a curious look and then shrugged. "I hope she doesn't."

Fergus grunted softly in agreement.

"Evelyn's probably been exorcised, too, if that note means anything."

"Yeah . . . " Fergus said and trailed off. He caught a flash of red from out of the corner of his eye. "Hey, can you go ahead and see if Raja's returned? I'm gonna get something for us to eat."

Terry hesitated, studying him, but nodded, disappearing into the shadows between buildings. Jane came out of the alley, hurrying over.

"Haven't found Evelyn, have you?" he asked.

She shook her head. Her face was drawn and sallow. She tried to pull her hair out of her face. "First Audrey, now Evelyn . . . "

"You mean, first Flynn."

She stared at him without comprehension. "What about Flynn?"

"Deirdre told me everything."

She continued to stare blankly. "She's the one who killed him, isn't she? Did you kill her?" she asked, her voice catching and eyes seeming to bulge a little.

He took a step back from her. "No."

Jane said nothing. She stood watching him for a long time. He thought about leaving, but somehow, he couldn't seem to escape from her stare.

In a bid to make her just go away, he threw out, "*Your* people ordered it. Your precious Fand. Maybe even you. Niamh are the ones behind it, and you're one of them, so don't act like I let him or you or anyone else down by leaving her alone."

"I didn't order it. I would never . . . I *loved* Flynn. I still love Flynn. I would never do that." For a moment, her expression bordered on manic, and then she looked away. "Are you going to kill me, then?"

"No. It's not gonna fix anything, and he wouldn't be happy knowing I did something like that, so no."

She stared at him for a moment, her eyes turning red and glistening. "Why couldn't you kill her?" she demanded, grabbing his arm and giving it a shake. Her nails bit into his skin. "It's not fair. She killed him. She should die!"

Fergus gently peeled her fingers away. "No, it isn't fair, but I'm still not going to do it."

She relented, clutching her hands to her face. Tears slipped through her fingers as she sobbed quietly. "Flynn was right about you. He said that you were the kindest person he knew." She gulped back a great sob, trying to keep her nose from running and then pressed her hands harder to her face, so that he could barely understand what she said next. "But I wish he wasn't," she managed, half-choked with tears. With that, she turned and ran off down the alley she'd come from.

He watched the shadows between the buildings swallow her up and thought he probably should have warned her about the Knights, but then decided he'd worry about Evelyn first.

• • •

Raja was there when he got back. He was sitting with his head between his knees. His dark, wavy hair fell over his face. Terry sat across from him, chewing his lower lip. Three hurried over to Fergus, looking worried. Shrugging faintly, he walked past her to dump a pile of convenience store delicacies on the floor.

"Eat up."

Raja didn't lift his head, but the other three began to pick through the assortment. Fergus walked over to him, starting to reach out and touch his shoulder, but hesitating.

"Hey," he tried.

He caught Terry watching him as he slowly unwrapped a meat pie. His mouth twitched sympathetically when he caught Fergus's gaze. He shook his head, and Fergus took that to mean he'd already tried, so he sat down with the others and began to quietly fill himself up on the greasy food. No one said anything. Raja hardly moved at all. Pip and Terry concentrated on their food, but Three was fidgeting. Finally, she spoke up.

"Pip recognized your map."

"Your map?" Terry asked.

"Oh, right, sorry!" Three immediately said, clutching her mouth.

Fergus sighed. "I found it in Flynn's room," he said, reaching out to take the original from Three as she spread her copy on the ground.

"It's a floating island. Well, not really. It's more like a kind of port in the middle of the ocean where a bunch of people live in house boats."

"Where is it?"

"A long way east from here. It'd take a really long time to get there, even by airship. It's near where we come from."

"Is there anything else there besides that port?"

"I don't know," she admitted. "It's hard to get permission to dock there. Well, that's an understatement, actually. It's mostly pirates in those parts, so they demand a lot. But you know, the port never goes very far, so maybe there is something holding it in place?"

"I couldn't afford the airship fare," he said, sighing.

"You could always come with Pip and me. Team up for a while? We earn more than enough to travel on."

"I'll pitch in, too," Terry said. "I'm guessing this is about Tír na nÓg. If we can actually find it . . . " He sounded a little wistful, though Fergus wondered if he hadn't just said it to try to get Raja's attention. That seemed like a pretty good idea.

"We could leave all this behind," Fergus added quietly. "It might be nice."

"I want to come, too," Raja suddenly said, not looking up. "We have to find it before the Knights do. If nothing else, we can try to protect that from them."

No one said anything for a minute, and then Fergus nodded. "Well, how about it, Three? That's six extra hands."

She pulled on her lower lip as she looked between them. "We'd have to find a captain who could even make that first leg . . . Money, too."

"We'll find a way," Fergus said, feeling confidence slowly blooming. "Let's find it," he said, voice rising a little, despite Terry's warning glance. "Let's go to Tír na nÓg!" he declared, pumping his arm.

Three grinned. "All right! To Tír na nÓg, then!" she echoed.

Pip nodded once, staring at his meat pie. Fergus looked to Raja, who at last raised his head. He nodded slowly, staring into the distance. Finally, he turned to Terry.

"To Tír na nÓg," he agreed and reached out to ruffle Fergus's hair.

Fergus stared at him for a moment and then his mouth quirked. Maybe he'd never see Ursula again, but perhaps it was for the best. He wouldn't miss New Peiling, at least. Without Evelyn, there wasn't much to say about Everyday Resources. Besides, he and Terry were probably still wanted men. If they left, they could finally live freely. Plus, it seemed Terry had chosen him over his mother's ghost. That was a rather curious thing unto itself, and somehow, he felt very warm thinking about it. His mouth twitched again, trying to form a full smile. He crammed a meat pie into it, tucking the map into his pocket, and rubbed his fingers on his jeans. Then he reached over, lightly punching Terry in the shoulder, and grinned.

GLOSSARY

Banshee: A female fairy that foretells death with her cry.

Cait Sìth: A cat fairy with a white marking on its chest.

Gancanagh: A male fairy that seduces human women, causing them to die of love for him.

Gytrash: A large black dog fairy with glowing eyes. Sometimes considered a harbinger of death; at other times a guide.

Kelpie: A fairy that appears as a black horse, luring travelers onto its back and dragging them into the water to eat them.

Púca: A shape-shifting fairy that often appears as a black horse. It sports a fondness for taking drunkards on wild rides across the countryside.

Selkie: A fairy that appears as a seal, which can shed its skin to become a beautiful woman. If a man steals its skin, he can force the selkie to marry him.

Tarbh Uisge: A gentle water fairy that appears as a black bull with no ears.

ABOUT THE AUTHOR

Addison Lane was born and raised between a small town in the Deep South and the Big City. Though wanderlust ever calls, she presently resides on the East Coast, where she's a mild-mannered web designer by day and literary crime fighter by night. *Hanging Flynn* is her first novel.